THE BONE GATE

Lesser Known Monsters: Book Two

← ME

RORY MICHAELSON

PLZ COME ON SOCIAL
MEDIA AND SEND ME A PICTURE
OF YOUR PETS? IF YOU DON'T
HAVE PETS MAYBE JUST DRAW
ME A PICTURE?

LOVE

rorymichaelson.com

LESSER KNOWN
M&NSTERS
BOOK TWO

THE BONE GATE
LESSER KNOWN MONSTERS: BOOK TWO

E-book edition ISBN: 978 1 8381660 5 2
Paperback ISBN: 978 1 8381660 6 9
Hardback ISBN: 978 1 8381660 7 6

Cover design by Dean Cole ©
Illustrations by Axel Toth (Urban Knight Art ©)
Cover images © istockphoto.com

CONTENT NOTE

This book uses British English conventions, spelling, and grammar. Some colloquialisms may appear, but hopefully this just gives you some new and funny words to use in real life.

Please be aware this story contains sexual content, as well as themes or events of anxiety, depression, ableism, psychological abuse, dysphoria, queerphobia, and major character death.

The content of this story may be upsetting or distressing, but stay with me. The themes of this series will always be hope, love, and inner strength. We may travel through darkness to get there, but we will get there together.

For you, who never stop fighting for the right to be yourself.
You are needed.

ALSO BY RORY MICHAELSON

The Lesser Known Monsters Series

Lesser Known Monsters

The Bone Gate

The Little Book of Lesser Known Monsters

EXCITARE

Eighteen months ago, Oscar Tundale's friends **saved the world**. That was, of course, only after Oscar almost ended it. A careless word striking a **dangerous bargain** was all it took, with a **monster** who wanted to save her own.

The problem is, actions tend to have **consequences**.

So now, Oscar finds himself once more in a cemetery, on a mild springtime night in Prague. He courts **danger**, as if and as well as it is his lover. But they have yet to realise one thing from that fateful night in **London**...perhaps the world has not stopped ending yet.

❧ I ❧
ASSAULT OF THE EARTH

UNFINISHED MEN

O scar ran as fast as he could.

Faster than he'd ever been able to before.

Well, practice makes perfect...and I've had plenty of that.

He darted through the crooked tombstones and behind the pale building with the jaunty red roof. His backpack bounced against his spine through his thin jacket; he could feel the weight of the rusted hilt rattling around uselessly. That thing hadn't done anything since the night with the world parallax in London, but he still kept it close. 'Keep it close in case it doesn't make things worse,' the Bean-Nighe had said. He could always use things not getting worse.

Oscar burst around the corner, the lights of the city sprawling into view through the tall bars of the perimeter fence. Prague. *Well, at least it's pretty here.* He couldn't help but imagine what it might have been like to be here under different circumstances. The last few months had been a blur. All long travel, strange locations, and full of—

A huge clod of stone and soil shattered into pieces against the wall beside him, kicking off a cloud of dirt, forcing him to duck away and cover his eyes. A massive form emerged from the shadows.

The creature opened its mouth, a yawning maw of earth and clay, and let out a gasping moan as it lumbered forth. Yeah, full of *that*. *Monsters.*

The thing's thick arms reached out, misshapen earthen fingers grasping at him. Oscar took a step back, readying himself. It must have been eight feet tall. "I've seen bigger." Oscar forced a grin, even as panic threatened to pull the edges of his nerves to tatters.

The creature ambled forward, raising an arm. Its body heaved. A swelling mass of earth bulged through its leg as it channelled from the ground beneath its feet, and bubbled up to its arm like a loaded missile. Oscar was already moving as it began to spew from its hand, running back the way he came. He heard the shower of soil and stones behind him and the dry, gasping moan of fury.

Oscar pumped his legs, running off the path into the small copse of trees nearby. He didn't know how long he could keep this up, but at the same time, his heart pounded with dreadful excitement. *Oscar Tundale, Fearless Monster Hunter.*

The earth burst open before him, showering him with debris. Oscar let out a scream in a very un-Monster-Hunter fashion and raised his hands to protect his face from the incoming soil shower. Stopping his forward trajectory proved too much, and Oscar lost his footing on the ground beneath him, falling onto his backside with a jarring thud.

Blinking, he watched as the monster heaved itself up from below.

Gaeant. Terrakinde. An Earth Elemental.

He knew it had several other names, but they had all escaped his mind almost as fast he'd learned them. What mattered right now was that it was here, and it wasn't happy.

Oscar scrambled back, avoiding a thudding stomp from one of the monster's thick legs as it lurched toward him. "Wait!" he cried out hoarsely.

Maybe I'm not ready for this. Should I call for him?

The gaeant stomped again.

Oscar twisted and rolled, pushing himself to his feet so adroitly, he surprised even himself.

No. I can do this.

One huge fist rushed toward him.

Closing his eyes and clenching his teeth, Oscar danced back, feeling a rush of air and spray of dirt as it passed close by. *I'm doing it! I*—

A massive crumbling hand caught his arm. Oscar's stomach sunk. The grip closed like a vice, painfully squeezing him from wrist to elbow and pulling him into the air.

Oscar felt ridiculous, his legs cycling desperately, mouth gaping like a fish. But he only felt ridiculous for a moment. Then, he felt *terrified*.

A whistling sound sang in the air. Oscar opened his mouth, taking a breath to cry for help.

THUNK.

Oscar fell to the ground, and the bulk of the gaeant's arm shattered to pieces on and around him. One heavy clod landed on his chest, winding him.

The monster twisted, letting out a dusty wheeze, dark round eyes searching the night for its attacker. Its stumped arm was swelling, regrowing from the broken earth beneath its feet.

Oscar rolled away, blinking the dust out of his eyes, and saw *him*.

He looked...*terrifying*.

Oscar grinned.

Taller than when they had met, his dark hair had grown a little longer over the months spent travelling. Now, it hung loose and wild, framing his pale features, angled jaw, and delicate nose. His eyes flickered like flames in the darkness, lighting his handsome face ghoulishly. He smiled back at Oscar, flashing a mouth full of pointed teeth. Oscar's heart soared.

Here he was, just on time. Like always. Oscar didn't think it was possible to love him more.

The gaeant staggered forth, and thrust both arms toward Dmitri. Its body trembled with building force. Oscar was about to open his mouth to cry out for Dmitri to move when the first volley of earth cannoned loose. Huge clumps of it sprayed out of the monster's massive fists, hurling through the air at Dmitri.

Dmitri flowed with the darkness, a swirling blur of movement. Dodging under one of the monster's outstretched arms, he snatched at the handle of what he'd thrown. The large, curved tooth was deeply buried in the bark of the nearest tree. Dmitri snarled as he tore free the axe that had taken off the gaeant's arm. It had bitten so deep into the wood that his muscles bulged with the effort, straining the sleeves of his snug vermillion shirt, as the tree groaned and shook. Oscar shivered in the show of power as Dmitri snarled and the blade came loose.

Wait, did I just swoon?

The beast let out another rattling roar, dust billowing from its jaws, raising its heavy arms toward Dmitri once more.

Burning eyes and a singing blade soared through the night.

Oscar closed his eyes as the axe struck home across the thing's face. He'd seen Dmitri fight a few monsters now. Tentacles and eyes, barbed limbs, or teeth like knives. Things that regrew, inflated, and burst. Be that as it may, one thing remained true: *stabbing something in the face is usually a pretty safe bet to end a fight.*

There was another thud as something fell to the ground; Oscar peeked to see the thing now on its knees, its head and one of its arms missing. Dmitri swung, again and again, broad blade biting deeply into its shoulder, then chest, a look of cruel determination on his face and sweat on his brow. Oscar turned away, walking back around the quaint little building. The skyline of Prague unfolded before him, but behind, he could still hear the dull, grizzly thudding of the axe.

Not for the first time, Oscar wondered at the changes in his life this past year. He'd gone from nervous care assistant on a children's ward in London to world travelling, adventure having, Monster Hunter. *Well, maybe Dmitri did most of the monster hunting, but it certainly does feel like I'm in the thick of it too. Okay, running away from the thick of it.*

Prague wasn't the beginning.

Paris. Lithuania. Buenos Aires. Lima. Beijing. Rome.

Dmitri had taken Oscar to places he wouldn't have been able to point to on a globe. They had travelled through rain and storms, searing heat, and deep, wet jungle. All in search of clues about other world parallaxes. They had destroyed two potentials and found lots of monsters that wanted to stop them and even more monsters drawn to the hum of Oscar's blood. His ancestral touch from the other world, Theia.

Oscar sometimes struggled to separate the places they'd been in his mind, let alone put all of them together with what his life had been before all this. Who *he* had been. He stretched, night air catching at his hips where his T-shirt lifted. He unhitched his backpack and set it on the grass beside him. From the way Dmitri had been chopping, he may be waiting a while.

Oscar sighed and was just wondering if the ground was too damp to sit on when he realised the hacking noise had stopped. He was about to turn, when firm hands gripped his hips, and hot breath rushed against his neck.

He froze still, skin rising in goosebumps.

"What's this? Delicious prey bringing itself to my cemetery?" The deep voice rumbled, slightly breathless, lips tantalisingly brushing the flesh at the side of his neck like a butterfly's wings, his scent charred cedar spiked with fresh sweat.

Oscar swallowed, his heart skipping a beat. "You are mistaken, fiend. I am not prey, but a fearless Monster Hunter."

The monster chuckled, the heat of his breath blossoming across Oscar's throat once more. "Well, little Monster Hunter—"

"Fearless," Oscar repeated stubbornly.

He felt Dmitri's smile against his skin. "Well, fearless little Monster Hunter. You have vanquished me with your perfection." One hot hand slid under Oscar's T-shirt, large enough that it almost crossed his chest completely, fingertips catching his left nipple. The other ventured lower, pushing into the seat of his jeans and squeezing him as sharp teeth grazed his throat. "Perhaps I will feast upon you...but only for pleasure."

Oscar shivered, a helpless moan escaping him as Dmitri squeezed his nipple.

"Would you like that?"

Dmitri was always like this after a hunt.

Oscar swallowed thickly. "I would."

Dmitri chuckled again, his hands pushing the denim of Oscar's jeans over the rise of his hips. They fell loosely around his knees, underwear following in short demand.

Oscar gasped as the night air enveloped his bare bottom half. A low growl escaped Dmitri as he slid to his knees behind him, sending a thrill through every fibre of Oscar's being. The feeling of Dmitri's mouth against his most sensitive spot had a more mechanical effect, jolting Oscar's body and pushing his chest and face up against the railings as he was devoured.

IT WATCHED.

Watched as the darkborn toyed with the human, forcing mewling cries of pleasure. Deep within him, what was left of the man whose body it wore recoiled in disgust and fury.

Oh, he doesn't like that at all.

It smiled.

That kind of loathing was exactly how they had gotten here.

Hate, humans called it.

Such an amusing word. So short and simple for such a complex maze of nonsensically self-destructive energy.

But hate could be a useful thing, too.

Every action has an equal or opposite reaction. A term plucked from this withering mortal's memories, which it had consumed months ago. It was an accomplished idea for this pathetic world, if somewhat lacking in vision.

Everything was, is, and will be.

Hate was creation too. These fools just had no idea what it was they were creating.

The face that had belonged to the man called Harry Barlow smiled. It was a languorous and satisfied smile that the man himself would never have worn. Weeks of carelessness had caused this shell to degrade. Skin like crepe paper with a gruesome pallor, showed thick, dark veins beneath—eyes bloodshot and raw from all the times it forgot to make the stupid things close and reopen to wet them with its hideous serous mucus. Its fingers were raw and bleeding, and flesh covered in weeping sores and blistering rashes. It simply didn't have time for the kind of maintenance this vessel required.

The human cried out in pleasure as the darkborn claimed him.

It smiled again at that.

So primitive. That isn't how to fully claim a being at all.

It watched as their movements heated, mouths linking hungrily, hands desperately grasping at each other.

The human's essence sang louder. From a whisper to a moan.

It licked its cracked and bloody lips.

Soon, it would claim him completely.

And then, this will all be over.

2

THE MAGIC OF HOME

O scar stared out the window as London rushed by.
It had been just over a year since they'd left. Eighteen
months since the stone altar in the cemetery tried to consume his
essence. It had taken him months to recover. Then, a year of
running, laughing, loving, and screaming. How could the most
terrifying time of his life also have been the best?

At some point over the last year, between grand suites and
remote castles, Oscar had stopped asking Dmitri about money. It
turned out he had never been in the habit of spending it, and it
was possible to amass quite the piggy bank in...well, however long
he'd been alive. Another morsel of information his supernatural
lover seemed to plan on keeping to himself. Stock market growth,
he claimed. Just a few key shares in little companies. Like the
ones that made the phone in Oscar's pocket or the televisions
sitting in most households across the world.

Judging by the activity on the streets, London was returning
to some semblance of normality. The shops were open again, and
some people were walking around without masks on. Dmitri sat
in the driver's seat, long hair pulled neatly to the nape of his neck,
angular jaw stubbled above his crisp white shirt. His stormy grey

eyes scanned the road, the people. London had been his home for longer than Oscar could imagine. Sometimes he wondered just how much Dmitri had watched this place change.

Not long after the events in the cemetery, people started getting sick. Really sick. At first, they had thought it was a passing thing, but it just got worse. That's when everything changed.

Dmitri had been fraught when the sickness spread across London. Oscar had still been weak from the world parallax, and Dmitri worried he was unlikely to survive such a terrible illness. But Oscar never became unwell. Nor had Zara or Marcus. That was when they began to speculate that the illness may have been related to the world parallax. Dmitri suspected those who'd been previously exposed to the veil had a greater level of immunity. Dmitri's microbiology knowledge and skills had been useful as he studied the aetiology and epidemiology of the sickness and hypothesised that the disease's epicentres may have been where more breaches in the veil had occurred. Breaches could mean another world parallax.

Dmitri had brooded for almost a week before explaining to Oscar that he had to leave. He planned to use the sickness as a compass to search for more world parallaxes. He'd never expected Oscar to come with him; Oscar had never expected not to follow. The results had been mixed. There was nothing to link the illness to breaches after all, though they had found a couple more suspicious parallaxes out of two dozen sites.

Oscar's world had changed the night the strange little girl was admitted to the ward, her back cut to ribbons, and whispering that Dmitri was a bad man. From then on, life was a bottomless rabbit hole of mossy-skinned grave goblins and spooky waifs with a penchant for dramatic foretelling. Not to mention having a boyfriend who was some kind of dragon-wolf were-thing. That wasn't it at all, of course. It was all more complicated, yet simpler than that. Monsters were real, and Dmitri was what some called a Zburator. Born in this world to parents from Theia, the dark world balancing this one in energy and form. A Zburator that, right now, looked a little sulky.

"Are you okay?" Oscar asked.

Dmitri grunted, his face shifting back to neutral. "It's just strange. This place feels different now."

Oscar nodded. "Maybe it's you. I feel different, too."

A crooked smile played across Dmitri's lips. "You are different. You're getting better."

Oscar felt his cheeks colour at the compliment. He'd been training. Not on purpose to begin with, but as weeks passed, he asked Dmitri to help him get stronger and faster. With the song of Theia in his blood, monsters were drawn to him, so why not learn how to handle them a little better? At first, Dmitri had been against it, but a few close calls changed his mind. Now, he often hung back as he had with the gaeant in Prague—to let Oscar practice escaping, though he was always close enough to intervene should there be any real danger.

Oscar smiled. "I had a good teacher."

Dmitri's hand moved from the gear stick to Oscar's knee and gently squeezed.

The car pulled heavily as Dmitri steered to the right. The boot was fully loaded. A few strange relics and the broken remnants of the heavy clay man were loaded into different suitcases in the back. Those, and Dmitri's axe. He'd picked it up when they passed through Romania. A family heirloom he claimed had some kind of special property.

"Are you sure you're not grumpy because we didn't find more parallaxes?" Oscar ventured.

Dmitri grunted, that slightly sour cast to his face returning.

Oscar squeezed his hand. "We did everything we could. It's time to go home."

Those words brought a smile to Dmitri's face, though it didn't quite meet his tired grey eyes. "I like it when you say that."

Oscar felt colour rush to his cheeks. It had been an accident.

Had he meant London or had he meant Dmitri's house? Well, Oscar's house now, technically. "I like saying it."

"Are you nervous?" Dmitri asked.

"Nervous?"

"About being back. About what's next."

"Oh." Oscar chewed his lip, eyes wandering back to the window. "A little bit, I suppose." He had been in touch with Zara a handful of times and Marcus even less. He'd left his job at the hospital, and now he was back, so there definitely was a deep feeling of uncertainty. Would he go back to his old job? What was going to be the new normal?

"Do not worry," Dmitri said, as though he could hear his thoughts. "There's no rush. We can talk about what you want to do next. Anything you want."

Oscar smiled tiredly. "I'd settle for a cup of tea."

3

HOMECOMING

The spring sun hung low in the sky, and gravel crunched under the tires of the car as it pulled up before one-hundred and thirty-eight Kinmount Street. The house was just as gothic and imposing as when Oscar had first seen it, despite having had some major renovations. Oscar was shooing Dmitri away so he could pull one of the suitcases out of the boot himself when he heard the front door open. He'd barely managed to turn around when a huge, fuzzy bundle of grunting fur and slobber pounced at him.

Ed, mercifully, shifted as he collided with Oscar's chest, shriv-elling from a breed Oscar barely had time to recognise into some-thing much smaller—a dark terrier that made up for what it lacked in size in panting excitement. Oscar would have fallen flat on his back or dropped him if this had not become Ed's favourite game some time ago. Instead, he laughed, trying to keep a grasp on the wriggling puppy in his arms as he showered his face with wet kisses.

"He's been waiting by the door all day." Zara leaned on the porch with her arms folded, wearing some pleasantly battered pale dungarees.

17

Oscar laughed as Ed wriggled free of his arms and dropped paws first onto the ground. He bounded toward Dmitri and leapt again. This time, he bubbled and swelled in the air, dark fur shortening. By the time Dmitri intercepted him, Ed was as big a mastiff as Oscar had ever seen, all sagging flesh and heavy mass. Even Dmitri staggered slightly under his bulk. Ed, for his part, panted in his master's face happily. "I blame you," Dmitri growled with a grudging smile at Oscar. "He was never this playful before." Ed gifted his master with a lick that set his wide flat tongue right up the centre of his face.

Oscar abandoned the suitcase and rushed up the steps to grab Zara in an embrace. She looked different. "Your hair's long," he said, surprised as she squeezed him. The patch she had kept shaved on the side for as long as he'd known her had grown in, so it was barely noticeable. The brightly coloured streaks she had sported in various tones were gone too. Now her dark hair was choppy around her round tawny face, hiding the studs in her ears.

"Look who's talking," Zara snorted, flicking the wavy chestnut hair that now hung almost to his chin depending on how unruly it was feeling that day.

Oscar grinned.

"You're not becoming those boyfriend twins, are you?"

"No." He blushed. "It's just, everywhere was closed, or we were too busy."

Zara smiled, pulling him into another hug. "I know, same here. Half of London has been shut forever."

Zara hadn't mentioned the sickness much in their conversations, but work at the hospital must have been difficult. Children seemed to be relatively immune, but the ward had been under pressure to send support to the adult units and intensive care. That, along with her newfound supernatural responsibilities handed over by Dmitri since her near-miss with death, must have had her constantly busy.

"Is Marcus inside?" Oscar asked, leaning to peer over her shoulder.

Zara sighed. "No. He was supposed to be here, but he flaked."

"Oh, really? He's still doing that?"

Zara shook her head, looking troubled. "It's gotten worse. Even when we were all supposed to be staying home, I didn't know where he was half the time. I honestly don't know what's going on with him."

Oscar chewed his lip. It was true; Marcus hadn't followed through on more than half of the video calls they'd organised.

His thoughts were interrupted by the heavy thud of Dmitri setting a large suitcase beside him.

"Jesus, what did you buy?" Zara's eyebrows climbed. "Is there a body in there?"

"Yes," Dmitri said nonchalantly. Oscar cringed.

Zara stared at him dumbstruck for a moment before she burst into an easy laugh. "Good to see your sense of humour hasn't changed."

Dmitri cocked his head, confused. Zara only paused for the briefest of moments before embracing him in a quick hug that left him looking surprised.

"I've missed you." Zara smiled. "Mostly Oscar, but I'm happy you're back too, dogface. Pulling double duty is exhausting."

Dmitri grimaced. "Has it been eventful?"

Oscar thought they may have made it into the house before they started talking shop. No such luck, it turned out.

"Oh, some nights it's like I just lifted up a big fucking rock for the number of many-legged things scuttling around," Zara said tiredly. "I'll tell you all about it. But first, why don't you come into your house and make me some tea?"

OSCAR HAD BARELY SAT before Ed, now a soft-haired Scottie dog, scooted onto his lap and curled up. The sound of Dmitri rummaging in the kitchen still felt strange. Oscar had barely settled into the house before they had left, and the clean decor and warmth felt alien. He remembered it still as a derelict skeleton of a place that had tried to gobble up Marcus and led to everything else that happened.

"So, Oscar Tundale, traveller extraordinaire! Tell me everything." Zara smiled, sitting beside him on the sofa, her sparkling golden-brown eyes rapt with attention.

"Everything?" Oscar grinned. "Even the boring bits?"

"Even the boring bits. Maybe skip the sex scenes, though; they're the most boring. Too many dicks involved."

"I don't know; I think it's just enough dicks," Oscar answered quickly. Zara's eyes bulged before she snorted with laughter. Oscar felt his face heat.

"You've changed so much, Os. I mean, the hair getting longer is one thing, but you seem livelier. Happier."

"I am."

"Plus, I'm pretty sure when we hugged, I caught a feel of something under your shirt. I swear it was an actual bicep. Don't tell me you're going and growing muscles on me now, Booboo."

Oscar blushed again. It was true, months of carrying bags and running from a variety of weird and wonderful beings had him in the best shape of his life, but compared to Dmitri, he was still a gangly limbed beanpole. "Biceps might be a push, but Dmitri has been training me to fight monsters."

Zara's eyes narrowed. "Sounds...dangerous."

"He's always there, ready to step in. The world is more dangerous than we ever knew it was. It's important to me that I don't just always need to be rescued. I want to be able to save myself."

"I get that."

"I've gotten stronger, I guess. Since that night."

Zara grinned. "Me too."

Oscar leaned forward excitedly. "What do you mean? Can you do anything new?"

"Not exactly." Zara shrugged modestly but couldn't stop herself from smirking. "I mean, not like laser vision or flight, but I have better control and a couple new tricks. How about you? Any developments with the glowing sword of doom?"

Oscar sighed. "No, nothing. I stopped even trying after the first few months because nothing ever happens. It makes me wonder if there was a certain trick to it, like maybe it only works when there's an active world parallax nearby."

"Well, if that's the case, let's hope we can never confirm that theory," Zara said darkly.

Oscar grunted in agreement as Dmitri came into the room, carrying a tray loaded with a cast iron teapot, a few beautiful earthenware cups, and a bowl of small cookies.

Zara whistled through her teeth. "Hey, where did that come from? I didn't see them when I went rummaging through all your cupboards." She caught the guarded glance Dmitri shot at her. "Oh, don't worry, Wolfgang, I didn't go in your precious attic."

"It's dangerous," he growled.

"I said I didn't go in!"

Dmitri set the tray down and somewhat sulkily sat on the opposite couch. The house had been full of relics and no shortage of stashed weapons that had needed to be relocated during the renovations. They had all been hidden in the attic until they returned, giving him due time to get them in order and find new places to put everything.

"We got the tea set in Tokyo." Oscar hoped that might cut the tension.

"No way?!" Zara leaned forward to examine it excitedly. "Marcus is going to kill you for going before he got the chance. He's obsessed."

Oscar cringed. "I know."

"Was it amazing?" Zara picked up a cup examining its crackled glazing.

Oscar shot a look at Dmitri, smiling at the memory. It had been. But Dmitri's face was sullen, his eyes impatient.

Oscar sighed, leaning back and folding his arms. "Go on then. Get it out of your system."

Zara looked confused, but Dmitri needed no further prompt. "Please, Zara, tell me everything that has happened whilst I've been gone. What have you encountered, and what kind of measures did you take?" His words were soft but earnest, his eyes searching her for answers.

"Jeez. Checking if I did my homework?" Zara poured herself some tea.

Dmitri remained silent, but his eyes bore into her as she leaned back and took a leisurely sip.

"Well, I followed your list. I went to all the places you told me to check every night. Every. Night. Not a small amount of work, I would add. I came across a few things. Mostly smaller monsters. Flecks, as Oscar would say."

Flecks. The shadows Oscar had seen at the corner of his eyes his whole life. It hadn't been until the world parallax had opened that he learned they were real. Since then, he'd learned online that many people had seen them just like him. Dmitri said that some of them might have been sensitive to the veil, or caught glimpses where it was thin, but none of them carried the touch of Theia like Oscar did.

"They weren't much trouble; I smooshed them pretty good. There's just a lot of them. There have been two deaths. One I'm sure was them, the other is a maybe. It was too clean." The tiredness hidden in Zara's eyes rose to the surface. "Other than that and a weird pointy-headed thing in Stratford, nothing."

Dmitri frowned. "Nothing?"

Zara shrugged.

"That is unusual." Dmitri leaned back, looking troubled.

"That's what Gax said when I checked in with him. He said, all things considered, full-grown monster traffic was particularly low at the moment."

Gax. The disgruntled Bugge living in the nearby cemetery. Oscar remembered his croaky voice fondly. Plus, Gax had been the one to save them and tip the odds to destroy Ocampo when he rode in on the giant fire breathing Gwyllgi and tore her in half.

"Maybe they're scared of the flecks?" Oscar ventured.

"Unlikely." Dmitri sat back, retreating into his thoughts.

Oscar chewed his lip for a moment whilst Zara took another sip. "So, how is Marcus?"

Zara leaned forward and picked up a tiny cookie, nibbling it thoughtfully. "Even weirder than usual."

"He's out a lot?"

"Constantly." Zara rolled her eyes. "I mean, he wanted to come on patrol with me a few times, and I let him. He's been keeping a diary of different types of things he sees. Calls it his Taxonomy of Monsters. Some of the things he's got in there, I've got no idea how he found out. Been researching in some weird places if you ask me."

"Where does he keep it?" Dmitri's voice had a dangerous edge.

"Oh, it's secure, don't worry. He has it on an offline laptop that looks like it was unearthed from the Cretaceous period. He wanted all modern things to be unable to connect to it so that it was unhackable."

Dmitri grunted. "That's smart. Low-tech lockdown."

"Ugh," Zara moaned. "Don't say that word; you'll trigger me." She stuffed the rest of the cookie in her mouth.

"How's work?" Oscar ventured. "I mean, nurse work, not shadow smooshing work."

"Tiring," Zara mumbled through her full mouth, taking a few chews and washing it down with a swig of tea. "Understaffed, overworked, and the new consultant is pretty useless."

Oscar cringed sympathetically.

"Why? You wanna come back?" Zara brightened. "They'd take you back in a heartbeat; they're desperate for staff."

"Maybe." Oscar avoided Dmitri's gaze. *We still need to have that talk.* "Nobody asking where Ocampo went?"

Zara's eyes sparkled, and she looked down at her tea, shaking her head emphatically. "They mostly seemed glad to see the back of her. Everyone still acts like if they say her name three times, she'll be taken off the missing list. I don't even think they would be more scared of her if they knew she was a shadow riding mega-bitch."

Oscar smiled weakly. He had to admit, talking about her made him feel uneasy, and he had seen first-hand exactly how many pieces she'd been torn into.

"Anyway, you must be tired from all the travelling. I guess I should leave you to it." Zara moved to stand; Ed perked up curiously in Oscar's lap.

"Not at all," Dmitri said. "You should stay for dinner."

"Really?"

"He's not being nice. He's just going to grill you more about what you've been doing," Oscar translated.

Dmitri nodded, stern and guileless. "But I will buy you pizzas."

Zara pointed at him sharply. "Sold, to the too handsome man who can turn into a Dragon-Wolf."

Oscar grinned. "Plus, we need to talk to you about something for this weekend."

Zara cocked her head, curious.

"Well, since we've been away so much and need to make the place feel more like home, Dmitri suggested we have a gathering. A small one, of course, just a couple of people."

"Oh my God," Zara gasped, hands covering her mouth. "You're having a housewarming party? Does that mean we get to pretend to be normal?"

Oscar smiled and rolled his eyes. "Normal? What's that?"

4

THESE SCARS THAT BLEED

"Os, I could just carry it."
       "No, it's okay."
"Are you sure?"
"Yep."
"Your face is turning purple."
"Yep."
"Oscar, put it down."
"Yep."

Oscar dropped the suitcase the last few inches to the floor-boards with a heavy thud that made him grateful for the thick patterned rug covering their new finish.

"Jeez, Dmitri wasn't kidding when he said there was a body in there, was he?" Zara folded her arms.

"Gaeant body." Oscar shrugged. "Like a big, earthy, rock guy. Well, maybe not its body; it could be a leg. Or an arm. Or its other leg. I'm not sure, but whatever it is, it's really heavy."

"Wow. You made friends without me," Zara dead-panned.

"Yeah, he was cool. Shot out clumps of earth from his hands like cannons. Was about this tall." Oscar waved his hand vaguely as high as he could reach in the air.

Zara raised her eyebrows and hefted the suitcase easily with one hand. "Hey, it is kinda heavy. Where did you want it?"

Oscar's jaw dropped. "The landing's fine. Why couldn't I be the one to get possessed by a powerful ancient Indian ghost?"

"Because that would be cultural appropriation, Booboo," Zara shot back, striding through the hall. With both hands, Oscar took one of the smaller bags and followed. "Besides, you have the magic sparkle sword." Zara was already halfway up the stairs. "Full potential to be equally as fabulous."

"Not that it does anything when I want it to," Oscar grumbled, voice strained as he struggled with the weight of the bag. *Was this the gaeant's head?* "Plus, even when it did get swordy that one time, it was more like a sad little dagger."

Zara set the suit-cased remains carefully on the landing. ""Why did you bring back the chopped-up rock guy anyway? Kind of creepy to travel with chopped-up bodies, even monster ones. Maybe especially monster ones." She looked perplexed at the predicament the loss of normality had provided her with.

"Some guy in Slovakia said its body could be used to 'trace the dark.'" Oscar dumped his bag down with a thud. "We thought it might mean it would be good for hunting world parallaxes, but when we got close, it turned out it was just more interested in me than most monsters. Like a sniffer dog for Oscars. Since he implied it didn't have to be alive, we figured we'd just bring its bits back."

"Witchery." Zara scowled.

"Pretty much."

"So, did you see any other weird monsters on your travels?" Zara asked, grinning excitedly.

"You sound like Marcus."

Zara rolled her eyes, but the grin didn't leave her face. "An appreciation of the bizarre may have found its way to me. It's not like I have much choice but to be invested nowadays." She made her way back down the stairs, and Oscar followed.

"A heap, really. I mean, a few were flecks, but there was this thing in Thessaloniki with fingers like tentacles and a big old face the size of my whole body. It was super creepy."

"You need to stop name dropping all these cool places; you sound like someone who just came back from a gap year. It's insufferable," Zara shot back, trotting down the porch steps.

"You asked! Plus, I kind of did go on a gap year..."

"I believe it's pronounced 'gap-yah,'" Zara replied in her best toff voice, hefting another bag with one hand. "This one's even heavier!"

"Dmitri has been doing all the heavy lifting." Oscar frowned, trailing behind and stretching his back. Could he even manage another trip?

There was a sound from above as something scraped in the attic. Dmitri had been up there for the last hour making space.

"How has it been? With Dmitri?" Zara asked softly, setting the case back down and putting her hands on her hips.

"Great!" Oscar smiled. Dmitri could probably hear every word they said from up there. "Maybe we should check if there was anything else in the car before we move the rest of this stuff?"

Zara looked puzzled but followed him to the front door obligingly.

"NOTHING IN HERE." Zara peered through the back window of Dmitri's car before turning and leaning on it, arms folded. "What's going on?"

Oscar wasn't completely sure how good Dmitri's hearing was, but this ought to be far enough.

"Nothing! It's great. I mean, we barely knew each other, and next thing I know, we're together all day, every day, most of the time with no one else that can even speak the same language within a hundred miles. Well, the same language as me. Dmitri speaks like fifty languages, it turns out," Oscar finished glumly.

"So?" Zara said a little impatiently. "Is the novelty wearing off?"

Oscar frowned, shifting his feet with a crunch of gravel. "No, it's not that. Actually, the opposite. It's just intense. He always wants to know how I am, what I'm thinking. If I'm happy."

"And the sex?"

Oscar bared his teeth. "Constant. Like, it's amazing, and I love it, but sometimes maybe I just want to get out of the shower without needing to take another shower an hour later. Sometimes, I just want to read a book and eat pizza without it being—"

"A meat feast?" Zara offered.

Oscar tilted his head, confused. "You know I like margherit—ohhhhh, I get it."

Zara grinned. "No one likes margherita, Oscar; it's the vanilla ice cream of pizzas. And about the rest...well, Oscar, it sounds terrible. I have to say, it sounds almost like he adores you."

Oscar winced. "I know. And I adore him. He's kind and thoughtful and so very, very hot. I mean, seriously, sometimes I look at him, and my heart just gets all weird. But I can't shake this feeling that I'm not good enough for him. Like I don't know if it's me he loves or, you know, my *body*."

Zara looked flummoxed. "Oscar. I mean, you've packed on a little muscle, but I don't know what to say. I'm pretty sure Dmitri's abs have abs."

"No! Not my body. My *body*. The cells in me that carry the touch of Theia."

"Oh! Your little cricket-tune!"

Oscar nodded. That word always made him think of the Bean-Nighe now. Her gaunt, pale features looming out of the darkness, her round lidless eyes peering at him curiously, her voice a wandering lullaby.

Hello, Cricket.

Zara rubbed her chin thoughtfully. "Well, I have to say, after my close encounter of the weird kind, I do feel a difference in you."

Oscar's eyes widened.

"Don't worry, it's not like I want to jump your bones or anything. I'm still very much not interested in The Sex Pistols; I far prefer Pussy Riot. But there's something warm and welcoming about you. Like I want to squeeze you all the time. But it's hard to say. I felt a bit like that before I had this beefy ass Casper living in my body, just cos, you know—you're my Booboo."

Oscar chewed his lip and shifted on his feet, troubled. *So even Zara wants to be around me more. Maybe that's the only reason...*

Zara's face grew very serious, and slowly she reached up and took Oscar by the shoulders, staring him dead in the eyes. "I've been expecting this. Oscar, let me say this once. I'll say it slowly and clearly, so you don't forget. You deserve this. You deserve to be happy. You deserve to be loved. You deserve Dmitri."

Oscar's heart squeezed in his chest, and he blinked, feeling tears well in his eyes.

"I know you bottle things up, Booboo, and we talked about this. But please just remember, I love you, Marcus loves you, and even Nega-Tundale Paige loves you. Now, you found a guy with all the emotional availability in the world, just for you, so of course, that would send you into crisis."

Oscar smiled, wiping a tear from his cheek.

"Dmitri is obsessed with you. Learn to deal with it, Booboo. We all love you because you're you. Spiritually, physically, psychologically, and yes, cellularly you." She pulled him into a hug, and Oscar laughed.

"I love you, Zara."

"I love you too, Booboo. Just remember to love yourself as well."

Oscar nodded, stepping back, wiping his eyes.

He used to keep this side of himself quiet, not wanting to

burden others with his doubts, but the last few months, he had really been trying to open up. Tears weren't a thing that had come easily to him around others, and even now, he felt shame gnawing at him but pushed it away, smiling at Zara instead. "Thank you for the relationship coaching."

Zara shrugged, her eyes moving away from his uncomfortably for a moment. "It's okay. I'm not the best person to listen to for relationship advice, trust me. But I'm definitely an expert in Oscar."

Oscar grinned.

"Besides, Os, even if your magic money-maker does make Dmitri extra thirsty, that's as much a part of you as your eyes, smile, or personality. People fall in love for way dumber reasons than 'the combination of your human and supernatural cells sing to me ethereally.'" She raised her hands, wriggling her fingers for dramatic effect.

"I guess."

"Was there something else?" Zara asked, standing up straight.

Oscar shook his head.

"Well then, let's get back in there and move those bags. You don't want this place looking like a storage room for your house party! Who knows what the guests might say!"

A stone dropped in Oscar's stomach. He knew exactly what one of them would say.

"What?" Zara paused, looking back over her shoulder.

"There was one more thing, now that you mention it. Remember how when the sickness started, all those companies had to close, and lots of people lost their jobs?"

Zara's eyebrow raised curiously.

"Well, there will be someone coming to the house-warming party who you haven't seen in a long time. Well, I haven't seen them either."

"Shit," Zara groaned, her eyes widening. "You should have led with that! We spend our nights running from and fighting monsters now, and you didn't think to mention that the gnarliest bitch troll from hell is coming to your house-warming?"

Oscar winced. "I won't tell her you said that."

OSCAR WAS JUST DRYING the last of the plates with a tea towel when Dmitri walked into the kitchen. The larger man's thick arms coiled around him from behind, his long hair tickling Oscar's neck as he leaned down to kiss his throat.

"When are you going to remember there is a dishwasher, lubite?" Dmitri rumbled softly.

Oscar blushed. *Oh. That's right.* The first time he'd been in this kitchen, it had been a broken-down unused mess. The only sign of life had been a humming old refrigerator in the corner he'd been convinced held human heads and other body parts. Now, it was a sleek modern treat any urban homebody would kill for, with granite counters and sleek slate-grey cabinets framing a massive cooker and white subway tile backsplash.

"I might remember if we hang around long enough to use it." Oscar leaned back into his arms. Dmitri's body heat pulsed against him. He always ran hot. Anything from the beating sun to a glowing furnace, depending on his mood.

"We will, I promise." Dmitri's laugh was soft, vibrating against his back as he squeezed him tight.

Oscar wriggled free and turned around; Dmitri reluctantly loosened his hold to allow them to meet face to face. Well, chest to face unless Oscar tilted his head back.

"Zara seems well." Dmitri's stormy grey eyes fixed on Oscar's blue. "I was concerned the responsibilities would be too much for her. That she may struggle."

Oscar shrugged. Zara had not long since left in a cab. "I guess. I mean, her normal job involves a lot of responsibility too. She's the assistant manager on the ward now, so not only is she responsible for all the kids and families but looking after the staff too."

Dmitri nodded. "True. But in this case, when people die, it can feel very much like it is directly your fault. Like you should have done more to save them. And it sounds as though Marcus hasn't been around much to support her."

Oscar grunted. Everything Dmitri said was true, and it was horrible to consider. But the fact Dmitri had thought so carefully about Zara's wellbeing filled his heart with gratitude and love. "I'm just glad you two get on now. It was stressful when you hated each other."

Dmitri gave a lopsided smile that flashed a few pointed teeth. "I never hated Zara, she just hated me. Besides, I have to be nice to her. You've seen her fight—she's scary."

Oscar jabbed him in the ribs.

Dmitri chuckled. "Zara only hated me because she was worried about you. Because she loves you. We have that in common, so why wouldn't we be the greatest of allies?" He pulled Oscar closer, smothering his mouth with a kiss that took Oscar's breath away.

Dmitri deepened the kiss, his arms pulling Oscar up onto his tiptoes as his hands snaked down to his hips and squeezed his bottom. His tongue ventured into Oscar's mouth, and his body heat intensified against him as Oscar felt another part of him responding.

Breaking the kiss, Oscar struggled free, pushing Dmitri back against the island. Dmitri growled in frustration. The heat from his body was suddenly enough for Oscar's skin to begin to prickle and bead with sweat.

"So, Saturday, we have the house party." Oscar pushed away Dmitri's hand as it moved toward his throat. Instead, he slipped his own nimbly up Dmitri's shirt, running his fingers down the hard lines of his body.

"Yes." Dmitri's voice was low and husky, his hands drifting in the air, anxious to touch Oscar. One drifted too close, and Oscar slapped it away with a sharp tssk.

"Marcus, Zara, and Paige," he continued, his other hand now drifting down to Dmitri's belt, slipping over the top and pulling firmly, feeling the scratch of soft hair against his knuckles below. He also felt Dmitri respond against his touch, and the larger man let out a low growl. Oscar met his eyes, heavily glazed with lust as he nodded.

"And then it's just us. Doing nice normal things for a while. Then we'll deal with the gaeant parts, yes?"

Dmitri nodded again, so earnest, as Oscar unbuckled his belt, unable to suppress a smile at the innocent lust on his face.

"Good." Oscar captured his heavy bottom lip in the briefest of kisses. Dmitri leaned forward hungrily for more—only to be met with a restraining hand on his broad chest.

"Oscar," he moaned.

Oscar shushed him and slipped to his knees.

THE DITHERFOX

(VULPES TEMPES))

5

A HOUSE AS WARM AS HELL

"I'm coming!" Dmitri shouted.

Oscar paced the hallway anxiously, eyes fixed on the stained-glass window taking up much of the door. Dmitri had spent most of the morning loading the last of the suitcases into the attic. Except for the large clay man, the majority of the contents of their bags was now heaped inside the otherwise empty wardrobes in the recently decorated spare rooms upstairs. The gaeant's remains had been loaded into the attic—with some difficulty—on Oscar's insistence. He didn't want what was left too close whilst they were sleeping.

"They're going to be here soon." Oscar worried his bottom lip.

"Marcus and Zara will probably be late." Dmitri bounced down the stairs. He wore a midnight blue shirt that hugged the shape of his chest pleasingly, his sleeves rolled back to show those muscular forearms that made Oscar feel all gooey inside.

Oscar had opted for a simple emerald-green T-shirt and worn denim jeans. "Paige might be on time."

"She's an on-time person?" Dmitri stopped beside him, folding his arms.

"She's a does-whatever-she-wants person. She might be early, or she might not turn up at all."

Dmitri smiled. "I'm excited to meet her."

"This too shall pass," Oscar said glumly.

"How bad can she be? She practically raised you, and you're perfect." Dmitri planted a kiss on Oscar's forehead that made him blink but struggle to keep the scowl on his face.

As if on cue, there was a curt rap on the door. Oscar cast despairing eyes at Dmitri.

"Do you want me to answer, or should we answer together?" Dmitri asked, scraping a strand of hair that had escaped the knot at the back of his head behind his ear.

"No," Oscar sighed miserably. "Let me. I might need a minute with her before I unleash her on you." He began his solemn death march to the door.

When the door opened, Paige was tapping at her phone screen distractedly, cigarette pressed between her thin crimson lips. Her ice-blue eyes flashed up at Oscar, and for a moment, her face was a mask of surprise and confusion. She plucked the cigarette from her mouth and dropped it on the porch, pressing it out with one black heel. "Oscar? Why do you look like you joined a shitty band full of angry teenagers who don't want to clean their bedrooms?"

Oscar blushed.

That wasn't so bad, all things considered.

Paige pulled him into a brisk hug, filling his nostrils with the scent of the cigarette smoke on her coat and the sweet acidity of her perfume. She was just as willowy as Oscar but a little taller, though that may have been the perpetual stubby heels she favoured. *All arms and elbows,* she said their mother used to call it. Not that Oscar could remember. They had the same thin face, pointy chin, and long nose. Paige's eyes were a colder blue, and she'd dodged the smattering of freckles, gapped front teeth, and unruly chestnut hair from their father. Instead, a neat coif of raven hair was pristinely cut to her jaw. She pulled her dark jacket tighter around her bony shoulders. "Aren't you going to ask me in then? It's cold out here."

Oscar cringed. "Of course."

"Is this really where you live?" Paige asked, waiting for no further invitation and striding into the narrow space between him and the door. "It's like the house on fucking haunted hill."

"Yeah. I mean, I haven't lived here long," Oscar mumbled, with no other choice but to concede and let her in. Her heels clicked on the wooden floor loudly, her wide dark trousers only showing a flash of bare foot.

"Oh—" Paige stopped suddenly.

Oscar turned and closed the door with a click, affording himself a second to close his eyes and take a deep breath.

Paige was standing open-mouthed, black handbag hanging limply from her arm, staring at Dmitri.

Dmitri stood like a deer in headlights, eyes wide and mouth in an awkward half-smile showing the dental flipper he wore when around others to give the appearance of, well, human teeth. The dog-sharp teeth were now his standard after that night at the cemetery and could be quite unsettling for those not accustomed.

Paige turned sharply and shot a curious look at Oscar. "Who's that?" she said loudly, as though Dmitri wasn't standing right beside her.

Dmitri cleared his throat. "I am Dmitri. Oscar's boyfriend."

Paige's eyes widened comically. "Oh. Shit. Well, hello." She committed to an awkward sort of curtsy. Her handbag slipped free of her forearm, and she only just managed to catch it in her pale fingers before it fell. "I'm Oscar's Paige. Oscar's sister. I'm Paige," she stuttered, her pale cheeks coloured.

Oscar stared numbly. *What is happening?*

Dmitri smiled charmingly. Well, as charmingly as that flipper would allow. Oscar hated the thing.

"Can I take your coat and bag?" Dmitri offered smoothly.

Paige stared at him blankly for a moment as though unfamiliar with what those things were. "Oh, fuck, yes. Take them," she said, coming to her senses. She snatched off her jacket to reveal a wide-collared white blouse beneath.

Dmitri smiled, hanging it on the curled hooks by the door. "Can I offer you a drink, Paige?"

"What? Oh no." She guffawed, brushing her hair back. "Only if you have wine? Red?"

"Of course." Dmitri smiled, turning toward the kitchen. "I'm sure you and Oscar have much to catch up on. I'll bring it to you in the living room."

Paige watched him walk away, face slack at his broad retreating shoulders until he disappeared through the doorway. Then, her awed gaze turned back to Oscar. "What the fuck, Oscar? Where did you find him? Is he a robot? Some kind of Stepford husband? Is he a hired actor, and this is a prank or something? Why are you rich now?"

Oscar cringed, raising his hands defensively from the barrage of questions. "It's uh...complicated," he replied stiffly, using an old line of Dmitri's.

"I bet it is." Paige's eyes drifted back to the kitchen door.

"Come and sit down. I'll tell you uh, a little bit about how we met."

OSCAR WAS grateful when Zara showed up. Not just because he loved her, but because it gave Paige a distraction from wandering around the house, picking up every other ornament, and poking at things. She preened for a few minutes, staring into the large horizontal mirror that hung over the faux fireplace before prodding the thick bundle of dill hanging above it. Oscar chewed his lip at that. Dmitri had only put the mirror there for his sake and hadn't had a reflective surface in the house when they'd met. He'd made Oscar promise never to remove the dill, insisting that it was important for keeping out unwanted intruders. Paige's pre-occupation with the décor was, however, a relief compared to her ogling of Dmitri or the incessant comments.

"So, what's the deal with the European Catalogue model?"

"He's a doctor? Hot AND rich? What's the downside? Is the basement full of bodies? I mean, still, worth it."

"Jesus, Oscar, how did you bag that piece? If he is an actor you're paying to be your boyfriend for the night, how much did he cost? I have my purse."

"For fuck's sake, look at that arse. I'd have that without any dressing on the side."

Her constant comments left him at a strange juncture between uncomfortable and proud. When Zara turned up, the two greeted each other like rival alley cats forced to share the same space. The sides of Zara's eyes crinkled in an over-enthusiastic fake smile, and Paige's teeth were on such full display, a dentist wouldn't have needed to use a mirror to complete an exam.

"So, how have you been? How's work?" Zara asked.

The first blow, a not-so-subtle jab.

"Oh, I have my fingers in a few pies." Paige shrugged, sipping her wine. "That's the beauty of being self-employed. I don't have to run around at other people's beck and call."

Parry.

"Must be nice. I'm surprised there's much work around at the moment. I'd have thought the magazine industry was struggling."

Right hook.

"People always need art and fashion." Paige shook her head like she was tossing her unmoving hair. "It's just about being fluid. Making the move to more online mediums. That way, we can still help people who otherwise have no idea what they're doing." Her eyes travelled around Zara's fluffy purple sweater, threaded with sparkling strands, and her torn jeans. Her lip curled slightly. "It's a public service, really. Fashion police are over, but fashion first aid is in high demand."

Zara bristled, her forced smile becoming a little over-enthused.

Oh. Was that a direct hit?

"Dmitri, do you need any help?" Oscar asked loudly.

"I'm fine," Dmitri's voice echoed from the kitchen.

Oscar's eyes darted between his sister and his best friend nervously, a rat trapped between two vipers. "Coming!" he shouted, his voice cracking as he darted out of the room and made a beeline for the kitchen.

DMITRI LOOKED UP, brow furrowed, when Oscar walked in. A tray of freshly made nibbles was spread across a platter on the countertop. Oscar snatched one and popped it in his mouth whole.

"Hey." Dmitri grinned. "That's for everybody."

"I'm everybody." Oscar moaned, swallowing. It was delicious. "I don't know if I can do this. Please give me alcohol."

"That won't help."

"Paige is..."

Dmitri chuckled. "She has quite the vocabulary."

Oscar groaned. Of course, Dmitri would have heard everything she said from the other room.

"Is it nearly over? Tell me it's like midnight, and they all have to go home now."

Dmitri leaned forward and pecked him on the cheek. "It is barely seven." As he moved back, he looked thoughtful for a moment. "You only invited Marcus as well?"

Oscar nodded, causing Dmitri to grunt.

"Then it seems we will have a bonus guest."

There was a knock at the door.

～

Marcus' big russet brown eyes and beaming smile were so dazzling that Oscar almost didn't notice the person beside him. Skin even darker than Marcus', almost obsidian to his umber, hair a cap of tight dark curls, and large golden eyes fixed on Oscar with interest. The cerulean puffer jacket they wore went down to their knees. *Well, that certainly seems unseasonable.*

"Oscar! How long has it been?" Marcus pulled him into a rough hug.

Oscar squeezed him back, finding it difficult to pull his eyes away from the stranger who watched him with open interest, delicate features stoic and unfazed. "Uhhh, like a year?"

"More than nine months?!" Marcus snapped, thrusting Oscar back at arm's length and scanning him thoroughly. His eyes lingered on Oscar's narrow waist, and he frowned. "Still nothing, huh?"

Oscar sighed, grinning. "Come in, Marcus."

"Why, is there a whole litter running round in there? Is this the surprise? CAN I KEEP ONE?"

Oscar laughed, holding the door for his friend and plus one to come in. "No and no. Sorry, but I'm not giving you my firstborn."

Marcus harrumphed in a pantomime fashion, pulling off his jacket.

"Hi." Oscar shifted his gaze to Marcus' friend and was rewarded with that penetrating stare.

"Oh, this is my...friend," Marcus began awkwardly.

"Can I take your coat?" Oscar asked, holding out his hand.

The stranger just pulled the thick jacket close to their body and stared at him harder.

"That's okay. They prefer to keep their coat on," Marcus explained, scratching his head. The fuzz on top was a little longer now, but his neat fade remained.

Oscar nodded. *They. Copy that.*

"Nice beard." Oscar smiled, rubbing the wispy hairs on his own jaw.

"Thanks, man." Marcus beamed, stroking the thick growth on his cheeks happily.

"No more glasses? Did you get contacts?"

"Yeah, I couldn't run the risk of some monster dog swallowing my expensive glasses again." Marcus winked. "Speaking of..."

Oscar shot a nervous look at Marcus' companion at the open use of the 'm' word. They seemed completely unfazed. Instead, they peered up the stairwell curiously.

Had Marcus told them everything?

As if on cue, there was a scrabbling upstairs, and one of the doors rattled excitedly.

Oscar cleared his throat. "Ed is in the bedroom. We couldn't be sure that he would behave around Paige."

"Oh shit, the devil queen is here?" Marcus' eyes bulged. He burst into laughter. "Well, that makes it a party, I guess."

Oscar cringed. "She is, and I'm pretty sure her powers have grown since she lost her job in New York and had to move back. I think she may be dedicating all of her free time to evil now."

It had gone pretty quiet in the living room. *Maybe we'd better get in there and make sure everyone is still breathing.*

Oscar was about to suggest as much when Marcus' companion set off at a stride straight past him and into the living room. He looked at Marcus, tilting his head in confusion. "They seem nice?"

Marcus put a hand on his shoulder. "They are."

"Did they really want to come today? It was kind of a close friends and family thing."

Marcus' smile faded a little. "I'll explain later, Os. It's uh, complicated."

❧ 6 ❧

UNWELCOME GUESTS

Marcus perched, boots off and cross-legged, on the wide-armed sofa beside the window. The raspberry-coloured T-shirt he wore had simple white text across the chest reading *Sexy Trash*. Stiff upright and alert, the attention he paid to the room reminded Oscar of a meerkat. Dmitri sat beside Oscar on one sofa, doing his best not to look uncomfortable, whilst Zara and Paige sat on the other, as far apart as they could manage. Marcus' friend stood by the door, fiddling with the arms of their jacket and staring at each of the others in turn with open curiosity.

Two large trays of delicate snacks spread across the coffee table in the middle of the room, largely untouched due to the rigid atmosphere.

"Sooooo, what's with the jacket?" Paige asked, blinking at the unnamed guest.

The guest blinked back.

"I don't think they're interested in your fashion first aid," Zara mumbled.

Paige shot her a sharp look, then turned and eyed the mini-stereo on the side table beside her. "Shall we put some music on?"

She was already jabbing the play button with one finger. A lively electric synth beat pounded out far too loud, and a vocalist let out a joyful croon before Oscar could get there quick enough to silence it. He leapt from the sofa and bounded across the room, failing with the first two button pushes and succeeding with the third.

Paige's face was twisted with wry amusement. "Was that...disco?"

Oscar nodded, face flooding with colour. "Dmitri's favourite. He puts it on when he's cleaning."

Dmitri, for his part, nodded happily to confirm this.

"Right." Paige's eyebrows climbed, and she leaned back, rummaging in her trouser pocket. She deftly palmed a packet and had the slimmest cigarette Oscar had ever seen between her thin ruby lips before he caught her.

"Oh, don't smoke in the house, please." Oscar cleared his throat awkwardly.

Paige's red lips thinned markedly, and she puffed out her cheeks in disdain. "Then where?" she mumbled stiffly, gesturing with one hand as though this were the only place possible.

"Out the back door is fine. I can show you." Oscar moved to stand.

"Don't worry, I'll find it myself." Paige stood and strode to the door, where Marcus' friend lingered in her path. Paige waved a dismissive hand. "Move, please, you."

When Marcus' friend declined not only to move but to react in any other way than tilt their head in vague curiosity, Paige scoffed and stepped awkwardly around them to get by.

"What's your name?" Zara asked pleasantly.

The guest turned their golden eyes to Marcus. For his part, Marcus shifted uncomfortably on the spot, trying to peer through the door where Paige had departed. "They don't really have one," he said softly. "At least, not one you would understand."

Dmitri studied Marcus silently.

"What do you mean?" Zara asked, staring at Marcus. "What's going on?"

"Well, they aren't exactly from around here. They don't speak like we do, and—"

"Marcus," Zara said stiffly, "where did you find them?"

Marcus gave an awkward grin. "It's more like they found me."

"They have no scent," Dmitri grunted, and then his eyes widened. "It can't be..."

"Listen, I will ask them to share something with you all, but you have to promise not to lose it, okay?" Marcus' eyes were anxious. "Just with you guys, not Paige." He fixed his friend with a pointed stare at that last bit as if to remind them of this. They gave a slight, almost imperceptible nod.

Oscar was about to ask more when suddenly everything changed. His senses were overwhelmed in a way that took his breath away. His vision blurred at the edges, and his ears hummed and chimed like a tuning fork. Deep within him, he felt...curiosity. His eyes drifted to Marcus, and a sense of fondness that wasn't his own lapped over him. Blinking, he turned back to the mysterious guest and found them watching him with interest. As suddenly as it began, it ended. The withdrawal of the warm glowing energy made him gasp and lean into Dmitri's shoulder shakily.

"An ethernal," Dmitri growled. Oscar saw his eyes were alight, the beginning of flickering heat behind them.

Zara likewise had half risen from her seat, the barest luminescent glow forming around her clenched fists.

"It's okay. They just want to learn," Marcus whined. "They're harmless."

"Hardly," Dmitri breathed.

"What's going on?" Oscar asked weakly.

"Why don't you share with them what we would call a name?" Marcus smiled.

Oscar realised what was going to happen and was about to protest when the warm, engulfing energy washed over him again, not so tentative this time. Less like a lapping tide and more like a wave.

Familiarity, but unclear. Like a path decided but not known. A deep, certain knowledge unearthed, ancient but seemingly new as well.

The warm embrace ebbed away again. Oscar was ready for its departure this time, bracing himself against Dmitri and shivering slightly as it did. He noticed Marcus' guest was watching him again, a faint smile on their plump lips.

"They like you, Oscar." Marcus sounded excited. "They hardly like anyone."

"Well, they can keep their distance." Dmitri's voice was steely. "And no more of that emotional communication. I am not comfortable with this."

"Marcus, who is this? What is an ethernal, and why does this feel so dangerous?" Zara stood stiffly, glancing toward Dmitri as though taking cues from how to respond to this potential threat.

"That felt so...strange. That's their name?" Oscar said dreamily. "I felt like...like I was remembering something. Like I was hearing just the first few beats of an old song I loved but had forgotten all about."

Oscar felt a pleasant tingle run across his skin.

"They like that." Marcus grinned. "They said you can call them Song if you like."

"What? How do you know that? How are they talking to you?" Zara looked between the two, confused.

"They are soul-bonded," Dmitri growled darkly.

"Oh, now *that* sounds dangerous." Zara's disapproving stare turned on Marcus, who tried to give her his most charming smile in return.

"Paige is returning; let us discuss this more later." Dmitri's eyes were dulling back to their stormy grey, from flames to ash.

As if on cue, Paige appeared in the doorway, sidestepping past Song and returning to her seat on the sofa, where she sat stiffly, looking around the silent room. "Why the fuck is everyone acting so weird?"

∽

Song busied themself in the corner, where they found a large plant interesting them enough to examine its veined leaves as Dmitri observed them, expression unfathomable. Paige took the opportunity to change seats and was now sitting a little too close to Dmitri, regaling him with stories about New York to a very subdued response. Oscar, overwhelmed with curiosity, had moved to sit on the wide leather arm of Marcus' chair. Zara knelt beside them, her eyes bright with concern.

"Soul-bonded?" Oscar asked quietly.

Marcus nodded. "It just means we're linked. We can share things and communicate. It's really nice. I never feel lonely anymore."

"What's an ethernal?" Zara leaned closer.

"Ah, that one is definitely a discussion for when Paige leaves." Marcus grinned, scratching his head. "Besides, we have more important things to catch up about."

"You have questions about my travels and what things I saw? For your encyclopaedia?" Oscar asked.

"Taxonomy," Marcus corrected. "And yes, but also other questions I thought of whilst you were away."

"Like?"

"Like what's going on in the old weenie department these days? I know his teeth changed into fangs, but is there like a whole knotting situation now?" Marcus' eyes widened in anticipation.

"A *whatting?*" Oscar answered, confused.

"Come away, Oscar. Nothing good will come of this conversation for your sweet little mind." Zara grabbed his arm in preparation to drag him off.

48

There was a heavy thud from somewhere upstairs.

"What was that?" Marcus frowned, eyes shifting to the ceiling.

"Probably just Ed," Oscar said thoughtfully. *Though it is unlike him to cause a ruckus when he knows something important is happening.* Wondering, Oscar turned his gaze back to Dmitri, who was now sitting bolt upright, looking alarmed. "Dmitri, what's—"

"Paige, it has been a pleasure meeting you, but I think it is best if you leave." Dmitri had an uncharacteristic urgency in his voice. "I have...something bad has happened, and there is an emergency. You need to go now."

"Oh. Shit. Did I say something wrong? What's going on?" Paige looked around, confused.

"There's a fire...upstairs." Dmitri stood quickly, bouncing to his feet and shifting around the coffee table to move to the door.

"Wait, how do you know that? Why would that need only *me* to go?" Paige asked in angry bafflement. "What the fuck is going on?"

The thudding from upstairs got louder. Plaster showered down from around the light fitting.

"What is that?" Paige recoiled in her seat.

Dmitri cast a desperate look at Oscar. "Zara, would you kindly assist me, please? With the fire." And with that, he was gone.

Zara stood quickly, casting a worried look at Oscar and Marcus before following to the door. She'd barely gotten there when there was a massive crash from outside.

"What the fuck!" Paige shrieked.

Something careened into Zara, knocking her forcefully into the room and sprawling back onto the sofa, her head landing in Paige's lap and knocking her glass full of wine all over her blouse. "Jesus Christ," Paige howled, possibly more horrified by the claret on her shirt than the thing clambering on top of Zara.

It was the gaeant. *Only it wasn't.* This one must have only been about three feet tall, but its crumbling, muddy limbs were still strong on its squat and powerful body. It let out a wheezing cry as it raised a fist like a club at Zara. Paige finally registered what was happening and laid eyes on the thing, letting out a howling scream. She tossed her glass right at it, shattering it ineffectively on its earthen features.

Zara lashed out with a sharp jab and a glowing impression of her fist, four times the size of her hand, pummelled into the beast, sending it flying off her and into the top of the door frame where it shattered in two in a spray of earth and debris.

"Gaeant?" Zara panted, turning her head to look at Oscar still in Paige's lap.

"Uh-huh." His eyes shifted between the shattered remnants of the thing on the floor and Paige's horrified face.

"I thought those were big?" Marcus chimed, far too relaxed beside him.

"They are," Oscar said, confused. "I mean, it was. That one was barely the size of the other one's arm." He chewed his lip fiercely, then froze. "Oh no."

There was another loud thud from the hallway and a roar of anger that sounded like Dmitri.

"Oscar." Zara sat up, brushing flakes of earth off her jumper. "Exactly how many parts did Dmitri cut that thing into?"

7

THE DOMESTIC DISTURBERS

"S...seven. I think seven," Oscar yammered, eyes fixed on Paige, who was giving him a look of utter horror. He tried to remember.

Two legs, two arms, the head, and the body had been split in two, right? Or was it three?

"Fine." Zara's face became a mask of serenity, all business. "Stay in here; I'll go and help Dmitri. Don't open up the door unless I knock three times."

Oscar nodded mutely.

"This...*Song*. Can they protect you?" Zara asked briskly.

"We'll be fine." Marcus waved a hand, smiling, voice full of certainty.

Zara gave a single nod and rushed out of the door, slamming it shut behind her.

Paige, wine stain spreading further on her pristine blouse, was up in a flash and dashed toward the chair where Marcus still sat with Oscar beside him.

"Oscar, what the fuck is happening?" she snarled. It seemed fear was beginning to shift to anger.

"Uhhhh." Oscar searched desperately for an excuse.

"Don't even think about lying to me, you little shit. Every one of you knew what that thing was. I knew there was something dodgy going on when your boyfriend looked like *that*. What is he? A witch? Some kind of lich that wants to attach himself to you and drain you of your life-force in return for sexy favours?"

Oscar stared at her numbly. "What?"

"Oh, I've seen shit like this before," she snapped angrily. "I lived in New York, for Christ's sake. It all started when I fucked some guy who claimed to be a leprechaun after I'd had an edible, but Oscar, what the fuck is going on?"

Oscar shook his head as though doing so may clear his thoughts. *Paige...knows? About monsters?*

There was a loud crash from above and the sound of breaking glass.

"Oh, you're right in the shit here, aren't you, Oscar? I knew it!" Paige sneered. "Is this one here? This weird silent one, what can they do?" Her eyes were wild and frenzied as she waved a hand in Song's direction. Song watched her gesticulate with interest. "What is it that's even out there?"

Oscar's stomach twisted inside him. "I...It's something we brought back. From Prague. Dmitri and Zara will take care of it."

There was another crash from upstairs, and Oscar heard a loud growl. *That must be Ed.*

"I'm leaving," Paige said sharply, turning toward the door.

"No! You can't! They're out there, and they might hurt you. Zara said to wait here," Oscar pleaded.

"And what's she going to do? Terrify them with that fucking ugly jumper?" Paige snapped.

"You didn't see what she did to the one that smashed on the doorway?" Marcus asked.

Paige shrugged irritably, eyes scanning the cracked wood and marked wall there. "Knocked it off, I suppose."

Marcus laughed richly. "She kicked its ass. She's a regular

weird-whacker. Between her and Dmitri, they'll have this under control in minutes, so just take a seat, eat a snack, and hang out."

Paige's thin lips twisted in irritation. "I don't do what you tell me."

There was a heavy thud against the door.

Paige startled, twisting in the direction of the sound.

Another heavy thud followed just after.

"That was two knocks," Paige murmured hopefully. "Maybe it's Zara—"

The third knock was far more of a crash. The door splintered in its frame and split in half. Paige screamed loudly.

Song, who stood closest to the door, stepped aside, watching with interest.

"Marcus, you said they would help us," Oscar howled.

"I said we'd be fine." Marcus sounded unfazed.

Paige retreated, huddling behind the chair Marcus sat on, her fingers snatching at the latches on the windows.

"They're locked," Oscar shouted. "Only had them fitted recently, and the keys are in the kitchen."

"WELL, THAT'S NO FUCKING GOOD, IS IT!" Paige roared.

The split door fell aside as one of the mini-gaeants ambled in. Its hollowed eye sockets scanned around the room, slipping off Song and finding their way to Oscar. It let out a wheezing bark that sent a cough of dry earth free.

"Oscar," Paige whispered hoarsely.

Another small earth monster strode in beside it. This one was slightly larger, its limbs thicker and heavier. More than strong enough to break bones and crush throats.

"Two of them? Really?" Paige moaned.

In unison, the two gaeants set forth at a lurching run. One paused to thrust aside the coffee table with a powerful heave, scattering the snacks and drinks across the floor with a crash.

"OSCAR!" Paige screamed, making herself as small as possible.

Their pounding feet covered the space in no time at all, and with a powerful heave, they thrust themselves into the air, hurtling with the force of a cannonball at Oscar and Marcus. Oscar cringed, dodging to one side as quickly as he could, clumsily backing into the bookcase.

Marcus never moved. He sat calmly on the chair as the things bouldered through the air. And then they just...stopped. They hung frozen in the air, curled in on themselves, like tiny planets.

Oscar's eyes travelled back to Marcus. His hands were raised up before him, shaking slightly at the effort, a look of concentration on his face. "So..." Marcus cringed. "We still kind of have a lot to talk about."

THE LUBBER-FIEND

(HOMINUM PRODIGIUM)

8

MAGICK WITH A K

P aige sat on the floor, mascara smudged down her cheeks and covered in wine, her back propped against the flipped over coffee-table. She blew out a thick plume of cigarette smoke, then popped one of the fallen nibbles into her mouth and chewed it angrily.

"That's all of them." Dmitri dusted off his shirt, which was torn in several places. Other than that, and a split in his eyebrow already half-healed, he seemed fairly unscathed. His hair had come unbound and hung more than a little wildly around his face.

"I got three." Zara flicked a lump of plaster off her shoulder. "And we put what was left of them in the lock-boxes down in the basement. Even those sturdy little bastards shouldn't be able to break out of those if they reform again."

"Well, at least one good thing came out of all of this. Your jumper's ruined." Paige let out another noxious plume before picking up a toppled wine bottle from the floor. Finding it had some left inside, she hefted it and took a swig.

"I dealt with one, and Ed finished another. With the two Marcus handled, that should be all of them," Dmitri said.

"Hooray, we can count." Paige raised her bottle in a toast.

"Did we know that would happen? I mean not *that*, but that they could regenerate?" Oscar was curled up on one of the large sofas feeling shaken. He was plenty grateful when Dmitri sat beside him, curling an arm around his shoulders.

"I did not even suspect," Dmitri admitted. "Though now it does make sense. That is why the czarownica said it didn't matter if the creature lived or died. It would always just come back anyway."

"The who's a what now?" Marcus asked curiously.

"The witch we consulted in Krakow," Dmitri replied.

Oscar shivered, and Dmitri pulled him closer.

"Well, that's just great, isn't it? Fucking lovely." Paige smiled sharply and took another puff on her cigarette. Oscar hadn't had the strength to ask her not to light it indoors. "We all had a lovely time, ruined my three-hundred-quid shirt, and vanquished some weird little rock demons." She let off another plume of smoke. "Don't get me wrong. To ruin Zara's jumper, the shirt was worth it. I would volunteer it as tribute a hundred times over. The real evil has been defeated today with that jumper."

"Enough." Zara dropped onto the couch. "Aren't you in shock or something after seeing those things?"

"She knows about monsters," Oscar interjected. "She had some experience in New York."

Paige popped the cigarette out from between her lips for a moment. "Fucked a leprechaun," she said before popping it back in—as though that answered everything.

"Right." Zara frowned. "Maybe we should take you back to your hotel?"

"Nah, fuck it," Paige mumbled into the neck of the wine bottle. She took a gulp, then pointed at Marcus with her free hand. "He's in trouble. I wanna see what happens next."

Everyone's eyes shifted toward Marcus.

He sat legs crossed on the chair, Song beside him, eyes wide with interest.

"I helped," Marcus offered, flashing his teeth.

"With magick. Magick with a K. Not like, 'let me wrap you up in these hankies I had up my sleeve,' but real 'don't let the virgin light the black flame candle' bullshit." Zara scowled. "How?"

Marcus cast a searching look toward Dmitri for help.

"The soul-bond." Dmitri's voice was low and dark.

A tense silence hung in the air.

"Well, tell us what that is then, pretty boy. We're not all in the fucking know." Paige took another puff.

"You could call it magick, as it is perceived as such. At least to eyes trained by modern means. What it really is, is an exchange." Dmitri's gaze fixed on Marcus, who stared right back. "Song is an ethernal. They dwell in the space between realities. Neither here nor there. Shifting probability, influencing outcome, ensuring change. They are agents of chaos. Powerful and immortal."

Oscar stared at Song. They were watching Marcus now, with more than interest. *With devotion.*

"Give any being everything, and they will find what they don't have. They need it. In some cases, this results in a bond with humans. So they can experience their suffering," Dmitri continued.

"Do you know many other instances, Dmitri? I could only find two no matter where I looked," Marcus asked excitedly.

"A few," Dmitri admitted. "Though I have only seen it once firsthand."

"What does that mean? Experience their suffering?" Zara asked, her voice brittle.

"Once a bond is made, they perform an exchange. They anchor themselves to a human and feed upon their perceived and actual weaknesses. The imperfections and frailties they endure so they can experience it for themselves. In return, they give power. It is incremental, equivalent, and irreversible."

Zara's eyes flashed, and she looked angrily back at Marcus.

"It's not so bad, honestly! I just gave Song my short sightedness and a bit of my tiredness so far. It's actually really good—"

"Marcus, those things are part of what makes you human!" Zara snapped.

"Oh, you're one to talk," Marcus scoffed.

"What's that supposed to mean?"

"Well, shit." Paige popped her cigarette stub into the now-empty wine bottle. "Doesn't sound bad. Where can I get one of these ephemerals?"

"Ethernals," Dmitri corrected. "They only connect with certain individuals on this plane. Those with exceptional sensitivity to the veil. And it is nothing to envy. Once the process begins, it is constant. Only the ethernal themselves may end the bond. Either that or the one bound eventually loses their humanity."

"And then?" Zara's voice was more than a little shrill.

Dmitri's eyes fixed on Marcus again, filled with concern.

"I know what I'm doing," Marcus said. "Song and I have something special. They—"

"They love you," Dmitri finished for him.

Marcus nodded, face stiff.

"They always do."

"Wait, wait, wait." Paige turned around to look at Dmitri. "So why him? What makes him so fancy?"

Dmitri sighed. "Some are more delicate to the shift between worlds, even those who have not travelled between them or have the touch of the other within them. I suspected this may be the case, as Marcus has shown some sensitivity before. He notices some things before even I have sensed them. I first wondered back at the cemetery; he seemed to sense the Gwyllgi before even Gax."

"Wait." Oscar's voice was hoarse. "Is this what the Bean-Nighe was talking about? Why she kissed your forehead?"

"Bean eye?" Paige asked faintly.

"Bean-Nighe," four voices echoed in unison. Marcus chuckled softly.

"You didn't tell me about that, Oscar," Dmitri said softly.

Oscar blushed. "I forgot."

"It may have been," Dmitri agreed. "Though messages are rarely a straight line with her."

"Rarely a bloody zigzag either," Zara mumbled.

"So, this is nice and all, but I still don't have the sweet fucking foggiest what is going on." Paige folded her arms, leaning back. "Why is all of this happening, and why are you even involved with this shit, Oscar?"

Oscar looked around his friends and Dmitri in a silent plea. Dmitri simply took his hand and gave him an encouraging smile.

Oscar swallowed. "Our ancestor, Paige. We had an ancestor who was pulled across to the other realm, which some people believe is hell, but is really the other side to the coin of *this* world. The yin to its yang. The balance on its scale."

Paige tutted. "He got dragged there, and for all the luck of the Irish, he clawed his way back. Before he died, he managed to sow some seed with his poor wife, and they pumped out generations of babies that may or may not carry the skanky taint of the underworld," she finished in monotone.

Oscar froze. "Uhm, yeah."

"I got told all that by Mum when we were little. But I thought it was a load of bullshit she made up to make us feel special."

"Not quite," Oscar murmured.

"Visio Tnugdali," Marcus said thoughtfully.

Several sets of eyes turned his way.

"Twelfth-century religious text. Talks about the Irish knight Tnugdalus, progenitor of the Tundales. Chronicles his other-worldly visions."

Silence.

"What, did y'all forget I was a nerd?" Marcus shrugged.

"No one forgot, babe," Zara said softly.

Paige stiffened, turning her head angrily and rounding on Oscar. "Wait. Are you fucking telling me it's *you*?"

Oscar smiled weakly.

"Generations of Tundales? Soldiers, scientists, and bona fide heroes, and it's *you*?" Her face twisted with disgust.

Oscar's heart sunk.

"It is no gift." Dmitri's voice was stern. "It is a curse. He has been hunted. Searched for by those that seek to harm him or use him as a key to access that world at the cost of his life and countless others."

Paige scoffed. "Sure, right, I get that. But...Oscar?" She waved her hand at him as if to illustrate her point. "He's so...*bleh*."

Dmitri stiffened beside him, and Oscar put his hand on his forearm to settle him down. He had no such chance or luxury for Zara.

"Oscar has done more for people than you could even imagine, Paige. Whilst you were off living your dreams in New York, he was in London, working his arse off. Getting hunted and fighting to survive. I doubt you would have managed to show that kind of strength, given you are so..." She waved a dismissive hand in mimicry. "Bleh."

Needles jammed their way into Oscar's heart as he watched Zara's eyes flash with contempt. *She's so proud of me, and it's because she doesn't know.* He'd never told any of them, of course, least of all Dmitri.

He'd never admitted what happened that night the dark-eyed, girl-shaped monster, the acheri, had appeared in his flat.

I'm not strong like you think I am, Zara. Not like any of you think I am.

Paige snorted with laughter. "Oh, well, that explains it all a bit more." She turned, shooting a vindictive smile in Dmitri's direction. "What about you, Count Snack-ula? What are you, and why are you interested in my brother? Are you a good monster or a bad monster?"

"He's good," Marcus interrupted. "He's joined us. He's like our Scrappy-doo."

Paige smirked. "I'd say you're the Scrappy, and he's the Fred."

Marcus' eyes widened, and he pressed his hand to his chest. "Ouch."

"I love Oscar." Dmitri's voice was iron. Oscar's heart was beginning to race in his chest in the most unpleasant way. A way he'd not experienced in a long time. *Am I going to have a panic attack?*

Paige snorted derisively again. "Right. Because of his ambition and winning personality?" she sneered. "Or is it the magic in his blood?"

Oscar's skin turned cold, and his breathing became ragged. *Yep. Here it comes.* His vision was darkening at the edges, and he huddled his knees into his chest.

Dmitri pulled him close, almost entirely onto his lap.

His lips were at Oscar's ear, whispering softly. Oscar only caught parts, could only understand parts. He was speaking Romanian, Oscar realised, his native tongue, quickly and quietly. Oscar had no idea what the words meant, but threading through them, he heard one familiar word: lubite. *My love.* Oscar felt his breath coming steadier, matching Dmitri's own expanding chest against his back.

"I think you should go." Zara's voice was tinny in Oscar's ears.

"Gladly." Paige clambered to her feet, dusting off her trousers as she did. "This really is a fine fucking mess you've gotten yourself into, Oscar. You and your friends. I don't know what's worse: you and whatever *he* is, or this one selling his soul to that one with the coat over there for magic jazz hands. Hold that—maybe it's the sourpuss with a spirit stuck up her arse."

Oscar was only faintly aware of Zara's snappy retort because Dmitri had stiffened again beside him, then he heard it. The sound of the front door opening with a click, creaking on its hinges, and closing firmly. Then, sharp, clear footsteps.

Whatever Paige had been saying, she stopped short and turned to stare at the woman who entered through the doorway. A woman Oscar had never seen before.

She was beautiful in a pinched sort of way. She looked like the type of woman who would always want to speak to the manager no matter how good a job you did. Her light blonde hair was coiled on top of her head in two intricate rolls, and her pale skin was livened strikingly by her heavily blushed cheeks and vivid pink lipstick. She wore a long hounds-tooth coat that went all the way to the floor, with only the slightest glimpse of emerald-green pointed toes peeking from beneath. She clutched her white leather purse firmly to her chest as her eyes ran around the room slowly. Heavy blue jewels hung from her earlobes. Nothing about her matched per se, but everything went together uncannily.

Dmitri let out a noise that sounded close to a hiss.

"Well, I can't say I like what you've done with the place, Dmitri." She brushed aside a piece of rubble with one emerald pump. "Not as nice as it used to be, especially with these wretched humans strewn all over the place," she simpered, her accent prim and proper, a delicate English rose.

"Tildy," Dmitri snarled. "You are not welcome here."

"Oh, now, now. No need to be like that!" She waved a white-gloved hand at Dmitri daintily.

"Who are you?" Oscar asked, dazed, his breath finally finding its rhythm.

The woman's eyes, a crystalline icy blue, locked onto Oscar, and she examined him the way she might something ugly she found stuck to the bottom of her shoe. "I'm Tildy Darlington. Dmitri's wife. And who, might I ask, are you?"

INTERLUDE THE FIRST: WHEN DARKNESS MEETS

Harry Barlow, or Barloh as he'd been known on countless online conspiracy sites, was dead.

The thing that wore his body like an ill-fitting, moth-eaten suit moved his limbs like a putrefying meat puppet down the path beside the river. The memories of the man told it this was London's Southbank. It was empty, though the man's memories said the days saw it full of wretched humans and their ridiculous squawking offspring. What terrible creatures they were, spending most of their existence decaying slowly from within. Their thin threads of life held almost no power; the only pulsing beat sustaining its current shell was the deep hate the man had carried within. Hate stronger than most in this vile place. It had barely needed to submerge itself beneath his surface to bathe in it like an ocean of molten misery.

Most of the spiteful memories of this broken soul were not of interest, but one particular memory had drawn it here. A memory branded so deep it burned through every layer of the man's psyche. It just so happened that it was the end of a particular thread of power in this place that may just help. Not a strong thread, but it would lend purchase enough for now.

The thing that rode the man's remains knew everything he had known and more. It also knew what it was, why it was, and what it must do. It stared at the worn, dark steps leading down to the riverbank and sneered. In a blink, it shifted, dragging the man's remains through the shadows and reappearing down beside the river. Slowly, it strode in, and then it waited.

It waited for as long as it took until what it searched for grew near.

Eyes like oil slicks opened in the deep foul flowing filth of the city. Its essence thrummed. Several small fish nibbled at one of its rotting vessel's fingers, and the creature allowed it with disinterest. Then, a slick tendril tentatively passed through the murky depths nearby, searching. In a flash, it shifted and snatched the tendril in a decaying fist. The wisping, slick fibres pulled with all their might, but the corpse's face contorted in a grim smile, as it wound the thread around its hands, and began to pull.

The creature howled as she was dragged onto the shore.

She was a pitiful thing. Shrivelled and weak compared to what she should have been. A pale and sickly mockery of her ancestors. 'Jenny Greenteeth,' the corpse's memories named her. When the vessel had lived, been a child, she had drowned his father before his very eyes. Tried to drown him, too. Now, her dark eyes fixed on the dead body of the man that had come from that boy.

She snatched out with pale hands and ragged nails that tore the rotting flesh at its throat and cheek. Using her control of fluids in this place, she pushed her influence upon it. Water burbled from the corpse's throat and bubbled as it laughed wetly. She was trying to drown it from within. As if it needed to breathe.

That this creature had some small power was good, however. It moved to one knee and closed the corpse's fingers over the river hag's throat. She snarled, flashing mossy teeth. In return, the thing riding inside the corpse pulled on the shadows, drawing in their strength, and squeezed.

Her throat crushed easily between its fingers, the pale green flesh giving way and dark eyes widening as a thick, green liquid gushed free from her ruined neck. Another stream of sickly gore poured from the corner of her already slackening mouth.

It watched her die. It barely took a moment.

Something thrummed inside the corpse, a deep jolt of power. A roar of absolution.

It smiled.

Oh yes.

Some part of this man still clung deep within. His hatred must have been deeper than it had ever imagined. Good. The pulsing hate was a font of energy, like a pump of blood into these rotting limbs.

The human had hated this thing. Despised it. This creature, this Jenny Greenteeth, had ruined his life.

No. He had let it.

It lifted the human's rotting fist, full of the pulped meat of the river hag, and pressed it into the dead man's mouth. It gulped down the pulverised tissue as quickly as it could, whilst the power was still fresh. Theians *were* creatures of power, not like the mewling, festering animals of this place. Even weaklings such as this one bore the thrum of glorious energy. It was not much, but there was more of it yet.

And there was more to be found. More power in this world to be harvested, stronger beings that could be used. *And that was just the meat of it.*

Smiling, the creature pulled on the shadows once more and began tearing the river hag apart. There was work to be done.

❧ II ❧
A SHADOW & A THREAT

9

THE NAME OF THE DARK

The room exploded in a cacophony of voices.

Sometimes, when terrible things happened, Oscar felt like everything stopped. Like a moment was frozen, and he was helpless within it. This was nothing like that at all. Instead, Oscar had stopped. He couldn't speak, or move, or even think, but everything around him was just getting worse.

"Get out. I don't want you here," Dmitri snarled; his body was shaking with fury against Oscar's.

Zara's eyes were murder, fixed on the sharply dressed woman. "Who exactly did you say you were?"

Marcus was mumbling to himself; Oscar thought he might be repeating everything the woman had said as if trying to make sense of it. Paige stood in the middle of the room, eyes wide and grinning.

Oscar felt the crushing weight of their voices piling on top of him, burying him in their din. Tildy stood before them, still smiling faintly, her hands crossed daintily where she held her purse at her chest. There was a cruel sparkle in her eyes, and they were fixed entirely upon Oscar.

When he spoke, every other voice finally quietened, and the words were ragged in his throat. "What did you say?"

Tildy laughed softly, a sound like tinkling bells. "I'm Dmitri's wife, darling. And who are you? The new houseboy?"

Bile rose in Oscar's throat and wondered if he might throw up.

"She is not my wife," Dmitri spat, then his brow furrowed. "Not for a very long time."

"Till death do us part, my love, and we both still seem to be breathing," Tildy simpered, looking pleased with herself.

Oscar heard the sound of Dmitri's flipper grinding between his pointed teeth.

"Oscar," his voice was low and urgent. "Let me explain. Please."

Oscar turned his head, staring at him numbly. Dmitri's pale eyes never left the woman.

His wife.

"It was a long time ago. Very long," Dmitri said.

Oscar nodded. His throat was entirely too dry to speak anymore.

"Now, now, darling. That seems very close to revealing a lady's age." Tildy smirked. She looked around the room, arching an eyebrow. "I must say, your hospitality is not what it was. As an unexpected caller, I can forgive the mess, but you could at least have the houseboy fetch me some tea."

"Enough, Tildy," Dmitri barked. He shifted away from Oscar and stood. In a few short strides, he was beside her, his hand snatched out around her wrist, forearm bulging as he squeezed her with enough force to powder bone. Human bone, at least.

Tildy, for her part, looked positively thrilled. "Goodness, sweetheart, do control yourself in front of the guests. You're practically ravishing me on the spot." She added a conspiratorial wink to Oscar and whispered loudly, "He really is such a wild man when his passions take hold. Simply feral."

Oscar's stomach sunk even deeper. *This woman was Dmitri's wife. Dmitri was married.*

"I think I need to go." Oscar stood on unsteady legs.

"Oscar, please," Dmitri begged.

"I'll come with you." Zara glared fiercely at Dmitri.

Oh, well, there goes that budding friendship.

"I think that's best." Tildy's smile was sickly-sweet. "My husband and I have a lot to discuss."

"This is brilliant." Paige's eyes were sparkling with glee as she looked between Tildy and Dmitri.

"Stop," Marcus said suddenly. Everyone turned to look at him. Song stood behind his chair, their interest now drawn to the sky outside through the window. But every bit of Marcus' intense focus was upon the new arrival. "She's scared."

Tildy stiffened, the smug smile fixed upon her face. "I beg your pardon?"

"Terrified, actually." Marcus grinned; his eyes sparkled with mischief.

Dmitri growled and released her wrist. Oscar was sure he would see her flesh blanched or bruising from his grip, but it remained like unspoiled porcelain. Dmitri backed away cautiously, like a cornered wolf. "What's going on, Tildy? Why are you here?"

Tildy gave an uncomfortable laugh, eyes scanning around the room. "Well, darling, it's complicated, you see. Something seems to be after me, and I didn't know where else to go."

Dmitri stared at her. "After *you*? What would possibly be after *you*?"

Oscar caught something other than hatred in his voice in those words. Respect? He felt deep jealousy spread through his chest.

Tildy raised gloved fingers to her lips nervously. Her pale blue eyes were wide and slightly wild.

"Something bad," Marcus answered grimly. "Really bad."

73

Tildy's shoulders sagged. "You know, I really could go for that tea."

～

OSCAR WASN'T sure how long he had spent in the bathroom, sitting on the floor with his head between his knees, before Zara's voice came softly from the other side of the door. "Booboo, are you okay?"

"I'm fine." Oscar's voice croaked in a fair imitation of Gax, the cemetery Bugge who had a voice like a huge toad.

"Can I come in? I mean, unless..."

Oscar twisted his body, reaching up to flick the lock and move out of the way of the door at his back. The handle twisted and Zara slipped in, closing the door behind her. Her golden-brown eyes were deep with concern as she sat on the closed toilet lid and crossed her hands in her lap. Oscar reached up and twisted the latch again, locking those problems out, if only for a few more minutes.

Zara watched him patiently, waiting for him to speak for several moments. Oscar had nothing to say.

"I can kick Dmitri's ass. Or Tildy's," Zara offered. "Hey, I can do both, and I'll even throw Paige in as a special offer. Smash up two little bitches and get one free?"

Oscar gave her a woeful look.

"I'm sorry." Zara shook her head. "I don't know what to say. I've never been in this situation before."

"I don't know if anyone has been in this situation before," Oscar moaned.

"Fair," Zara agreed.

Oscar dropped his head back between his knees and closed his eyes.

"We can leave. Let them work out whatever is going on. Drink hot chocolate and watch trashy movies with hot people in them and rank them in order of preference. I'll make you a cheese toastie, and we can just lie in bed and sleep and complain. You don't have to do this. You don't have to be here," Zara said.

Oscar nodded, chewing his lip. "I think...I think maybe I do."

Zara's eyes widened in surprise.

"I mean, something is after her. It might have something to do with the world parallaxes. It could be related to everything else. Dmitri seems upset. He—"

"Has a wife." Zara's words cut in like a razor.

Oscar winced.

"Did he tell you? I'm guessing not, but seriously! I don't care whether he married her ten years ago or ten thousand, if the bitch is still alive, you tell the person you're dating."

Oscar gnawed his lip. He had no response for that.

"I don't know, Oscar. It's a shitty hand to be dealt, and I see what you're saying. All I'm telling you is you have every right to walk away from the table right now and come back with a fresh head. You can wait until there are fewer sharks in the water before you try to wade your way through it."

"Maybe," Oscar agreed sadly. "But maybe it's worse to not work it out right away. It could just be a big misunderstanding."

Zara huffed. "Misunderstandings don't usually include lifelong vows, but sure. Whatever you want to do, Booboo, I'm by your side. Just point if you want me to, you know, give anyone a bit of a light bashing."

Oscar smiled weakly. "Okay."

"Okay then." Zara reached out and held out her hand. "Shall we go?"

Those words made his stomach do a cartwheel. Oscar shook his head. "Just...five more minutes."

IF THE HOUSEWARMING had been strange and awkward before, it was a surreal hellscape now. The coffee table had been flipped right side up again and the majority of the snacks and debris picked up from the floor. Marcus remained in his seat by the window. Song perched on the arm of his chair, large golden eyes fixed on Ed, who sat in the shape of a spaniel on Dmitri's knee on one couch. Ed was shivering slightly and completely fixated on Tildy, who sat on the opposite sofa, delicately holding a teacup between her now ungloved fingers, revealing pointed nails lacquered navy. Her large coat was gone, displaying a pristine powder blue blazer with a ruffled white collar foaming around her throat. A matching powder blue skirt hugged her hips like a second skin, legs crossed, one emerald pump bouncing anxiously. She looked...*expensive*.

"Where's Paige?" Oscar asked gruffly.

"She went to smoke a cigarette out back. Said she...wait, what were her exact words? 'I need a break from this shitshow'?" Marcus chirped merrily.

"Quite the character, that one." Tildy smirked over her teacup.

"Oscar." Dmitri sounded forlorn. He gestured to the space beside him on the couch. Zara's eyes narrowed, but she did not speak as Oscar moved to sit beside him. Instead, she followed and squashed in at his other side, sandwiching him between the two of them. One of her hands quickly darted out to take Oscar's.

"Oscar." Dmitri's eyes were sorrowful and pleading. "I'm so sorry."

Oscar tried his best to keep his face stiff.

"Sensitive little flower, isn't he?" Tildy mused. "Not your usual type at all."

Dmitri growled.

"Oscar, is it? I'm sorry for making such a dramatic entrance; I truly am. But as your rather strangely insightful friend says, I find myself in somewhat of a pinch." Her words were clipped, and she shot a disdainful look at Marcus. "How exactly is it you knew about that anyway? Is it something to do with the one wearing the ridiculous coat beside you?"

If the pressure Oscar had felt in the air earlier from Song had been a gentle wave, this one was a whip crack. Fortunately, it was not directed at him. Tildy flinched, her legs shivering. *Sheer displeasure, disdain at being addressed disrespectfully. Threatening impatience.*

"Oh goodness." Tildy's teacup rattled in its saucer as she quirked an eyebrow, her voice quivering slightly. "An ethernal. My, my, Dmitri. You are keeping a strange crowd for a tea party these days." She took a sip of tea.

"Explain yourself, Tildy. You have no welcome here to wear out, so make it quick." Dmitri's voice was molten steel.

"Very well," Tildy sighed, setting down her cup. "The ethernal and their meal were quite correct. Something was hunting me. Still is, I believe."

"And what could be a threat to one such as you?" Dmitri asked.

Again, the words prickled Oscar. *Who was this woman to be so free from threats?*

"That's the thing, sweetheart," Tildy simpered. "I'm not quite sure. All I can say is, whatever it was slaughtered Alouicious and ripped Vander to shreds."

Dmitri stiffened.

"Friends of yours?" Zara asked sharply.

"Absolutely not," Dmitri replied. "But incredibly powerful beings. Stronger even than Lyn Ocampo was."

Zara's jaw clenched so tight, a muscle jumped in her cheek at the mention of the name.

"So, whatever killed them is strong enough to hurt you?" Oscar asked softly.

"So it would seem," Tildy bit off a tart reply.

Dmitri made a small, thoughtful sound beside him.

"There's something she isn't telling you." Marcus leaned forward, his gaze fixed on Tildy.

Tildy made an intricate show of ignoring him.

"Out with it, Tildy," Dmitri said firmly.

Tildy let out a withering sigh. "All I know is that it's old. Older than anything I've ever seen before. Older than time, perhaps. I made a narrow escape from the house where it finished Vander. It is a being of pure darkness. Almost like—"

"An Umbran?" Dmitri asked, confused.

Tildy swallowed and nodded, looking like her composure was suddenly difficult to maintain.

Marcus gasped, his head snapping around to look at Song. Oscar could only imagine they had shared some information with him through their link.

"Forgetting there's no way an Umbran should be on this plane, what would it want with you?" Dmitri asked. "What have you done, Tildy? Umbrans do not typically attack, let alone one of our kind."

Tildy offered a baffled smile, pouring herself more tea. "Your guess is as good as mine, darling. I haven't the foggiest."

Dmitri grunted.

There was a rattle of footsteps as Paige returned down the hallway and leaned against the shattered doorway. Her attention was on the phone in her hand, and she spared a disinterested glance around the room. "Well, this has been charming and all, but I think I'm going to go home and remove my fingernails with some pliers."

"Oh, I can do that for you, dear," Tildy simpered. "If only to repay the crimes you have committed against those shoes."

Paige's thin lips curled in irritation, razor-thin, and climbing right under her nose. "That's fine, thanks. I know a couple of other drag queens, and neither of them are the best nail technicians."

Tildy gave a rich and throaty laugh.

"So, what now?" Zara asked gruffly, folding her arms.

"We need to know more." Dmitri shook his head. "We have no idea what this threat is or what it wants. Perhaps Paige should stay here until we have a clearer idea of what is going on."

Paige rolled her eyes, and Zara sighed.

"It's time for another terrifying adventure," Marcus chimed excitedly. "We're back, bitch. The sequel; electric boogaloo."

"We should get more information," Dmitri continued, rubbing his hands together thoughtfully. "We may have to seek advice to decide how to proceed."

Zara groaned. "Seriously? Are you going to say what I think you're going to say?"

Dmitri nodded, his eyes meeting hers. "We need to talk to the Bean-Nighe."

10

AIR POCKETS

The bedroom door clicked shut behind Dmitri. He did not turn for a long breath, and when he did, his eyes were earnest and full of sorrow.

"Oscar, please forgive me."

Oscar dropped onto the edge of the bed. Every muscle in his body felt fit to spasm, tense beyond belief. Strangely, he hadn't felt this way through all the months of running from monsters. He hadn't really felt this way since before he'd met Dmitri. Well, since shortly after properly meeting him, at least.

"Are you angry?" Dmitri asked softly.

"I'm tired." Oscar's voice sounded beyond that word—even to himself.

Dmitri bowed his head and frowned sympathetically. "Tildy was a terrible mistake I made a long time ago. Before I ever met you. Well, it was before the Industrial Revolution technically."

Oscar shook his head. "I don't know what that means, Dmitri."

"Centuries."

Oscar's eyes narrowed. Dmitri had still never told him his age, but that was as close as he had come. *Centuries? Plural?* "I just...how could you not tell me you're married? Or were? It seems like something you should have mentioned."

Dmitri dropped beside him on the bed, watching him intently. The cool focus of his eyes had unsettled Oscar in the past, but he had come to learn that Dmitri wasn't weighing or measuring. He was simply giving him his full attention—something so profoundly unhuman he couldn't believe he hadn't realised the man was a monster sooner.

Downstairs, the voices were barely audible, but he could hear Paige's crisp tone cutting through the rest of the murmuring. She hadn't been happy to be told she couldn't leave. *Had Paige ever been happy to be told what to do?*

"There's too much I don't know, Dmitri. Even now. About you and the world I didn't know I lived in. I mean, I knew you had been with other people, but it's one thing knowing and another being presented with your *wife*." Oscar swallowed thickly after he managed to say the word out loud.

"Tildy was an incredibly dark time in my life. With her and the others she mentioned. Let's just say it was a tryst my better parts almost did not survive."

"And she's...what is she?" Oscar swallowed. "She sounds strong."

Dmitri regarded him levelly. "She is one who has done a good job containing tales of herself, but in the few accounts that have named her, she is what might be referred to as a Nix, though I believe in Scotland they call her Cirein Croin."

Oscar gave a short sharp laugh. "That doesn't sound so bad."

Dmitri shook his head and frowned darkly. "I'm afraid it is. The closest that can explain it in terms you might relate to are a dragon-like creature that nests near water."

Oscar gaped at Dmitri. "She's a *dragon?*"

"Not exactly." Dmitri shook his head. "But there are similarities, and they are not just limited to her demeanour."

Oscar fell bonelessly backward onto the mattress. *A dragon. How am I supposed to compete with that?*

"I never loved her," Dmitri said quietly. Oscar opened his eyes and looked up at the ceiling, where the plaster moulded into an ornate pattern like the petals of a flower around the hanging light fixture. "We simply hated in the same way for a time. Our wretched lives passed more easily together, dancing a pantomime of human gestures. It was a period of debauchery and despicable actions. The only feeling I have for my time with her is disgust."

"But you...had sex with her?" Oscar asked hollowly.

"Oscar, I don't understand."

Oscar groaned, covering his face with his hands.

"Why are you asking me this? Are you...jealous?"

"Yes. No. Yes, I am. I don't know, okay?" Oscar moaned, sitting up. Every part of him was tingling unpleasantly, vibrating in anticipation. "I just...I hate there's all these parts of you I don't get to know or have. And she's had a part of you that I never will."

"You do not want that part."

Oscar sighed. "She's so...how could you like someone like *that* and like someone like me?"

Dmitri reached out a hand to cup his cheek, and Oscar shied away.

"Lubite, I was with her in a time when I could not stand myself. My relationship with her was the sexual and emotional equivalent of self-flagellation. I have grown to be a better man." He shook his head. "A better *thing* than I was then. I do not deserve someone as good as you are, but I embrace the gift that you give me each day and try to be better. I am a drowning man, and your kiss is like coming up for air. That woman...my time with her was akin to a pig rolling in muck."

"Who's the pig?" Oscar grumbled.

Dmitri reached out again, placing his larger hand on Oscar's own. This time, Oscar did not move away.

"I am," Dmitri said. "I should have told you. I just never found the right time. I never would have imagined she would resurface."

"I don't want any more secrets, Dmitri." Oscar's voice was weak and small. Fragile. Too close to breaking. He hated himself for it. He hated the tears that rolled down his cheeks and how pathetic it made him feel.

Dmitri was perfect. Perfect except for the things Oscar didn't know, right down to the night he knew Zara would die but never told him. Because some things just *had to be*. The fact Zara had been revived with an ancient, powerful spirit was always meant to happen, but the fresh wound of Dmitri's silence had torn open that scar again. He sniffled, lifting his free hand to rub his tears away. Dmitri took it instead, pulling it into his own, so Oscar faced him.

"I know." Dmitri's eyes shone with unspoken emotion. "And I will do my best to share everything with you from now on. You are honest with me, and I will do everything in my power to do the same for you. I am trying, Oscar." The expression on his face was too close to pain.

A blade of guilt slid smoothly into Oscar's gut.

Honest with Dmitri?

That was a lie.

Every day, Oscar was keenly aware that not only did he withhold voicing the fear that Dmitri only wanted him because of the song in his bones, but also the truth about that night. The night Zara had died. The night the monster in the shape of a little girl had arrived, promising Oscar that no one else would be hurt if he just came with her. Everyone assumed he had been taken against his will. He never told them he had chosen to go to what would likely be his death. He never told anyone that he had given up.

Oscar swallowed. "I will try my best to be honest with you as well. I just...I need some time to take all this in."

Dmitri's face sagged, those stormy eyes suddenly looking ancient again. "Oscar—"

"We're not breaking up, Dmitri." Oscar squeezed his large warm hand with both of his. "I love you. More than I thought I could ever love anything or anyone. So much I don't know how I can handle it sometimes. But I can't pretend to be okay with this like everything is normal. I need some time to gather myself, especially if *she* is going to be around."

"I understand." Dmitri took a deep breath. "We should talk about Paige. I could try and make her forget if you wish to keep her far from this."

Oscar sighed. "I don't think so. I mean, even if you could and it worked, we don't know if it's safe right now. I think it's best to keep her close. Plus, she seems to distract Tildy a little."

Dmitri nodded. "Hopefully, she will not need to do that long. Not if we can find the Umbran and dispose of it rapidly."

"What is it?"

"It is an anomaly we will likely need help to deal with," Dmitri growled. "I had best explain in front of the others, though I suspect by now Marcus may already know more than I."

"IT'S NOTHINGNESS," Marcus was saying, his large eyes looking haunted as Oscar walked into the living room, Dmitri close behind. "Consuming but not destroying. More just absorbing and then redistributing."

"Umbrans are bottom feeders," Tildy said stiffly, a distrustful gaze locked on Marcus and Song squashed side by side in the chair. "Their purpose is to gobble muck and spit it back out as something more constructive. Mindless things with one sole purpose. I have no idea what would make one become so powerful. Why it would act this way, let alone why it is on this side of the veil."

"How do you know so much about them?" Oscar asked softly.

Tildy rolled her eyes. "I am Theian. Pureborn. Not some weak echo of my kind." Her eyes drifted to Dmitri in the doorway. "Delightful though they can be. Though I must say, dearest, the shadow does beat stronger in you now than before. I can practically feel you throbbing against me from here." She chuckled breathily. Oscar felt his cheeks burning.

Theian born. Like Ocampo had been?

"Song says the veil was sealed millennia ago." Marcus stared at Tildy with wide-eyed innocence. Then a wide grin spread across his face. "You're bloody ancient."

A snort of laughter escaped Oscar before he could stop himself, and Tildy's piercing blue eyes bore into him.

Oscar slithered to the couch and sat beside Zara with Paige crammed in on his other side. She was sipping at another large glass of red wine, watching with interest. Tildy dominated the entire other sofa to herself. Rather than sit beside her, Dmitri remained leaning against the wall by the broken door.

Tildy arched an eyebrow. "One should never trust a woman who tells her real age. That kind of woman would—"

"You *would* tell us anything. To get what you want, anyway," Dmitri cut in. "On with it. You did not come here to quote Wilde."

Tildy sniffed. "Well, that was an Oscar of quality."

Oscar shook his head, confused.

"At least this one is fairly cute, if not particularly bright, darling." Tildy sighed, smiling at Dmitri and earning herself a scowl in return.

"So, the Umbran feeds on waste and, what, shits glitter?" Zara asked impatiently.

Marcus was looking at Song, who was huddled beside him, their full attention on him, engaging in some kind of inaudible conversation.

"Why doesn't it just absorb everything?" Oscar wondered softly. "I don't get it."

"What feeds it doesn't matter," Tildy said ominously. "It does not crave nor sustain it. It is simply function. Nobody knows what an Umbran truly consumes—"

"Hate," Marcus interrupted.

Tildy's head snapped around to stare at him. "Well, except him, apparently."

"What do you mean?" Zara asked.

Marcus leaned forward excitedly. "They feed on hate. Other things too, but that's their main purpose. But that doesn't explain why this one would be hunting Tildy. Well, not completely anyway. Song has no idea what it would have to gain by killing Theians."

"At least some things can remain a mystery." Tildy crossed her pale ankles delicately.

Paige sighed heavily. "So, your plan is to go and see a Future-Witch that lives in a graveyard to tell you what the fuck is going on? Is attendance mandatory?"

Dmitri frowned. "I don't think so. It is actually better to split up."

"Oh, that always works out real well." Marcus rolled his eyes.

Paige sipped her wine. "Dibs on the home team. You weirdos have great booze, and I don't want to be wandering around the dark when there's a killer whatever on the loose. The pretty girl is always in the most danger."

"Oh, I wouldn't worry, dear. Your breasts are far too small to fit into that stereotype properly," Tildy said helpfully, earning her an acidic glance.

"If the Umbran is hunting Tildy, she should stay here. I have some artefacts in the attic that will keep the house masked from its senses or at least stop it from being able to get in. Zara, Marcus, you visit the Bean-Nighe to get more information."

"I'll go with them," Oscar added quickly. Dmitri's eyebrows

shot up in surprise. For a moment, Oscar expected him to challenge him, but instead, he just gave a stiff nod.

"Very well," Dmitri said. "But you must ask the Bean-Nighe—"

"It doesn't matter what we ask her," Marcus interrupted. "She will only tell us what she wants to anyway."

Dmitri paused, frowning thoughtfully. "At least try to steer her to tell you what she knows about the Umbran. Anything that may reveal why it's here and why it is killing Theians."

Marcus nodded.

"Well." Paige drained the last of her wine, then reached for the half-empty bottle on the table. "Let's get this party started, bitches."

THE MIND-WYRM

(VERMIS MENTIS)

11

THE DEVIL YOU KNOW

The evening was cool for one so close to the beginning of summer. Oscar's mind travelled back to a colder evening when they had walked down this street. The memory of his feet dragging through autumn leaves, Zara beside him, and Marcus roving a few steps ahead. Before everything had gotten so much...fuller. Now, he had Dmitri waiting at home, and Song trailing behind. The strange little ethernal was examining the ground as they followed, apparently fascinated by the cracks in the pavement.

Darkness had not yet taken full hold, and they would need to wait until the night deepened to risk passage into the cemetery. It wouldn't do to have anybody see them using the parallax in the wall both Zara and Marcus claimed they had long since mastered opening.

"You definitely throw the best parties, Os." Marcus grinned. "I don't remember the last time I had so much fun."

"Maybe you had the part of you that understands what fun is sapped out of you already," Zara said sharply.

"I don't think that's possible. Song only takes imperfections, and my sense of humour is beyond godly."

Zara huffed out a breath, completely unmollified. "Why didn't you say anything, Marcus? How long has this even been going on for?"

Marcus' grin turned to bared teeth with an uncomfortable gaze. "A little while. I mean, Song only became corporeal a couple of months ago, but I sensed them before. Apparently, I've been transferring energy ever since that night at the cemetery."

"After we saw the Bean-Nighe?" Oscar asked, shocked.

Marcus nodded and spun around, leading the way again. "Song said I was sensitive to the veil before. They think maybe that's why I am kind of hypervigilant about disturbances to natural order."

"That's a long way of saying paranoid," Zara replied.

Marcus ignored her. "The night when Ocampo tried to feed Os to her pet rock, some barrier between it and me snapped. Song says that's when they felt my aura reaching out. Reaching beyond. And I think that's when I manifested for the first time."

"Manifested?" Zara repeated dully.

"Used magick," Marcus clarified, looking back over his shoulder. "Affected the metaphysical world with my energy in a less than regular way. Or more than regular, I guess, depending on how you look at it."

"Wait," Zara demanded, "what exactly did you do?"

"I uhhh..." Marcus stopped again, turning. His eyes drifted to Oscar and away again as the two stopped behind him. "If I understood the Bean-Nighe and Song right, I think I may have helped Oscar activate the glow stick of death he murked that little girl with."

Oscar's mouth suddenly became very dry. "What?"

"Nina, the unfriendly ghost." Marcus rubbed his beard. "I think I helped you puncture that spooky lil' bitch."

Oscar swallowed. "I haven't been able to do anything with the hilt since."

Not since the night he had stabbed the acheri.

That was probably the most useful thing I did. Maybe ever. I thought I saved Marcus' life, but he's the one that made me do it?

"Dmitri has been trying to help me figure out why I couldn't make the hilt work all this time." Oscar moaned.

"I'm not saying you don't have some kind of touch with the old shining stab-aroo, Os, but I think I may have added some vodka to your fruit punch." Marcus winced apologetically.

"Don't tell Dmitri." Oscar sighed miserably. "That's so embarrassing."

"Don't worry, buddy. I think he likes you; he won't care." Mischief sparkled in Marcus' eyes. "Besides, once someone has seen your butthole, what else do you have left to feel ashamed of?"

"So, this ethernal." Zara cleared her throat. "Song started taking from you then? An inter-dimensional god was feeding on your humanity? And you never thought to mention it?"

Oscar felt a stab of defensiveness on Marcus' behalf. "I guess we all have secrets sometimes."

Zara's mouth shut so quick her teeth clicked, and she looked like she might choke on her tongue.

Marcus grimaced. "Not straight away. I think I was just kind of skimming the surface. Gathering and shifting residual energies. Song only started properly trading with me a few weeks later."

"And what would happen if I..." Zara's eyes drifted to where Song trailed behind them, clenching her fists. Song stopped their examination of the concrete beneath their feet, raised their eyes, and stared straight back at Zara with interest.

"Oh, don't even think about it," Marcus said quickly. "Song isn't someone you really want to consider getting all *Zara smash* with."

Zara grunted, narrowing her eyes at the ethernal, who smiled back placidly in return. "They seemed pretty placid when the gaeants were causing trouble."

Marcus shoved his hands in his pockets, taking a deep breath as Song came and stood close beside him. He took their small dark hand in his smoothly. "They knew I could handle it. If I was afraid, they might have been. Song can't read thoughts, but they can feel strong intentions. What I can do now is barely an echo of the power inside them."

"They're that strong?" Oscar turned to stare at Song, who had picked up a dry twig from the ground and turned it in their fingers curiously before popping it into their mouth. They spit it out with a look of utter disdain.

"We're talking god-tier shit, Os. They can't impact this world directly; that amount of power exertion would cause them to discorporate like smoke being blown away by a blast of air. They'd barely impact this reality before they lost their body entirely, probably for days if not weeks. But with me as their conduit...well, let's just say I'm not the weakest player in the game anymore." Marcus winked.

"I don't like it, Marcus." Zara shook her head. "What Dmitri said before about losing your humanity...what does that even mean?"

"Don't worry." Marcus beamed. "Song cares about me. They see me for who I am, not who I want to be or who I was. The exchange takes decades in the recorded cases I've found. The ethernal finds a companion and indulges in their negative experiences of the world. Pain, sorrow, regret, shame, crooked teeth, acne scars. All the rubbish stuff until they've taken it all. And then, when it's all gone, people don't die. They just become...*more*."

"It sounds suspiciously like they become less," Zara said darkly.

Oscar grunted in agreement, though he wondered if Song might want to take some of his extra freckles or the small gap between his front teeth, or maybe his bad posture.

"No way," Marcus said. "I'm more myself than I've ever been. I lied back at the house. There *is* more I gave Song. Enough to sate them for years at least."

"What are you talking about?" Zara's voice was thick with worry.

"They feed on things their connected human sees as flaws in themselves." Marcus' eyes glistened. He turned his face away to look up at the faint whisper of the rising moon on the horizon. "I gave them something that didn't fit right with me from before I was born."

Zara shook her head, confused.

Oscar gasped. "Wait, do you mean..."

Marcus grinned nervously. "It was a strong physical change. That's why I didn't tell Dmitri; I knew he wouldn't approve."

"Marcus," Zara breathed in realisation. "Did you use an omnipotent being to change..."

Marcus nodded. "Yup. Though I can't say it's smooth sailing. I really had to rethink some of my wardrobe. Plus, I smell way worse now. I guess it's the extra slugs and snails and puppy dog's tails."

"Fuck," Zara breathed, slowing down in a daze. "That's—"

"I'm so happy for you, Marcus." A warm rush of affection rushed into Oscar, flooding every part of him. He turned and saw Song watching, a smile on their lips.

Marcus blindsided him from the other side, wrapping his long arms around him in a hug. "We're glad you understand." Marcus wiped at his eyes again.

"Shit. I mean, Marcus, I'm happy too, but this is a lot. I want you to know that I support you," Zara stammered; her eyes were shining. "I don't know what to say. I mean, you know we thought you were already perfect as you were, right?"

"I know." Marcus' voice quavered, and Oscar squeezed him tighter. "But now I get to feel perfect too. I thought about it. Hell, I thought about it before I ever knew I would have the choice. Way I see it, a hundred different people would probably make a hundred different choices if they were given the same options, every one of them valid. What Song takes is my perceived imperfections, right? So, I could have tried changing my feelings instead of my body, but I figured that what made me *me* was more what was in my head than what was outside of it."

Zara swallowed, a tear rolling down her cheek. "I understand, and I'm happy for you. Please, just be careful, okay?"

Marcus barked a laugh. "Said the girl who has a ghost that likes to smash things living inside of her."

Zara clumped together with them in a hug, laughing. "Yeah, I guess none of us can lecture the others on lifestyle choices right now."

Oscar felt the faintest of touches at his side and turned to find Song there, large eyes like burnished gold fixed upon him. Another feeling flooded him, admiration with a bitter edge of something sharp and barbed. Was that...envy?

Marcus laughed. "Song wants to be in on the group hug too."

Oscar opened his arm and welcomed them into their huddle of love. Their small and slender body seemed at least two-thirds padded coat, and they felt neither hot nor cold as Oscar embraced them and his best friends together.

The nagging buzz of a vibrating phone broke them apart, and it took a moment of pocket checking for Zara to identify herself as the origin. "Okay, enough of the love-in. I actually need to nip back home before drama-palooza recommences."

"Oh?" Oscar asked, confused and still disentangling himself from Marcus' and Song's arms.

"Yeah, they were short at work due to sickness. That was them calling just now. I need to make sure they've sorted out cover for the next few days. I'm useless without my laptop. I'll be real quick. Just loiter around the dead parallax, and I'll catch up in no time." She was already tapping buttons on her phone to order a cab.

"You don't have to come. Song and I should be able to manage...well, just about anything bad that happens at all, really. I'm pretty sure I could deal with the Gwyllgi right now." Marcus sounded disturbingly hopeful at the prospect.

"Well, since we're all big pals with that thing now, let's hope we never have to find out." Zara grimaced. "See how it looks when you get there, but don't take any risks, all right?"

Oscar nodded in agreement. They hadn't seen the Gwyllgi, guardian of the veil, since the night it tore Ocampo apart. The bulky hellhound built like a huge bull, with large slabs of raw skinless meaty muscle and a jaw that ran three-quarters around its vast head, wasn't something he had the urge to run into ever again, regardless of their current *terms*.

ZARA'S booted feet pounded up the stairs to the fifth floor. Ever since the Ghatokacha had been passed onto her by Nani, she had taken the stairs every day and never gotten out of breath. Hell, she took every chance she could to use up the throbbing energy inside her. She had never been the physical type before, and now she couldn't help but wonder how much faster she would have felt at home in her own skin if she'd felt this kind of strength inside when she was younger. It didn't seem right that after she had almost died, she felt more alive than ever before.

They had been ready to withdraw care when her family

arrived, and Nani Anjali gifted her with her inheritance. Well, cousin Rami's technically, as he reminded her every few days—but fuck it. Rami would never have worn this so good.

Strength, stamina, and resilience. Those were the perks. Those and the massive spirit she could manifest from her body, strong enough to shatter stone. It had taken a while before she started to realise some of the costs.

Irregular sleeping patterns.

Short temper.

Strange bursts of energy.

Vivid dreams of lives she'd never lived, places she'd never been, fights she'd never had.

Ravenous hunger.

Increased sex drive.

Well, maybe that one wasn't so bad.

It wouldn't have been so bad if she hadn't been prone to her temper before, but now she caught herself grinding her teeth and clenching her fists at the slightest provocation. The boundless energy that dwelled inside her was always raring for a fight.

Zara thrust the key into the lock on the flat she shared with Marcus, twisting carefully; she had snapped three keys and had to pay for as many locksmiths in the last six months. Opening the door, she basked in the momentary pleasure of being home. It wasn't much, but it was hers. Well, hers and Marcus', but that only made it more home— secrets aside.

Slamming the door behind her, Zara tossed her keys onto the kitchen counter and strode in. She didn't bother to switch on the lights; between the fresh moonlight through the window and her now better than perfect vision—another perk—she could more than find her way to the kitchen table. She had just flipped open the laptop screen when a voice spoke. A voice that really shouldn't have been there. Crisp and cool, amused by her presence in her own home.

"My, my, whatever could you be doing here?" the voice said dangerously.

Zara spun around, eyes widening.

From the shadows by the bedroom, a figure stepped. The sound of her heels clipping rhythmically on the laminate flooring sent a shiver up Zara's spine. A snug, midnight blue dress hugged her slim body, tight as a snake's skin, and her angular features sharpened in a smile.

12

PIECES OF MATE

Oscar hugged himself, regretting the decision to not bring a coat. It really was far too cold for this time of year.

"Gax?" Marcus called for at least the fifteenth time. For good measure, he used the stick he was holding to rattle a nearby bush.

They had gotten into the cemetery not long after Zara had left. Marcus had accessed the parallax, pressing on the specific bricks to grant access with unsettling dexterity. When he saw Oscar's expression, he shrugged. "So, I came back a few times. Wanted to chat with Gax, and saw the Bean-Nighe a bit."

The thought sent a shiver down Oscar's spine. After everything that had happened here, he could not imagine choosing to return alone. Sometimes he still woke up in the night, frozen stock still and sweating bullets, convinced the bed was trying to pull him in to open a gateway and end the world just as the sapping stone had tried to.

It happened far less after he started spending every night with Dmitri. Even coiled in his uncomfortably hot embrace through summer nights or warmer climates, Oscar just turned the air conditioning up to max and enjoyed the restful sleep. He wasn't the only one. Dmitri often talked about how he hadn't slept the way he did with Oscar in more years than he could remember, maybe ever. He found his presence comforting and complete, allowing him to go into a deep, restive state he barely knew he could.

"Gax!" Marcus shouted again.

Song helpfully rattled another bush, burying their face in it to peer inside with those golden eyes. They almost seemed to glow in the darkness. Song caught Oscar watching, and a brief feeling of curious pleasure washed over him, then was gone just as quick.

Whilst Song continued to indulge their curiosity in the foliage, Oscar made his way over to Marcus.

"Don't you feel weird being here?" Oscar mumbled.

"Why?" Marcus cocked his head. "Because of that one time Zara dealt with the world parallax and was all like," his voice took on a shrill tone, "you know what we are, babe? We're rock destroyers."

Oscar frowned, confused. "Has Gax ever been this hard to find before? I mean, I thought he could sense everything that happened in the cemetery?"

Marcus shrugged. "Sometimes he's busy. He reads a lot. But yeah, he usually pops up faster. I've visited him a bunch, so we've become kinda chummy."

Oscar's eyes widened.

"He's a cool guy!" Marcus grinned, then shrugged. "Well, cool weird-little-goblin-thing."

Marcus steered them down a narrow path flanked by worn tombstones covered in moss. "He does usually show up pretty quick, though. He likes to pretend to be all annoyed like I've disturbed him, then talks my ear off for hours."

"And the Bean-Nighe? Is she still in the same place?" Oscar wondered aloud. He remembered the Egyptian-styled pathway with deep gated tombs the Gwyllgi had chased them to. The lank orange hair and pale orbs for eyes as she had emerged from the shadows within.

Hello, Cricket.

"Once she was," Marcus said. "Two other times, the entrance was up on the big mausoleum to the east, but every other time, she's been in different places. One time, I had to jump into the pond! Went straight through the surface and landed in her cave but was still wet as anything. She thought that was hilarious."

"Wow." Oscar gnawed his lip. *He really has been here a lot.*

Marcus had always had a fascination with the uncanny. This included conspiracy theories. From benign and seemingly point-less ones, like bees not really being what made honey, to more far-fetched conspiracies like Prince Charles being Dracula. Dmitri had done nothing to help that one by repeatedly avoiding the subject. After that, even Oscar struggled to decide what was real and what was absurd anymore. When the reality of monsters had been exposed to them, Marcus had thrown himself into it with reckless abandon. *Maybe a little too reckless.*

"So, how are you holding up?" Marcus prodded another bush lazily as he strolled ahead. "With the whole, being the other woman gig?"

Oscar blushed. "Dmitri said he hasn't seen or heard from her in years. Hundreds of them, it sounds like."

"Did he tell you how old he was yet?" Marcus interrupted quickly, eyes flashing with interest in the moonlight. That was now a long-standing game between Marcus and Dmitri. Marcus had found newspaper cuttings about a vampire in Highgate in the seventies, then Spring-Heeled Jack stories from the nineteenth century, which he swore fit Dmitri's description. Dmitri had been nebulous with his answers but agreed if Marcus could guess his age to the year, with a maximum of one guess per week, he would confirm if he got it correct. Of course, Marcus had taken to this game like it was his new full-time job, and peppered him with oddly specific questions until Dmitri learned to ignore anything that may trace back too easily.

"Nope." Oscar shrugged. "But it sounds like his time with her was a different life. I understand. I just wish that he had told me."

Marcus grunted in agreement. "That's the great thing about Song and me. We don't have any secrets. They let me feel everything and share with me whatever I want to know. Obviously not just everything in general, or ya know, my head would explode."

Song was lagging behind, studying a gravestone with interest.

"Do they uh...have an age?" Oscar asked.

Marcus' face crinkled in a smile. "It does not work like that, my man. Time is just an illusion. A way for humans to try and organise their experiences and perception of events to help them process data. To Song, time isn't something that's really happening to them; it is something happening to things around them all at once, each with their own relative trajectory, almost like a location rather than a singular stream. In their incorporeal form, they are basically a conscious collection of cosmic energy. Constantly living and dying, being reborn as the same and different forms. This form isn't really Song. It's more a projection of them based on how they see themselves right now. They manifest it into this world made up of matter collected from the living cells around them. It burns up a hell of a lot of energy."

"I'll bet." Oscar hoped he didn't sound as confused as he felt. "Can they get hurt?"

"Their form can get harmed or broken apart, but they don't feel pain. Not physically, at least. They've tasted my pain, so they know what it is as a point of reference."

"And do you, uh..." Oscar looked back at Song, who was now on their knees, pulling up a handful of grass then letting it fall into the evening wind a pinch at a time.

Marcus' eyes widened, and he started laughing. "Do I boink with the omnipotent being that feeds on my weaknesses and provides me with supernatural abilities?" He wiped his eyes merrily. "That's kind of a personal question, Oscar."

Oscar shrugged, feeling his cheeks colour. "It never bothered you before."

"Well, things change." Marcus winked. "A gentleman never tells. But I will say this, imagine your mind being laid open, exposed to secrets of the universe like a house-cat basking in the blazing sun—bathed in knowledge, ecstasy, and purity. Imagine being completely together in every sense of it, lost in each other, like you don't even want to emerge from the cocoon of wholeness you created from your minds, and it lasts forever, but no time has truly passed..."

"Sounds...nice?" Oscar swallowed.

"It's everything," Marcus said dreamily, watching Song.

Song stood up, dropped the rest of the grass, and fixed their gaze on Marcus, that faint smile on their lips again. Oscar felt a warm glow of happiness within him at the way they looked at each other.

This time, it didn't didn't come from Song.

THEY REACHED the Egyptian Alley by the time the full moon was finally visible above the tall, thick trees. Oscar kicked a heavy stone in front of him as Marcus and Song walked just ahead.

"Let's check the tombs here and then the big mausoleum. I reckon if we don't find anything, we should just call it a night. Maybe Gax has his lady friend over."

"Lady friend?" Oscar asked, surprised.

"Dandeli. She lives in one of the pub cellars nearby. She's hilarious." Marcus grinned.

As they made their way between the tall, gated tombs, Oscar passed Marcus and pushed against one of the gates.

Locked.

Oscar sighed, looking back at his friend, who shrugged. Song was wandering around the entrance of another one of the crypts.

"Okay, this really is pretty weird," Marcus said.

Oscar frowned. "Maybe the Bean-Nighe is somewhere else in the world? Dmitri said she doesn't just appear here."

"And took Gax with her?"

Oscar shrugged.

"Nah, this place is his home. More than. He hasn't left in over three decades." Marcus rubbed the hair on his chin. "I haven't been here in a couple of months. Not since..." His eyes travelled to Song, who pushed a gate, this one was unlocked. They wandered though and out of view into the tomb.

A moment later, Marcus' eyes bulged, and he turned and dashed toward the gate that Song had passed through.

"What?" Oscar rushed after him. "Did Song find her? Did they find the Bean-Nighe?"

Marcus disappeared into the tomb but was back in a flash, his face dusky and grey. A thin sheen of sweat formed on his brow. Behind him, Song walked out of the tomb. Their large, burnished gold eyes were sad, watering on the verge of tears. One of their hands was raised, a thick slimy glob of dark green goo dripping from it.

"What's happening?" Oscar breathed, ice in his belly.

"It's Gax," Marcus managed, visibly trying not to heave. "He's dead."

THE CAB PULLED UP OUTSIDE MARCUS' and Zara's block. The cemetery venture had been much shorter than expected, and Oscar had texted Zara saying they would come and pick her up.

The journey was tense. Marcus was withdrawn, clearly shaken and upset. He had gotten friendly with the Bugge, and Oscar couldn't blame him. Gax had been fun, if gruff, and he had saved all of them. Oscar had tentatively peered inside the crypt and saw what remained of him. Gax deserved better than to end up splattered all over the inside of one of the tombs he so adored. *So much better.*

Song was completely fixated on Marcus, a look of concern upon their face. They reached out and took Marcus' hand in their dark fingers, and Marcus seemed grateful for their comfort.

As they got out, Oscar pressed the button for the lift, watching in silence as the light counted backwards down to the ground floor.

"I just can't believe it," Marcus said, forlorn. "He was so clever. So quick. He could disappear in a flash. What could possibly do that to him?"

Oscar swallowed. Tildy's words had replayed in his mind ever since he saw the inside of the tomb.

Whatever it was, slaughtered Alouicious and ripped Vander to shreds.

He had almost thrown up after he saw the mess, and even now, a deep, sick feeling had settled in his guts.

The elevator pinged, and the doors slid open. The three of them crammed inside, Song taking great interest in pressing the correct button as the doors closed.

"We need to get Zara and head back to the house. For all we know, the Umbran could have found the Bean-Nighe and—"

"Don't say it," Marcus wailed. "She's too strong. She can see the future. This thing...it can't be powerful enough to do that, can it?"

Oscar knew from the hopelessness in Marcus' voice what the answer to that question was. From whatever Song had shared with him, Marcus knew it could.

There was another *bing*, and the elevator doors slid open on the fifth floor. After the weeks he spent recovering here, this almost felt like second home to Oscar now.

Almost.

Song moved ahead, straight to the correct door.

They froze, and beside him, Marcus tensed.

"What is it?" Oscar asked, startled.

"Something's happening," Marcus breathed, rushing forward.

"Is it the Umbran?"

Marcus waved a hand, and something clicked inside the door. Oscar belatedly realised his friend had just opened the lock with a wave of his hand. He was right behind Marcus when he forced it open, slamming his hand against the light switch and bursting the room into blinding light.

There was a flurry of movement, too fast for Oscar to fully catch, a rush of bare flesh and snatched blankets. Zara panted, clutching a throw that had been on the sofa around her nakedness. It was barely big enough, and Oscar averted his eyes, embarrassed. On the floor, another figure crouched, lithe and beautiful. She wiped her mouth with the back of her hand, smiling. She adjusted the strap of her dress where it had come loose, threatening to expose her otherwise fully clothed body.

"Oh, hello Oscar. Fancy seeing you here." Doctor Ocampo smiled.

INTERLUDE THE SECOND: A GENTLEMAN CALLER

The Umbran watched from the darkness.

It was almost completely cloaked in the shadow of night, the dark pulled in around itself like one might a blanket on a cold day. It was strong enough now that it could draw deeply on the shadows, even ride them almost as smoothly as if it were in Theia itself...not that the body it inhabited made it any easier.

It had consumed several of the darkborn of this realm now. Darkborns were all it would call them, for none had quite the power of a true Theian. The power the river creature's flesh provided had been the best. Not only for the strength its cells brought, but also the morbid exaltation from this host's memory which pumped an echo of sour hatred from its core even beyond death. The others it consumed had been soft and ripe from their time in this world and easily plucked, but with their combined power, the Umbran was finally beginning to feel alive in this place. Their energy allowed it to reknit its host's festering flesh back together with cords of darkness. To bolster and strengthen its limbs and joints, weaving shadow over bone, sinew, and muscle, augmenting it beyond what any human could ever manage—living or dead.

The dark, unnatural energy patching the corpse together also went toward plugging up the festering stench the Umbran had begun to find distracting. The way its insides had been liquifying was truly beyond inconvenient, but it managed to encapsulate that swill for now at least.

In the building ahead, the Umbran sensed power.

More power than it had fed upon so far, though still not yet enough. The strength within would nourish this form further when consumed, and that was not to speak of what their bones would contribute to the coming peace.

The Umbran moved closer.

Voices from within.

In one of the horrible, garbled tongues of this realm.

It narrowed its eyes, straining the vessel's dead organs and filling them with power. Through the window, it saw a Theian. One it had almost taken before. It throbbed with tempting power.

The Umbran licked its black, cracked lips.

"Dmitri, darling, surely you can't hold a grudge. It's been so long," the Theian said. It held the shape of a human woman. How shameful. She was strong, at least for this realm. The Umbran had only sensed two stronger presences in this place.

"It could have been millennia, and I still wouldn't be able to stand the sight of you," the other snapped. He was not as powerful as the Theian but would still make a fine meal. The acidic hate bubbling within its chest told it the owner of this body had despised this darkborn every time it laid eyes upon him. The Umbran knew from the vessel's shattered memory that this was Dmitri Roburt Tza. The one that held the affections of the human with Theian cells within—the answer to this painful riddle.

"But we had such fun!" the Theian purred. She strode to him, running one long fingernail down his angled jaw.

"Do not touch me." He shivered and stepped back.

"That's not what you used to say," she cooed.

The Umbran felt a wet growl bubbling in its throat. These foolish children. It would not wait any longer until it ended them. It took a single step forward and stopped.

No.

Something was wrong.

A pressure in the air, unmistakable as it was subtle, pushed out from the house. Another step closer and the Umbran would have felt the feet of its vessel begin to grind back on the very earth beneath it.

The Umbran let out a low growl.

"So, you still just linger around humans?" the Theian's voice shifted. From honey to poison. "Playing house? Like being mortal is so special that you wish you weren't blessed to be what you truly are?"

"Human or not, Tildy, I am happy with who I am, what I have, and the company I keep. When could you last say the same?" Tza sneered bitterly.

The Theian, Tildy, pierced the air with a sharp laugh. "Oh, you've always built castles on quicksand, darling. How fragile is this little world you have constructed for yourself? How much does that whimpering little howler monkey clinging to you even know about what you are? What you've done?"

"He knows enough," Tza snapped.

"Does he?" Tildy smiled, unperturbed despite the man towering over her. "Does he know why you found him in the first place?"

Tza froze, his face unreadable.

"Just because we weren't together anymore doesn't mean I stopped keeping up with your activities, love." Tildy sighed, approaching him once more. For a moment, it looked as if she might caress his jaw with one long nail again, but instead, she clutched his jaw, fingers biting deeply into his flesh, and pulled his head down to her own level. Tza tried to wrench his head free, but her nails bit deeper and blood ran down his neck. "You wish to act as though you are better than the rest of us, but you are still a slave to other's whims. I could liberate you, you know. Set you free of this poorly conceived cage you have set yourself within. All I have to do is tell him."

She released him, and Tza staggered back with a low growl, his hand coming up to touch the rapidly healing, superficial wounds on his face. As if the real wounds weren't caused by the words she had just said.

The Umbran felt a deep pulse of hate throb from within and was almost overcome with the desire to feed, dragging the shambling corpse close against the push of the house.

"I...I would tell him myself if I could." Tza's voice was ragged. "There is no secret I wish to keep from Oscar, nothing I believe would keep him from me—"

Tildy's cackle cut him off. "Oh, darling! You are hilarious! You speak like one of them now! Do you have any idea how naive that sounds? Have you learned nothing of these listless mouth-breathers? Yes, he would probably stick around for a while, at least; that's what they *do*. They hold grudges and harbour resentment and make themselves oh so miserable until they wander off somewhere else or just die. He might stay, but do you honestly think he wouldn't wonder? That doubt wouldn't gnaw holes in his guts every time he laid his eyes upon you? You should save yourself the pain and be done with it. He is not worthy of you and the wonderfully terrible thing you are."

Tza staggered back as if struck, glassy horror in his eyes. Hate pulsed within him like a swollen, throbbing artery.

"I do not love you, Dmitri. I do not even particularly like you, and I never did. You were just an interesting toy I used to scratch an itch. You have only grown more insufferable with time, and frankly, I wouldn't be here if that thing out there wasn't trying to suck the meat off my bones. But that doesn't mean I can stand to see one of us down on his knees for a lowly, pathetic, snivelling human."

"Enough," Tza growled.

"The irony is that in playing human, you make yourself weak, and that's the very thing that will make you lose him."

Tza tensed at the threat in the words. His muscles stiffened, and his eyes began to glow.

Tildy shrugged. "In any case, I will be quiet now, darling. I was simply being honest."

"You have never been honest, and you know nothing of Oscar." Tza's voice was filled with more spite than meaning.

Thick saliva ran down the Umbran's chin at the ripe thrum of malice radiating from the darkborn, and it took another step forward. The ward, or whatever it was that was repelling its body, was strong...but the Umbran's hunger was rapidly becoming stronger.

There was a spark of light from the steps on the porch, and the Umbran froze, its dark, shining eyes flashed over the flickering flame and the long pale face it illuminated.

The human woman had a cigarette between her lips, and the end glowed like a burning eye as she sucked in, scowling through the smoke. "You alright there, mate? You look a bit shit."

The Umbran stared at her stiffly, tilting its head with a creak of stiff, brittle joints.

The woman puffed out a lungful of smoke. "If you're here to see Dmitri or Tilly duchess of fancy-pants or whatever-her-silly-fucking-name-is, I wouldn't bother. They've been bickering for ages; they didn't even notice me come out here."

The Umbran abruptly sensed that the searing hate bleeding from Tza had disappeared, and the voices inside silenced. The ward pressed harder against it now, threatening to force the decaying meat from its bones if not for the shadow clutching it together.

The front door burst open.

"Paige, what's going on?" Tza barked, dashing out with an axe hefted over one shoulder, the Theian behind him, eyes alight with crackling blue energy.

The Umbran hissed.

Not yet.

I am not strong enough yet.

But soon.

And with that, it melted back into the night.

13

THINGS THAT GO BUMP IN
THE DARK

Oscar stumbled back, tripping over his own feet and landing painfully on his bottom.

"Marcus, stop!" Zara cried, jumping forward to stand in front of Doctor Ocampo.

Oscar looked up. To his right, Marcus stood with his fingers poised menacingly in the air, no sign of his usual playful smile or twinkling eyes. His face spoke murder. Song loomed behind him, eyes fixed on their soul-bonded with concern.

The throw Zara clutched before her threatened to slip and expose her even more. Her face was panicked but glowing, skin dewy and flush in the dim light.

She and Ocampo had been...

Ocampo stepped from behind her, snatching a crochet blanket from the old chair nearby and casting it over Zara's shoulders. This one was much larger, and Zara immediately clutched it around her like a threadbare cloak.

"I smell power." Ocampo smirked at Marcus, whose hands were still poised in the air, shaking.

Shaking with fear or with the effort of holding something back?

"Whatever your friends would do to me, I no doubt deserve it." Ocampo's dark eyes, like obsidian hammers, found Oscar's.

She can't be. This can't be. Doctor Ocampo is dead.

Oscar had watched her get torn to pieces. What hadn't been gobbled of her remains by the Gwyllgi had been incinerated by Dmitri in his Zburator form.

"In any case," Ocampo drawled, "the cat is out of the bag. Now we just have to see which way we skin it."

"Zara, what the fuck is going on?" Marcus' voice was brittle.

"I'm sorry," Zara gasped, pulling the blanket tighter around her. "It's complicated."

Oscar looked at her, seeing the way she glanced at Ocampo nervously, almost protectively.

Complicated? No. It isn't.

"You died," Oscar's voice was a harsh whisper.

Ocampo shrugged. "I am not so easy to kill, I'm afraid. Something your little wolfling might have known had he taken the time to learn about me. So long as my head remains, I can regenerate whatever has been taken of my body. In fact, I spent a good deal of the sixties with no body at all. Regrowing it can be quite a chore."

"Thank you for explaining how to make sure you don't come back next time," Marcus snarled.

Ocampo smiled grimly. "As I say, no less than I deserve. But you may wish to stay your hands for a few moments longer. I bear information you will wish to receive."

Oscar struggled to his feet, his knees shaking beneath him with the effort.

His stomach twisted and lurched every time he looked at her. The woman, the monster that had traced his family line for centuries only to try and use him to open a gateway between Earth and her own world, the place humans might consider hell, Theia. The woman who had promised to kill everyone he loved if he didn't comply.

I will make a gift of their entrails and torn faces, heaped in a pile with the eye of the one you hold dearest on top like a cherry. Perhaps I will have you eat it. Push you into the depths of madness before I bend you to my will.

Oscar shuddered.

"Zara, what exactly is happening here?" Marcus demanded again.

Zara's mouth gaped like a fish pawed from its bowl by a curious cat. Her eyes travelled the floor desperately, and she began to gather her clothes, awkwardly clinging to her blankets still.

"You're fucking her?" Marcus spat. Oscar had never seen him get so angry.

Zara's eyes were wide and watery. "You don't understand."

Marcus snorted. "I'm familiar with the anatomy. It's pretty straightforward."

Zara was pulling on her jeans, taking care to keep herself covered. "Lyn has changed. She knows what she did that night was wrong." She turned to snatch up her jumper.

Ocampo snorted derisively, and Zara's eyes flashed toward her in warning.

"Wrong?" Oscar asked hollowly. "It's more than wrong. She tried to kill me, Zara. She tried to merge our worlds and kill countless others."

"You think I don't know that?" Zara snapped, turning her back and pulling on her fluffy purple sweater. "She *did* kill me, Oscar. At least, she was the one who asked Nina to do it. I get it."

Ocampo's dark eyes shifted to her own feet, her lips pursed.

"But...it's different now," Zara stumbled, struggling to find the right words.

"Now you're diddling her?" Marcus interrupted flatly, his eyes shining. "Or now you have a monster living inside you?"

"People in glass houses shouldn't throw stones." Zara's eyes sharpened and met Marcus'.

The air seemed to shiver between them, thick with tension. Like a clear jelly set wobbling with the tap of a teaspoon.

"I will not apologise." Ocampo's sharp voice cut through the air. "Not only because I think it would be worthless, but because I do not particularly regret any of my actions."

Zara's bared her teeth angrily.

"I do, however, acknowledge circumstances have changed," she continued. "There was information I was not party to. The game was lost, and the pieces cannot be reset. A different game has commenced, and so we may find ourselves in a more co-operative position on this occasion."

"Jesus, you can't even pretend not to be evil for a minute," Marcus spat.

Ocampo frowned. "Perhaps I do regret one thing. I thought I could save my world, but now I know the world I knew is already dead. I spent far too much time and effort trying to save it. I suppose that relates to my other...indiscretions, but I believed I was doing the right thing at the time."

Theia was dead?

When Oscar had asked what Dmitri found beyond the veil, what Theia was like, he'd never answered him clearly. He said he felt an oppressive force like he was being force-fed far beyond his will. Like the air itself was oil, filling him beyond capacity. And then he had fled. Fled back to this world to save Oscar.

"What do you mean dead?" Marcus' voice was almost a whisper.

"The balance has long since shifted, and Theia has changed from what it once was. That is why the taint is spreading. Why the Umbran is here."

Ocampo's words drove into Oscar like the spikes of night she had flung in the cemetery. His jaw clenched so hard it ached.

"You know about the Umbran?" Oscar swallowed, and he sidled to stand behind Marcus. His friend's fingers were still frozen like claws in the air, his russet eyes fixed on Ocampo.

"I am sure I've forgotten more of Umbrans than you shall ever know." Ocampo sniffed. "But of this one, and why it is behaving the way it is? I have some small knowledge."

"Then spill it," Marcus snapped. "Before I spill you."

Zara's mouth opened and a helpless, miserable sigh was all that escaped. Her eyes were wide and shining with concern. The way her gaze shifted between Marcus' hands and Doctor Ocampo...

She's afraid. Afraid Ocampo is going to get hurt.

"How long has this been going on?" Oscar managed.

Zara's eyes gave him his answer. Wide and guilty.

A while? Maybe months? Zara has kept this from us for months.

Oscar reached out and put his hand on Marcus' arm. "I don't want to be here anymore." His voice sounded very small.

Marcus nodded once, eyes only leaving Ocampo to flash toward Zara. His hands did not lower. "Agreed. But I do think Zara had best take her new special friend to see Dmitri. It would be an awful shame for something terrible to happen like last time, but I think we need to know what she knows. After that...well, I'm sure he'll know what to do with her."

Ocampo gave him a toothy smile that didn't meet her eyes. Those black eyes that drifted to meet Oscar's once more, staring into them unfathomably.

"As long as I don't have to be near her," Oscar moaned. "I don't trust her."

"Agreed," Marcus snapped. "Hard to know who to trust nowadays."

Zara rolled her eyes, arms folded. "Don't be so dramatic, Marcus. You entered a secret pact with a divine being who's sapping the imperfections from your soul so you can perform magick. It's not like any of us can take the high ground here."

Marcus' back stiffened, and his eyes narrowed. Finally, he lowered his hands, but his tone stayed razor sharp. "What Song and I have doesn't hurt anyone else. Doesn't risk anyone but me.

I'm not the one boinking the bitch that tried to end the world, Zara."

Ocampo cackled softly. "He's got you there."

Zara shooed away her words with a sharp *tsk* and wave of a hand.

Ocampo folded her arms. "Had my plans been realised, the world would have been full of powerful monsters, and I would have ruled with fear. What you need to ask yourself is whether that is really any different than what you have now? At least I would be clear with my intent and not have chosen my victims based on wealth, colour, or creed."

Marcus barked a cold laugh. "Yeah, all people eaten equally. Lovely."

Oscar wasn't sure if it was he who couldn't meet Zara's eyes or her who couldn't meet his. All he knew was between Ocampo and Tildy, things were only going to get worse.

❦ 14 ❦

HOW'S YOUR HEAD?

The cab ride back to one hundred and thirty-eight Kinmount was miserable. Oscar's thoughts alternated between swelling panic and crushing betrayal. *Zara.* After everything they'd been through together, after everything they'd done, she had kept something like that secret? Something like *her*.

Oscar had never thought for more than a moment that he would ever see Lyn Ocampo again. A woman who terrorised him even before she revealed herself as an ancient and terrifying monster. He *had* dreamed it, however. On those rare nights when he found himself back on the altar in the cemetery in his nightmares, sometimes she was there. Watching and smiling, her eyes as black as eternity.

For all the inner turmoil Oscar felt, beside him, Marcus seemed to be wearing his own turmoil on the outside. He was a bundle of hysterical fury. Oscar had tuned out his rambling about how he should have known and how strangely Zara had been acting these last few months after he began to repeat himself a third time. Twice, he came close to saying things the driver might have found more than a little alarming, and Oscar managed to interrupt him long enough to stop him. After a while, Song placed

119

their hand on top of Marcus' and the tirade had stopped, his eyes finding the ethernal's and not leaving them again. Oscar wondered if they were having some kind of silent communion between them and felt oddly like an intruder in the back of the car.

In the stiff silence, Oscar took out his phone and typed a message to Dmitri, pausing and worrying his lip for a moment over how to give all the information before deciding some things were better left in person, and thumbed send.

Gax is dead. Ocampo is alive. She knows things about the Umbran. She is on her way to the house now with Zara.

— OSCAR

Oscar's phone started buzzing in his hands almost immediately. It was only a short attempt, three rings before it stopped. Oscar began to send another message to try to explain he couldn't talk right now, that he didn't even know what to say, when a message came in from Dmitri.

Come home, lubite. I am waiting for you, and everything will be okay.

— DMITRI

Oscar felt a bubble of emotion inside him pop, and a warm flush of gratitude spread over his skin. Sometimes Dmitri seemed to know exactly what he needed. No doubt he had even cut the call attempt short, realising Oscar might not have the words yet.

Right now, there was nothing he needed more than Dmitri's warmth, his strong arms around him, and...

The memory of Tildy's cold blue eyes and pink lips curling in a sneer hit him like being dunked in a bath of ice.

Oscar felt his breath shaking in his chest, his pulse pounding at his throat, and his skin prickled uncomfortably. *Not again.* He closed his eyes, taking a long, deep breath through his nose and out through his mouth. Then another.

Then he responded to Dmitri, thumbs feeling only a little numb.

On our way, will be back soon.

— OSCAR

Oscar stared at the screen. *What if Zara and Ocampo beat us there?* Maybe Dmitri needed to have more information before they arrived. *So, he doesn't have the same shock we had.* Oscar's mind flashed back to watching Dmitri in his massive Zburator form, shaking Ocampo like a chew toy in his jaw. He quickly typed an extra message and tapped send.

Ocampo and Zara are TOGETHER.

— OSCAR

Dmitri didn't respond, but Oscar didn't worry too much about it. He was, after all, quite old-fashioned in many senses and did not favour communicating that way. He *was* constantly photographing Oscar, but often avoided being photographed himself on almost every occasion.

Oscar had wondered for weeks before he finally asked why.

I do not change, lubite. I looked the same in the past as I will look in the future. Who I am and how I have grown is not reflected in my face or my age. I keep it in here. He had taken Oscar's hand and touched it to his chest.

Oscar thought he understood, but now after Tildy had arrived and all the things she had been saying? Oscar knew Dmitri had a dark past. He'd been a completely different person. What must it be like to see that same face when you looked in the mirror?

Maybe that was why he didn't like his picture taken.

WHEN THEY ARRIVED at Kinmount Street, the cab driver refused to drive up the bumpy drive to the house. Oscar, Marcus, and Song got out of the taxi and made their way on foot. When they rounded the corner and the house came into view, the windows cast an ominous yellow glow onto the cars parked in front. Just Dmitri's sleek black car and Paige's funny little yellow rental. No sign of whatever Zara and Ocampo might arrive in.

Sitting on the steps with her legs crossed and cigarette in hand was Paige. "Alright, bro?" She exhaled a plume of pungent smoke.

Oscar met her eyes, hoping some of the silent struggle in his own might deter her from pushing him any further.

"Christ, what's wrong with you? Who died?" Paige scoffed.

Marcus grunted, and Oscar felt a fresh wave of sorrow.

"Oh, shit." The smirk slid off Paige's narrow face. "Someone really did carc it. Who?"

"No one you know," Oscar said numbly.

"Though if you'd met, I bet he'd have loved to give you a hug," Marcus added.

Oscar opened his mouth to comment but then shut it again

quickly at the sad smile Marcus sent his way.

Gax's skin had been highly toxic to humans. Paige would have been dead in seconds.

"I had to come and sit out here." Paige took another puff. "At first, I wondered whether those two needed to fight or fuck, but now I know which." She inhaled.

Oscar's skin turned cold, and his heart twisted in his chest.

Paige let out the smoke, puffing it toward Song, who traced a finger through it curiously with no offence taken. Paige scowled slightly at the undesired response. "Turns out, he really likes you, Oscar. Wonders never cease. Not long after she called you a sickly little street urchin, he went upstairs and fetched an axe. He's had it next to him ever since, and every time she opens her mouth, he just stares at the axe. She's stopped saying much. Not exactly a fucking buzzing cocktail party."

Oscar's heart unclenched. He imagined Dmitri's eyes burning, his thumb tracing over the blade of his axe as he stared at Tildy. *Why does that thought make me strangely pleased?*

"It's not going to get any better," Marcus warned starkly. "There's another guest on the way that might make Tildy look like Mary Poppins."

Paige's lips curled in a grimace.

"I'd better go in and talk to Dmitri." Oscar started up the steps beside Paige.

Paige cleared her throat. "Are you okay?" she asked stiffly. She didn't look directly at him, and it took Oscar a moment to notice she was speaking to him. He must have looked bad for her to ask that.

"I'm fine," he said weakly. "I just need to tell Dmitri what's been going on."

Paige gave a single nod, eyes on her cigarette. Oscar moved on and opened the door. Just as he was closing it behind him, he heard Paige start to quiz Marcus.

"So, Jazz-Hands, tell me what happened at the cemetery."

∾

DMITRI SAT on the wide leather chair by the window, his hair now rebound, and his axe indeed resting across his lap. His jaw was clenched with frustration but his eyes filled with relief when he saw Oscar.

Dmitri shot a stern look at Tildy. "You, stay here. I trust you will behave."

Tildy tilted her head, sapphire earrings tinkling musically. She offered Oscar a simpering smile before looking back at Dmitri. "Darling, you know I'm at my best when I'm bad, but just this once, I shall endeavour to be boringly good."

Dmitri bristled, but Oscar found that, strangely, he didn't care. His head was too full for any more *Tildy* right now. Beyond bothering about her allusion of some kind of ownership over Dmitri, he walked past her, thrilled by his own nonchalance, and reached down to take Dmitri's hand. Feeling its warmth in his own, the familiarity of his touch filled him with energy.

Oscar looked at Tildy. She smiled again, eyes heavily lidded. She obviously wanted to exude superiority. Power. Beauty. Control. But knowing what the Umbran had done, Oscar saw something different now. He saw uncertainty and fear.

Oscar swallowed. "Don't worry, Tildy. We have someone who can give us more information about the Umbran. Hopefully, we will make sure you're safe, and you can be on your way soon. Until then, you're welcome to stay with us as long as you need to. Anyone who is a friend of Dmitri's is a friend of mine."

Tildy's eyes widened, and her smile froze in place, becoming rictus.

Dmitri's face slackened slightly in surprise, then his eyes sparkled and a ghost of a smile flickered on his lips. "That is very kind of you, Oscar." He stood, hefting his axe, and squeezed Oscar's hand. "We will be back soon, Tildy. Do not be too afraid until then; I believe the ethernal is outside, and the malachite ward stones should keep the Umbran away."

Tidy's smile twisted, and her teeth gnashed. For a moment, Oscar wondered if they might shatter in her mouth.

"So gracious," she managed, voice strangled. "I shall await your return with anticipation."

∽

DMITRI CHUCKLED SOFTLY as he pushed the office door closed behind him.

Oscar had no idea what this room had been before, but now it was a comforting juniper green, with bookshelves stacked to almost overflowing and a huge oak desk at its centre. He was desperate to go through all the books and read as many as he could. Language would be a barrier, but Dmitri promised to read the others to him.

Lamps gave the room a warm glow, casting it upward onto the pale ceiling, where the twisted lampshades cast a pattern similar to looking up through the branches of a forest. Dmitri had placed something that made this room always smell like sage and cedar, and only laughed when Oscar asked what it was. It had taken him a whole day to find a small, murky stone on one of the shelves, powerfully exuding the scent.

"That was amazing." Dmitri grinned, flashing his pointed teeth, flipper apparently discarded now that Paige knew the truth. "To think, I spent decades with her, and yet you learned how to get under her skin in ways I could not in hours."

Oscar shrugged his shoulders uncomfortably. "I wasn't trying to annoy her. I meant it."

Dmitri's eyebrows raised as he strode around the desk and took a seat on the tall-backed captain's chair. The studded leather was darker than seaweed. "You would have her here? Under your roof, knowing who and what she is? What she has been to me?"

Oscar sighed. "You can't really hate her, Dmitri. Not after being with her for that long. You might hate the part of yourself that she brought out, the part that she let you be. But without her then, you wouldn't be you now. She obviously cares for you. When she was afraid, you were the one she came to for help. I just don't think she knows how to ask nicely."

Dmitri's face softened, and his eyes shone. "How can you be so good? You amaze me every day."

Oscar blushed, leaning against the edge of the desk. "I'm not exactly a hero like you or Zara. I can't even save myself yet."

"Saving yourself is the hardest thing anyone can do." Dmitri smiled tiredly. "Far harder than being a hero."

Oscar chewed his lip.

Dmitri sighed, the smile fading from his face. "I am sad to hear of Gax's death. He was a friend."

"I know," Oscar said softly.

"And Ocampo." His eyes glittered angrily. "I thought I'd been...thorough."

"She said it was her head. As long as that survived, she could come back."

Dmitri grunted; he looked as though he were committing that to memory. "And Zara knew about this?"

"They're together."

Dmitri looked confused.

"Like we're together."

His eyebrows climbed. "Oh. That is a surprise."

Oscar grunted in agreement. "Given the whole Zara punching her in half for trying to end the world thing, yeah."

Dmitri sighed, linking his fingers behind his head. Whenever he did this, Oscar's eyes pulled to the curve of his biceps and the swell of his chest. Sometimes Dmitri looked so good it was practically obscene.

"Are you okay?" Dmitri asked.

Oscar sighed, stepping closer. "I'm shocked. Disappointed.

Scared."

Dmitri nodded gently. "I understand. I fear leaving Zara alone may have been a mistake. Pushing that kind of responsibility on her seems to have affected her judgment."

He trailed off, eyes widening in surprise as Oscar stepped forward, climbing onto his lap to sit facing him. Oscar captured his bottom lip in a gentle kiss, earning him an appreciative growl.

"I thought you needed space?" Dmitri's lips traced Oscar's, as light as a feather.

"I did," Oscar said. "I've had it. And now, I need you. I need to feel something different from all the other things trying to make space inside me right now. I need to feel you instead."

The hungry look in Dmitri's eyes sent a thrill through Oscar's belly as his large hands traced up his thighs and gripped his bottom. Dmitri kissed him roughly, his stubble scratching on his jaw.

Oscar broke the kiss, biting his lip as he unbuttoned Dmitri's shirt, pushing it open. "I'm still angry you didn't tell me you were married." Dmitri's scent, like charred wood and citrus, filled his nose. Oscar ran his hand over the contours of his chest, and Dmitri's eyes ignited with glowing flames. "But I forgive you, so long as you don't keep any more secrets from me in the future."

"I promise." Dmitri's voice was husky with desire.

Oscar wiggled, feeling the larger man's excitement against him, earning another growl.

"How long until the others arrive?" Dmitri purred, pulling Oscar against him, making him feel his heat.

"Long enough." Oscar pulled up his T-shirt. It wasn't even over his head when Dmitri lifted him, sitting him on the edge of the desk, mouth latching onto his nipple.

Oscar gasped as he was pushed back. Dmitri's dexterous hands unfastened his jeans and pulled them loose as his hot kisses trailed down Oscar's belly, until he was engulfed in Dmitri's welcoming mouth.

THE
FUTAKUCHI-ONA
(CAPUT MORTEM)

15

THE PRESSURE COOKER

Oscar was still drying himself from the shower when he heard the front door open. Dmitri had cleaned up first, and Oscar was grateful he was the one downstairs to intercept Ocampo instead of him.

The uncomfortable knowledge that he still wasn't sure what to say to Zara clawed its way back to the forefront of his mind, and he swallowed the lump in his throat. He would say whatever needed to be said, and they would figure it out. This was Zara. She was *family*.

But preparing himself to get dressed and go back downstairs was harder than he'd anticipated. With every article of clothing he pulled on, it was like he was donning one of the problems waiting for him downstairs.

Paige.
Tildy.
Ocampo.
The Umbran.
Zara.
Gax's death.
The Bean-Nighe missing.

Is Marcus okay?

Closing his eyes, Oscar tried at first to shove all of that away, and told himself that he could just deal with everything one thing at a time.

One thing at a time?

It's all happening now. Here.

Oscar sat on the edge of the bath, clenched his jaw, and pulled on a sock. He tried to imagine he was pulling on armour instead of a problem.

There was too much for him alone to handle, yes.

But I'm not alone.

Zara would help. No matter what had been going on, Zara would make things better. Marcus would probably make everything a mess, but then somehow manage to start unpicking things and figure it all out with that giant brain of his, especially now that he apparently had the power of a god at his disposal. And Dmitri...

Oscar slowly exhaled, feeling the tension in his shoulders lessen. Dmitri would be there. Patient, solid, determined, and protective.

Everything would be fine.

Oscar smiled and opened the bathroom door.

BY THE TIME Oscar got downstairs, Zara stood by the open front door, arms folded with a scowling gaze fixed out beyond the dark porch. Oscar peered out and caught a glimpse of Dmitri and Ocampo standing close together. Ocampo's face was severe and cool, as always, her posture relaxed and languid. Dmitri, in contrast, was speaking, low and urgent, his body tense like a wolf about to pounce.

Oscar heard a light shifting behind him and turned to find Ed, a tiny terrier, standing in the kitchen doorway, peering fretfully out.

"It's okay, Ed. She's not going to cause any trouble." Oscar said, failing to even convince himself.

"Oscar," Zara said.

Oscar took a steadying breath and turned to meet her baleful eyes.

Zara reached out and took his hand, pulling him closer. "Can you stand here with me for a bit, please? I want to be close. In case he decides to..." She trailed off worriedly, attention wandering back out the doorway.

"Would that be such a bad thing?" Oscar said sourly.

Zara sighed, then puffed out her cheeks with a breath as she folded her arms. "Maybe not. She's not been a good person, or even a good monster. Trust me, when I found out she was still alive, we fought. A few times, actually. She probably could have killed me once or twice, but she never did. It was a whole Dread Pirate Roberts situation. Eventually, I stopped fighting and asked her why she wasn't really trying to hurt me. And that was what she really wanted. To talk."

Oscar shrugged. "And?"

"She fucked up. She might be older and stronger than most things on the planet, but she made what she thought was the right decision, and it wasn't."

"No shit," Marcus said.

Oscar and Zara turned their heads to find him leaning against the living room door frame, idly pushing at a bit of broken wall left on the floor from the gaeant's attack.

"She tried to end the world," Oscar added, unable to stop himself.

Outside, Ocampo was speaking. She had that steely calm that she'd always exuded, absent of the acid Oscar was used to having directed at him.

"She did. But she was trying to save her own world," Zara said.

Oscar shook his head.

"Are you telling me you wouldn't fuck over a world full of monsters if it meant letting everyone on earth live?" Zara asked.

Oscar paused, puzzled. "I don't know."

Marcus folded his arms and scowled.

Zara sighed. "Neither do I. Look at the shit we do. Who's to say humans are any better than them? All the rape, and murder, and bigotry. Lyn's bad, and she's done some shitty things, but she thought she was acting for the greater good. She knows she was wrong now, no matter how stuck up she is about saying it. She's been tracking the Umbran, and she can help us."

"I don't trust her," Oscar said simply.

"Me neither," Marcus added.

"I don't even know if I do completely," Zara admitted.

"Then why are you sleeping with her?" Marcus said coldly.

Zara let out a long breath and chewed on that for a few minutes. Oscar watched the pair of powerful beings standing outside. Dmitri was speaking again. His tone seemed calmer now, but his body was still tense.

"I was all alone." Zara's tone of voice pulled Oscar's full attention back to her. She sounded fragile. Zara hardly ever sounded fragile. "I was alone and scared of what I am now. What it meant. There were monsters I had to fight and kill with you and Dmitri gone." She turned and looked at Marcus. "You were off doing your magick self-discovery. People were dying, and I felt like it was my fault, and I didn't have anyone. Not you, not Marcus, not anyone." Zara brushed a tear from her cheek. "When Lyn and I finally talked, she helped me. She helped me to better understand who I am. *What* I am. I don't know what I would have done without her."

Oscar swallowed.

Marcus finally nodded. "I get it. I don't like it, but I get it. You just have to understand it's kind of a shocker. I mean, to start with, she used a ghost kid to make you deader than Thomas Jay dancing on a beehive, then you punch her in half. Next thing you know, we walk in, and y'all are getting some WAP—"

"I think that's enough of a recap," Zara cut in.

Marcus shrugged.

"I'm sorry. I don't expect you to understand, Os. I felt alone. Like I'd been left behind, and I had to deal with everything alone, I just—"

Oscar's heart swelled, and he wrapped his arms around her before she said any more. She sniffled wetly into his neck.

"I'm sorry, Oscar. I know it's fucked up, but it happened. And yes, she's a bitch, but she's not *that* bad."

"Not that bad?" Oscar laughed. "Did she put that on her online dating profile?"

Zara laughed, wiping her eyes.

"Is it serious?" Oscar asked.

Zara looked out the doorway again to where the two now spoke. "I don't know. I mean...maybe? It's messy but intense."

Oscar nodded, remembering the first time he'd been with Dmitri. The knotted disbelief, and comfort, and yearning. Zara and Marcus had been there for him then. Well, Marcus had. Zara had threatened to smash Dmitri's face if he did anything too evil. "I get it."

"So, am I still cancelled?" Zara asked, looking between Oscar and Marcus.

"You're good for now." Marcus nodded, a smile splitting his face.

"We should start a support group or something," Oscar mumbled.

"Or a website," Marcus offered brightly. "I'm thinking *OnlyFangs*."

Oscar's eyes caught movement from outside. Seemingly done with their conversation, Dmitri turned and began to make his way up the steps, Ocampo trailing behind him, acting less the meek invitee and more regal guest of honour.

"Come, lubite. We must speak," Dmitri said gently. His glance at Zara was loaded with disappointment, and his voice was stiff. "You too."

Zara blinked, the faint smile she'd worn before sliding from her face. "Sure thing, boss."

～

OSCAR COULDN'T HELP but recall the first time they had sat around the dining table in this room together.

The dining room was a far cry from what it had once been. The dingy moss-coloured walls and dusty old furniture were gone, replaced with navy walls that contrasted with the honey floorboards and light rustic table. The table which Oscar, Zara, Marcus, and Dmitri sat around now. Some things were different, of course. Oscar took the seat beside Zara, who had taken his hand and squeezed it gratefully as soon as he did. He almost expected Dmitri to be mad, but when he met those stormy eyes, all he saw was understanding.

At least until Tildy took the seat beside him; then Dmitri's eyes dulled with anger. Tildy looked quite pleased with herself, given that reaction, until she met Oscar's eyes, and then she looked like she might have just swallowed a bee. It took Oscar a moment to realise that if Dmitri could hear everything that happened in the house, Tildy had probably heard, well, everything that happened in the office.

I thought Dmitri had been particularly...vocal.

Oscar blushed, and couldn't help a smile from creeping onto his face when Tildy's apparent discomfort deepened as he watched.

Paige leaned in the doorway, refusing to take a seat, and instead tapped impatiently on her phone. It seemed she'd made a new friend, because Ed was in the form of a Yorkshire terrier, attempting to innocently lean against her leg. "What are you doing, Dog-thing?" Paige grumbled but made no attempt to avoid his affection.

Nearby, Song stood, amber eyes owlish, watching Ed with interest.

"Well, this is nice," Marcus said brightly.

The palpable tension in the room rippled before uncomfortable silence settled over Oscar like a too-heavy blanket.

Zara cleared her throat. She didn't seem to be able to meet Dmitri's eyes. "Lyn told you everything?"

Dmitri, however, had no such problem, his eyes drilled into her averted gaze as he spoke with a pointed tone. "She did, though it would have been useful to have the information sooner."

Zara folded her arms. "I couldn't be sure you wouldn't get hairy on the situation. We all remember the last time you and Lyn saw each other."

Dmitri's tone was level. "As I recall, you were the one to finish her off."

"In any case, you weren't around. I was going to tell you, but it was kind of hard to explain. So, I put it off a little." Zara seemed to be struggling to not sound sulky, and she failed.

"You may have put us all at risk. And not just with your appetites." Dmitri's gaze shifted to Ocampo. "This knowledge could have made a significant difference, but you delayed by weeks or even longer."

Ocampo sighed softly. "Don't be dramatic, mongrel. Let us get to the point."

Dmitri scowled but took a deep breath and spoke again, his voice calm even if his eyebrows were so drawn together, they almost touched. "Theia is a ruin. Pulverised by a shift in energies at work for centuries in our absence."

"What are you talking about?" Tildy asked, sitting up stiffly.

"I entered some months ago through a world parallax. Created by *her*." Dmitri nodded toward Ocampo. Tildy's eyes widened hungrily. "It was for mere moments, and I'd never seen Theia before, and I did not know what it should have been. I had no idea there should have been more. It was barren. Except for the darkness."

Ocampo raised her chin regally. "Our world was a great civilisation. Ancient and wonderful. But my fears were all too right. This world has destroyed ours. Poisoned it and putrefied it with imbalance. Only it was not a dreaded future, but a loathsome past."

"Imbalance of what?" Marcus asked. He looked at Song, but their attention too was on Ocampo.

"Hate," Ocampo said simply.

Oscar and Marcus looked at each other, confused.

"Energy can neither be created nor destroyed," Ocampo said. "So tell me, what becomes of the energy of hate?"

Oscar frowned. "I don't understand."

"The impact hate has in this world is merely a by-product of the energy created, not a quantifiable endpoint. Even destruction gives place for new rebirth. Hate simply *is*. Hate is one of the forces which travels beyond the veil. There, it is used and transformed. It became energy for sustenance to some in that world, part of the life cycle. A portion of that energy was then transformed and shifted back through the veil to the human world."

"So, what changed?" Marcus asked.

"Humans," Tildy said stiffly. "It was the humans' fault, wasn't it?"

Ocampo nodded once. "Some centuries ago, a group of druids sealed the veil to prevent the passage of Theians to this place. Before that, passage was free but rarely taken. Some of my kind enjoyed coming to this realm and being worshipped as gods, others to feed, but humans became increasingly competent at harming us. The druids' barrier should have acted as a stopper between worlds, sealing them apart. But of course, they were inept. They *were* human, after all."

"Gods," Marcus mused, enraptured. "The gods were just monsters."

"Wait," Paige interrupted loudly, apparently realising who Ocampo was at that moment. "Is this saucy bitch the one that tried to murk Oscar?"

Ocampo's voice cut cleanly through Paige's inquiry. "The humans did not so much create a barrier as they did a valve. A one-way system in which energy could be transferred beyond but not return."

"Isn't that a good thing?" Oscar asked.

Ocampo's eyes narrowed in irritation. "A pressure cooker of hate?"

"Maybe it makes the monsters all soft and delicious?" Marcus offered hopefully.

Ocampo ignored him. "With the energy unable to be transferred beyond its natural outlet, a process as old as time was impeded. A key component to a functioning ecosystem removed. No, it is not a good thing. One of the mechanisms through which energy from this realm was processed, was Umbrans. They were not an intrusive force in Theia, more like a cleaner fish of sorts. A functioning component of a healthy ecosystem. With this obstruction, it appears they have become gluttonous and malevolent. It seems they must have begun to consume more and more until there was only ruin remaining."

Zara shook her head. "You didn't tell me that part."

Ocampo's eyes drifted to the floor, her sharp features softening slightly. "I did not know it all to begin. After opening the world parallax, I only began to suspect. I had to contact those with different talents to my own to confirm."

"And now an Umbran has passed through? Is the valve broken?" Oscar asked, struggling to comprehend what this meant.

Ocampo shook her head. "Not broken. Since it was opened, places where the veil is thin are letting out bursts of pressure. None of these could contain an Umbran. They have grown too bloated and powerful with hate. This one, or part of it, must have passed through on the night of the world parallax and found a vessel so full of hate, it could take purchase."

"No shortage of those here," Zara drawled.

"But what will it do?" Marcus asked.

Ocampo's eyes flashed over to Dmitri.

"We do not know," Dmitri said darkly. "It may seek to consume more hate...or something else. What we do know, is it's strong. Too strong. We have no way to stop it, and it is somehow growing stronger."

"What kind of strong are we talking?" Zara asked, folding her arms. "Stabby, smashy, or bity? I want to be prepared."

"All of the above, I'd wager," Ocampo replied grimly. "Compared to the power I was granted on the night of the world parallax, with enough time to grow, the power of the Umbran would make that look like a sad echo. The manipulation of darkness is a high power to Theians, granted only to the most elevated of our kind. This creature would have the power to control darkness as if it were part of its own self and form it into living weapons of its bidding."

"Great," Zara grumbled. "More shadow boxing."

"Won't it consuming the hate make the world a better place, though?" Oscar asked hopefully.

Ocampo laughed, an incisive bark.

Dmitri shook his head. "No, lubite. It will only make it hungrier. Always hungrier."

A chill ran up Oscar's spine.

Marcus leaned forward. "Song doesn't know anything. They said when they try and peer through the veil, it's like looking into a dark window. Like trying to look through the surface of a pond, but the water's covered in oil. They know it wasn't always this way, but they haven't been able to get in since the seals were made. Apparently, there was some falling out between Theians and ethernals near the beginning. Song doesn't remember the details."

"So, what's our move?" Zara asked, ever the pragmatist.

"We don't know what happened to the Bean-Nighe. She may be our only guide on how to proceed," Dmitri began.

"There is another," Tildy cut in, though from the look on her face, the helpfulness brought her no pleasure.

Dmitri scowled. "Betty Blumpkin."

A malicious smirk split Tildy's face. "Indeed, though I know she will have no interest in helping you."

"Why? What happened?" Oscar asked.

"I killed a friend of hers. A gretchling that was targeting schools," Dmitri answered firmly. "She is generally a neutral force, not usually dangerous, but she is also not particularly reliable."

"And the Bean-Nighe was?" Zara snarked.

"She may be all we have," Tildy said.

Dmitri gave a grudging nod of agreement. "We don't have time to waste. We have to try and find the Bean-Nighe and, failing that, Betty Blumpkin. We should try to be both places at once. The motives of the Umbran are unclear, but if it is hunting Theians, it will surely be drawn to the most powerful of them. I suspect the Umbran may still be searching for the Bean-Nighe. She is more elusive than we know."

Marcus swallowed. "You think it was at the cemetery when we were there?"

"I don't know," Dmitri said. "But it's a risk we must take twice."

"And Betty Blumpkin?" Oscar asked, enjoying the sound of the name on his tongue.

Dmitri's scowl returned. "Unreliable but not dangerous. Well, unless she wants to be. She's based in Soho in the guise of a drag performer."

Paige stuck her hand in the air excitedly. "Oh fuck, dibs on that team."

～

Zara stood, stretching. "I'm stepping outside. I need some air."

"I am going to check the wards, then will join you in a moment. We need to talk," Dmitri said sharply before standing and walking briskly out. Song wandered out after him with Ed closely in tow. Oscar wondered if perhaps the mimick-dog could smell their power and thought it safest to stick close by. He was not a cowardly creature, but Oscar had to agree that there were far too many terrifying beings under this roof right now.

Zara looked like she might not want to leave the room anymore, but stood and made her way into the hallway regardless.

"I need a drink." Marcus sounded a little strange. "Come with?"

"Okay," Oscar agreed.

They'd just passed outside the dining room door when Marcus grabbed Oscar's wrist, grip like a vice. "Wait!" he hissed and leaned his lanky frame to peer back through the doorway.

"What are you—" Oscar began.

"Shh. I want to see what happens when the bitches of Eastwick are left alone. It's like mixing mentos with Coke and dynamite. Shut up and watch."

Oscar leaned in, peering over Marcus' shoulder.

"Lyn," Tildy said in that simpering voice. "It's been ages. Literally Ages!"

Ocampo flashed a rare smile that didn't quite meet her dark eyes. "It has. Last time I saw you...was it Paris?"

"It was." Tildy giggled.

"Where in Paris?" Paige interjected curiously. "Have you been to Louvre-Tuileries?"

There was a moment of stiff silence before Tildy responded. "Darling, of course I have! But this was quite some time before that became such a wonderful spot."

"You must be Oscar's sister." Ocampo leaned forward, her sharp eyes assessing. "What a shame about your blouse."

"Oscar's fault," Paige retorted snidely. "He fucked about with some little rock men and ruined everything as usual."

Ocampo's eyes widened in amused delight, and Tildy's tinkling laugh rang out.

Of course. They have some common ground.

Marcus turned to Oscar, face slack with shock. "Wow. I mean, I didn't expect that."

"What?" Oscar said miserably.

"They cancelled each other's bitch signals right out."

All three women's eyes shifted to the pair of them in the doorway, and Marcus and Oscar froze.

"You two," Zara said firmly from the kitchen. "Get in here. Stop goading the monsters."

Oscar and Marcus couldn't move fast enough.

❧ III ❧

THE SPEED OF DARK

16

MERRY MET

The dull throbbing bass from various bars filled the veins of the small backstreet with life, even if there wasn't anyone to be seen. Down a grotty alley that had taken them three passes to find, Oscar wondered why anyone would choose to live here, let alone anyone with power.

The dull metallic number six on the black door had come unscrewed at the top. It hung upside down like a crooked nine, its edges bubbled with rust. Knocking on the door revealed two things. First, its wood was hollow with rot, and second, it wasn't locked or even fully closed at all.

"Careful," Zara warned.

Oscar saw the light building in her eyes that told him the power that lived inside her was stirring.

Paige scoffed. "Of what? Tetanus?"

"You think it's here?" Oscar swallowed. "The Umbran?"

Zara peered into the dark corridor, its walls dark with patches of mould. "It could be. I don't know. Just be ready to move. If there's one thing the unholy trinity agreed on, it was that if we see it, we run. But even if it's not here, we still don't know enough about this Betty Blumpkin."

She was right. There hadn't been time to discuss it. Dmitri seemed to think she was safe, or at least safe enough that he'd rather Oscar went looking for her with Zara's protection than go back to a place the Umbran had already certainly visited. Oscar had wondered if Zara was so tense because Dmitri trusted her to protect him, but he thought it was more likely because Ocampo would be accompanying Dmitri to the cemetery.

Despite the trust that had grown between Zara and Dmitri, his eyes still stared cold fury at Ocampo for what she'd done to Oscar. The way she'd left him for months after.

A pang of bitterness washed through Oscar's guts. *Why doesn't Zara hate her for that too?* He smothered it. Zara loved him, and he knew better than anyone that things like love were complicated sometimes.

Oscar felt himself roughly pushed aside, and Zara gasped as Paige strolled into the dank and mouldy hallway as if it were her own home. He half expected her to flick a lazy wrist and toss her keys into the upended traffic cone that looked half melted on the floor.

"BETTY!" she hollered loudly. She pushed a hand into her jacket pocket and pulled out her packet of cigarettes.

Zara exchanged a look with Oscar, confusion mixed with amazement.

Paige popped a cigarette into her mouth. "Oi! Betty fucking Blumpkin. We need to talk with you."

"Paige, we have no idea if—" Zara began.

Paige flicked her lighter. The flame cast a dull glow on the hallway as she sucked it into her slim cigarette before it flickered back to darkness.

Oscar's skin turned ice cold; he saw the air around Zara glow as strength poured into her.

"Paige. Get back," she commanded.

Paige cast an irritated look at her.

"What do you want with Betty Blumpkin?" the voice from the

shadows said. It was barely more than a whisper, but it carried. Paige jolted with surprise, taking a few awkward strides back toward the door.

Oscar had only seen her for a moment...at the end of the corridor loomed a figure—tall, thin, and corpse-white.

Zara stepped forward, putting herself between Paige and whoever...*whatever*...was hidden in the darkness.

"We were sent by Tildy Darlington." Zara's jaw was clenched so tight a muscle jumped in it. Oscar thought he could feel the air vibrating slightly as the spirit inside her hummed with energy.

It didn't feel like this before. Has Zara gotten this much stronger?

Oscar thought about the useless hilt in his backpack. It wasn't like he could even use it to fight, despite what he once believed. Even *that* had been Marcus' new and incredible power.

He could almost see the shape of the figure in the darkness now. She seemed to be leaning against the filthy wall with her arms folded. "And what do you want with her?"

Oscar swallowed. "We need help with an Umbran. We need to know how to get rid of it." He took a step forward into the corridor.

Zara put out a hand, barring his path, glowing eyes flashing in his direction. Oscar got the message. He'd messed up again. Too much information. Too many cards laid down. This could be Betty Blumpkin, or this could be the Umbran. It could be anything in-between. His heart pounded at the thought.

The figure moved smoothly, stepping forward, and emerging from the darkness. She was beautiful. Youthful features like a doll, punctuated with silver and gold piercings at the nose, eyebrow, lip, and ears, and short hair as white as snow slicked back on her head. Her eyes were thickly lined, her lips the same dark colour: purplish black on her alabaster skin. Her appearance alone would have been striking, but she stood taller than Zara, maybe even a shade taller than Dmitri. Her lithe body moved with sinuous grace, dark jeans showing legs like drainpipes, leather jacket rolled up to reveal long pale forearms, black nails, and thick chains at her wrists. Her irises were red as blood.

"Christ, it's a goth. I should have guessed, lurking in the dark like that. Probably just been listening to some very sad music and writing a poem," Paige mumbled.

Amusement flashed in the woman's crimson eyes.

"Are you Betty Blumpkin?" Zara asked.

The tall woman shook her head. "Come with me."

BETTY BLUMPKIN WAS the least convincing drag queen Oscar had ever seen.

Her frazzled electric blue wig barely pushed her just over five feet tall and sat askew on her round, little head, showing tufts of dark wiry hair peeking out at the sides. Her dour, sagging face was painted in bright clownish colours that paid ill-attention to detail, seeming to hope the colourful aqua shadow around her eyes and blood red of her lips might distract from her rosy, pockmarked skin. She wore a dress that reminded Oscar of the gaudy doll his aunt Joan used to put on top of the toilet rolls in her bathroom. Grubby rose and chocolate tulle petals puffed out around her, torn and threadbare like a toddler's ballerina dress after playing in the mud all day.

Paige snorted in barely suppressed laughter when they entered the room. Bare and filthy, it felt cold despite the mild evening. Oscar assumed that the few tall, grimy mirrors propped around the edges of the room were for Betty to observe herself.

"What?" Betty barked, raising both hands and waggling them in the air with stubby fingers. "Whaddaya want?" Her voice was a deep, rattling wheeze, thick with an American accent.

Zara paused and looked like she was composing herself for a moment before she spoke. "Are you Betty Blumpkin?"

"Yeah. Now, what the fuck are you doin' here?" Betty growled, stalking across the room on stubby legs, the back of her grotty gown trailing on the floor.

"We need help. With the Umbran," Oscar said hopefully, peering from behind Zara.

"Don't we all, kid." Betty barked a laugh. She stopped her pacing and turned around with her arms folded, forearms thick and hairy. "But why should I help you?"

"Do you know what it wants?" Zara asked.

Oscar couldn't help but wonder why Tildy sent them here. This didn't seem like any powerful monster Oscar had ever met before, least of all the Bean-Nighe.

Betty chuckled, waving a hand at the tall, pale woman who'd brought them here. She leaned against the wall, her narrow face unamused. "Get a load of them. Persistent, ain't they?"

"As persistent as we need to be," Zara said, grinding her teeth. She wasn't glowing now, but Oscar could still sense that thrumming energy from her. The spirit inside her was practically bouncing on the spot. He hadn't seen her use her powers since the gaeants at the house, and he wondered if the warrior spirit inside her had been unsatisfied with how quick that fight had been over.

Betty laughed again, the sound like an unclogging drain. "Pull the other one. You ain't a threat, kid. The wards would never have let you in if you had violent intentions. But I can't help ya. I don't see the future; I only see what already went down. It's that bitch with the eyes you want." Betty gestured to her own beady eyes, mouth twisted in disgust showing small browning teeth.

Zara scowled. "I know."

"There has been an Umbran before. Not as strong as this one. It was before the gaps in the veil shut up shop. Around the Crusades. Fat chance of getting rid of this guy the same way as they did." Betty shrugged.

"Why?" Oscar asked.

Betty narrowed her eyes, walking toward them with a

disturbing grin on her face. "You're a cute one, ain't ya? And I know where you've been from the smell of ya. How is old Spring-Heel?"

Oscar shook his head, confused, stepping further back behind Zara.

"Spring-Heel. Pterolykus. The beast of all the fuckin' moors." Betty stalked closer on her stumpy legs, voice growing louder.

Oscar saw Zara tense, and the air seemed to crackle around them. He caught movement on the floor in the darkness. *Was it just a rat?*

"DMITRI," Betty barked, cackling. "You got his stink all over ya!"

There was a flash of movement, and something pinched Oscar's bottom. He yelped, jumping in the air. Zara apparently saw something slipping away in the dark and stamped down, narrowly missing.

Then Oscar saw it.

A long translucent tentacle slithered back under Betty's dress. She had a wide closed-lip smile on her face.

"What did you do?" Zara growled, raising her fist.

"She pinched me," Oscar whispered shakily.

Paige snorted with laughter.

Betty shrugged again. "He's got a nice ass."

Zara stepped forward.

"Keep it in your pants, girlie. I can see that thing inside ya spoilin' for a fight, but you ain't gonna find one here." Betty waved one of her hands and walked away.

"Don't touch him again," Zara warned.

"You met my bodyguard." Betty gestured at the tall, white woman. "Vandle. Or as some of you idiots call her, Bloody Mary."

Oscar's memory prickled. *Bloody Mary, as in...*

"The bitch that pops out of mirrors and kills you when you say her name three times?" Paige asked dubiously.

Oscar stared at Vandle. She showed no reaction.

"Eh," Betty grunted. "She did a bit of that back in the day. A few can travel by mirror, so it wasn't all her. Just mostly."

Vandle smirked, a curl of dark lips and flashing red eyes. A chill ran up Oscar's spine.

"Dmitri said this wasn't going to be dangerous. We are going to have words when we get back," Zara grumbled lowly. Then she spoke more loudly. "If you won't help us, then—"

"I didn't say won't. I said CAN'T," Betty barked, biting off another coarse laugh.

Oscar reached forward and touched Zara's shoulder. She glanced back and met his eyes briefly, communicating silently.

This was a dead end.

"Alright, Betty, enough bullshit. If this hungry umbry thing gets stronger, what happens to you?" Paige asked, her voice sharp and inquisitive.

Betty froze, her beady eyes fixing on her. "Same thing that happens to everything else," she growled, then mashed one tiny fist into her other open palm. "Smoosh." Spittle flitted from her lips.

"And there's nothing you can tell us? I mean, even in terms of self-preservation?" Paige continued. "Not that you aren't a woman of obvious quality." Her eyes shifted around the filthy room, and Oscar could hear the sneer in her voice.

Betty smiled genuinely for the first time. "I can't help you because no one has seen the relic they used to destroy the last rogue Umbran in aeons. Thing like that needs a willblade to kill it." Her dark eyes shone.

"Willblade?" Zara asked.

"A blade forged of pure control and resolve with the power to part night and day. It could not be wielded by any but those that held the touch of both and was nothing but a useless hilt in the hands of any others."

Oscar watched Betty cautiously, eyes trained on her gown for any more of those tentacles.

"Oscar," Zara breathed, looking back at him and widening her eyes.

Oscar looked back at her curiously.

Zara widened her eyes again, and Oscar's jaw dropped in realisation. He began to fumble his backpack off his back.

"But like I said, one hasn't been seen in centuries. There's no chance you're just gonna—"

"Is this it?" Oscar asked, pulling out the rusted hilt the Bean-Nighe had given him and holding it in both hands.

Betty Blumpkin froze. Her mouth hung open, still forming her last word. Her eyes flashed to Vandle.

Vandle was fast. As fast as anyone or thing Oscar had ever seen. Her long body sprang from its lazing position against the wall into full rapid movement. An uncoiling spring.

But Zara was already full of adrenaline. She stepped between Oscar and Vandle and let her strength take form. She lashed out with a fist, the glow of the spirit bursting out from her closed hand, hammering through the air where Vandle was. *Had been*. Vandle was gone.

"Okay," Paige's voice was stiff and fragile. "Maybe everybody just needs to calm down for a minute."

Zara slowly turned.

Beside Paige was a mirror casually propped against the wall, so dusty and dull, it was barely even visible. Vandle loomed behind her, long fingers closed around Paige's throat, one black nail tapping threateningly at her neck.

"Hey!" Oscar cried out. As his attention was drawn away, he felt something hot and slick touch his hands and snatch the rusty object from between his fingers.

By the time he looked back, Betty was slipping the hilt into her hand from one of the tentacles now retreating back under her dress. Her beady eyes sparkled. "Well, well, well. You shoulda said you'd brought me a gift."

17

THE BE TEAM

Dmitri's eyes slid smoothly over their surroundings, drinking in details like reading a familiar book. His vision was as sharp in the darkness as it was in the day, sharper perhaps with no light pounding into his eyes. If he were to let himself change, and allow the heat that was always waiting hungrily to blossom from his chest, his eyes would glow, and he would see even clearer, smell even stronger, and practically feel the hum of movement around him.

He focused, allowing just enough of the constant pressure inside him free. Like carefully unscrewing a bottle of shaken fizzy drink to allow the gas to hiss out without the contents fizzing free...only if the shaking were done by an earthquake and the beverage was magma.

It was worse since he'd crossed over.

The fire inside him was hungrier than ever before, desperate to sear away everything that made him more man than monster, and somehow being in this place made it worse.

They were at the other side of the cemetery from where Oscar was nearly taken from him. Dmitri could still feel the scar

153

of it—a tightness in this place, like stretched skin over an old wound, closed but forever changed.

Dmitri shut his eyes, allowing his senses to reach out. The heat inside him that used to flicker just out of reach, ready to be billowed, now pounded at his gates, desperate to be set free.

He let a little out.

It pulsed into him like molten fire.

It was just enough that if he opened his eyes, he knew they would be glowing now. If his teeth hadn't been left permanently sharp from the last time he changed, they too would have turned.

The lava spread through his veins. His flesh itched with the need to move. To fight. He steadied his breath. His senses blossomed, revealing his surroundings more clearly.

Dmitri's grip on this place was nothing like what Gax had held. Bugges bonded with a domain entirely. This was closer to scrying rather than becoming one with the map.

He focused on his breath.

Felt the night stretch out around him.

The gentle vibrations in the earth.

The immense but contained pressure of Song's power nearby.

The touch of the moonlight.

His own beating heart.

"Have you fallen asleep?"

Dmitri's breath hitched, and he opened one eye.

Marcus stood before him, head cocked with interest, a bemused smile on his face.

"I'm trying to concentrate," Dmitri said, trying to sound patient.

"Why?" Marcus shook his head, grinning.

Dmitri opened his other eye, but only to allow himself to scowl properly. "Why am I concentrating?"

"Yeah, and why does it look like that when you do?" Marcus seemed to be trying not to laugh now. "You looked like you were really hungry or something."

"Wouldn't surprise me. When was the last time you had a good meal? The nineteenth century?" Ocampo's voice was smooth and cold, and it sent a chill over Dmitri's skin—no small feat, given that if his skin were any hotter, he might give off steam on a cool night.

"Not all of us need to feed on newborns," Dmitri tossed back, refusing to look at her.

"Oh, I don't eat newborns, mutt. I've always had little taste for such cruelty. The only humans I have fed upon in some time have been those freshly dead from other causes. Well, and one fellow who told me I would look prettier if I smiled more."

"Sounds like he had it coming," Marcus grunted.

Dmitri scowled. Marcus quipping with the manananggal made him uncomfortable, but asking Marcus not to be playful would be like asking the wind not to blow. Still, he could see the uncomfortable shift to the boy's russet stare and hear the keen edge to his voice that told him Ocampo had nothing near his trust. It didn't unsettle him the way that Zara's gaze upon her did.

In truth, Dmitri wondered if he was being a hypocrite. A long time ago, he'd done crueler things than Lyn Ocampo had to people just as innocent as Oscar. That she had done those things to Oscar, made that feel impossible. This woman had tried to end that sweet, uncertain smile and dull those bright cornflower eyes, and that still felt a crime beyond forgiveness. He would tolerate her if it helped their cause. He had done worse.

The ethernal stood not far away, head tilted, owlish eyes fixed on the half-moon. From the fact they and Marcus were at ease, Dmitri was quite certain the Umbran could not be here, but still, he wished he'd brought his axe. Leaving it with Tildy had been the smallest kindness he could muster. It wasn't as though she needed a weapon, nor did she know how to unlock that one's full potential. That would take speaking its name, a truth only he and one other knew. Still, it was the nicest thing he could bring himself to do.

Even with no sign of the Umbran, it was best not to let any guards down, though. Not after what had happened to Gax.

"You two should not treat this so lightly. Based on what Tildy told us, I do not expect the Umbran will accept defeat easily," he growled.

"Well, if it won't accept de-feet, do you think it will accept de-hands?" Marcus waggled his fingers and grinned.

Dmitri turned away, stifling a groan, and led the way deeper into the cemetery.

OCAMPO PARED off in the darkness, slipping into the night silently. Dmitri understood, but knowing that she preferred to hunt alone did not make him feel any more relaxed about having her out of his sight.

"Dmitri, you said you knew a bit about ethernals?" Marcus asked sheepishly from behind him.

Dmitri grunted. *Of course he had questions.*

"Song said they couldn't explain it all to me because—"

"Because they could not limit or stopper the knowledge, and it would likely overwhelm your mind and leave your brain leaking from your nostrils," Dmitri finished for him.

Marcus gave a high and nervous laugh. "Yeah, pretty much."

"I know enough." Dmitri moved a tree branch aside and, after passing under, held it up for Marcus to follow. Song hesitated some distance back, their eyes fixed on Dmitri with interest, but made no move to follow.

Fine. They can make their own way through.

"Ethernals, from what I gather, are all much the same and completely different at once. Part of a singular, like various facets of a single fact, they exist in mutual understanding all at once, but each represents a unique experience of the greater being's interaction with the space and time around it. They are intrigued by the ineptitude of mortals."

"Song finds it fascinating that humans are so bad at communicating their needs," Marcus agreed. "They can't understand why we try to fit feelings into things as unclear and incomplete as words. They sent me the image of crying babies over and over for like the first two weeks I met them. They didn't understand why the parent didn't just know what it needed, or understand that sometimes the baby didn't *need* anything, it just wanted to cry."

"I suppose mortal solutions to communication are particularly inelegant to something such as an ethernal," Dmitri said. "The one I met in the past believed art was the most efficient and effective modality humanity had discovered."

Marcus' eyebrows climbed. "Good to know. I'll take them to the Tate. What else?"

"They are selfish." Dmitri checked behind him. Song still had not followed, but Marcus seemed unconcerned. "Interested only in their experience of the world. Their experience of their time with their tethered."

Marcus grunted. "I don't think Song is selfish—"

"And they are terrifyingly powerful. I know of no other being carrying the same knowledge, experience, or abilities of their kind. None that remain anyway. There is little wonder they and those like them have been considered gods."

Marcus gasped. "There you go with that god stuff again. You know, I'm really going to have to get you to elaborate later. I have a feeling I may need to expand the taxonomy I'm making quite a lot."

Dmitri opened his mouth to answer but heard the soft sound of movement up ahead. The hot scent of fresh death grew thick in the air. "Hush. There is something here." His dark coat billowed behind him as he picked up speed.

Dmitri rounded the corner of a mausoleum, weaving between two tall tombs and dashing through a small copse of trees. That was where he found Ocampo crouched on one knee, examining the body.

Dmitri's eyes moved over it quickly, recognising it almost immediately. A dark spike of dread pushed into his chest.

"What is it?" Marcus had just arrived behind him, eyes bulging when they found the mass of torn flesh and sinew. Nothing but a pile of meat scraps now.

Ocampo rose to her feet, dusted off her knees, and her eyes flashed toward Dmitri's, mouth a thin, grim line before she answered. "A bad sign."

Song arrived a moment later. Their eyes took in the corpse, and they sent a brief feeling out. The urge to get closer to the death. To witness the parts breaking down and becoming one with the earth. To watch the energy return.

"No." Dmitri shook his head.

Ocampo swallowed. "It is still warm."

Meaning the Umbran is close.

"We need to find the Bean-Nighe," Dmitri growled. "It has grown too powerful."

Marcus stared at the mass of flesh on the ground. "There is just so much. What was—" He gasped as the realisation arrived. "The Gwyllgi. It's the Gwyllgi."

Dmitri nodded, face dark.

"There are no signs of a struggle. Whatever killed it was far more powerful than it was. Otherwise, the Gwyllgi would not have been felled without a fight. I say this having *encountered* this creature firsthand," Ocampo said, her eyebrow twitching.

That was a diplomatic way of saying it had eaten half of her.

"The Gwyllgi was the gatekeeper. A force strong enough to guard the space between Earth and Theia. I didn't think anything could do this." Dmitri's voice was hoarse. "And I don't understand why. The Gwyllgi was a guardian, not a being compelled by hate."

"The Bean-Nighe," Ocampo said crisply. "Does she have any other means of contact? I doubt if the Gwyllgi was felled so swiftly, she would be able to stop it. It may be we must give up on her altogether. She may have been slaughtered six ways from Sunday by now."

"No other means," Dmitri answered. "Her realm is the between. Entered and exited at her will. I doubt she would risk breaching it with the threat of the Umbran looming outside."

Marcus shook his head. "I saw her a few weeks ago. She said some strange things, but then, she always does."

Dmitri's gaze turned on him intensely. "What did she say exactly?"

"Just asking after you and Oscar mostly. She wanted to know how he was. If he'd grown braver. No, she didn't say braver. Truer?"

Dmitri frowned. "Truer? I do not understand. Oscar does not lie."

"Everybody lies." Ocampo smiled. "Most of all, humans. It's just a matter of about what."

Dmitri flashed her a dangerous glance.

"I don't know," Marcus continued, trying to remember. "She also wanted to know about Zara. She hadn't been able to read her before because she was going to die. She wanted to know how strong she was."

"Strong enough." Ocampo's eyes travelled to the warm heap of leftovers on the ground. "Though perhaps not for this."

"I thought it was weird because she never really makes sense. Normally, she wants to talk about things like rocks and dolls. Things that could have been if someone had been just a minute later out the door." Marcus shrugged at Dmitri. "You know what she's like."

"Sounds hideously whimsical." Ocampo's voice was acid.

"She can be frustrating," Dmitri agreed. "But she is a powerful ally, though she prefers not to take sides. Was there anything else, Marcus?"

Marcus looked at Song. "Is there some way you can help me access my memories in greater detail?"

They just stared back blankly.

"Hmph. I don't think so," Marcus grunted.

"Do not seek to trade parts of yourself so eagerly," Dmitri warned. "You already have more power than most humans could ever imagine."

"I only have the stoppy and movey powers so far." Marcus shrugged. "Super memory would be pretty sweet. I still need to practice more with what I can do to see if I can get better. I feel like it's like trying to thread a needle whilst wearing boxing gloves."

Dmitri grunted. "Regardless, it may be best for us to go back to the house. I do not like leaving Tildy there alone, even with the wards and Ed keeping guard."

Marcus' eyebrow quirked, and he smiled mischievously. "Worried about your old wife? Are there others? You gotta be careful; they might make a club and come after you. I saw it in a film."

Dmitri gave him a sullen scowl. "More worried about the house and Ed. That woman is rarely up to any good, particularly when left unsupervised. I'm not entirely sure if the Umbran wasn't after *her*, that she wouldn't be following it around with viewing goggles and cheering on its horrors."

Marcus winced.

"I was tempted myself," Ocampo drawled, examining her nails. "But it seems it has a greater taste for the blood of ours than humans."

"I almost forgot you were evil before you said that," Marcus muttered.

Ocampo smiled sharply. "I wouldn't say it's an evil intention as such. I'd just rather be the visitor than the animal housed at the zoo."

Dmitri pulled out his phone and thumbed in Oscar's contact number, holding it to his ear.

No answer.

Oscar was busy then.

Interest burst through the air from Song, and Dmitri turned to see what had piqued their curiosity.

They stood not far away, attention fixed between the trees, where the night met shadows from the branches and the tall mausoleum beside it, casting a patch of earth into inky black.

A cold sensation prickled across Dmitri's flesh, and he dropped his phone, stepping forward. "Get back," he growled.

Song looked up at him and cocked their head in confusion.

Then, a row of dark spikes jammed into their chest from the shadows on the ground.

❧ 18 ❧

THE SAME PARTS

Oscar's phone buzzed in his pocket as his eyes shifted between Betty Blumpkin, who now clutched the rusted hilt greedily against her chest, and Vandle, who tapped her dark pointed nail gently at Paige's throat.

Bzzt bzzt. Bzzt bzzt.

It was the only audible sound in the room other than Paige's heavy breathing.

"Christ, kid, you've just been carrying this thing around like a lucky teddy bear?" Betty chuckled. "It's beyond priceless, and that's just talkin' money."

"You said yourself it was the only way to stop the Umbran," Zara snarled. "There's not much point in you getting coin for it if you're dead and have nowhere to spend it."

Betty laughed that coarse rattling laugh again, waddling to the other side of the room. "It's not just *having* the sword. You gotta have the touch of both worlds, as well as the cojones to use it too. Full conviction or it don't work right. Nothing less for something sharp enough to part night and day, huh."

"What are you talking about?" Oscar's voice cracked, his eyes fixed on Paige.

Her own were wide with panic, but her mouth was a stubborn line, and her chin jutted out the way it always did when she wasn't getting her own way. She swallowed slowly, staring back at Oscar.

Betty stepped between them and jabbed one stubby finger at Oscar.

"Well, kiddo, conviction you might not always have, but the touch of both worlds? You got that, pounding out of ya like a deep bass. The question is...can you use it?"

Oscar swallowed, remembering the faint glow of the blade that night in the cemetery, and the way he'd driven it into the swirling mass of darkness they had called Nina before it could kill Marcus. She'd burst into a thousand motes of darkness and vaporised.

Enough to part night and day.

"I've done it before." The words died in his throat even as he said them.

He hadn't done it. Not really. Marcus had made it happen.

Betty grunted. "You don't sound so sure, kid. I'm guessing your use of this thing has been about as reliable as a public toilet's hand soap dispenser."

Oscar cringed.

"I figured. You're kind of a shrinking violet. Surprised you got Dmitri's interest. I remember back in the day, he had more of a taste for the terrible kind." She grinned.

Oscar swallowed. "I know. I've met Tildy."

Betty cackled. "She wasn't even the worst of 'em. But hey," she raised her hands, "variety is the spice of life, I guess. Some people like some yoghurt after their chilli peppers. Gotta cleanse the palette."

"What are you going to do with it?" Zara asked stiffly.

Betty turned the hilt in her hands, her face thoughtful. "That's what I oughta ask *you*."

Tension rippled through the air between the squat drag queen and the glowing nurse.

"Not to be a pain." Paige's voice sounded strangled. "But can we just go? This is the worst drag performance I've ever been to."

Betty flashed her a toothy smile, then cast a long look at the rusted hilt. "You." She pointed it toward Zara. "You should be the one."

"What?" Oscar whispered.

The hilt pirouetted through the air in a slow arc as Betty tossed it.

Zara's hand shot out to snatch it cleanly in its flight.

Paige coughed, and Oscar turned to see her clutching her throat, no sign of Vandle behind her. He caught the flicker of movement in the mirror beside him and tried to track it, finding nothing. He looked back to Betty just as Vandle dropped softly behind her, feet making no sound at all as she landed.

From above.

Oscar looked up.

All over the ceiling were mirrors he hadn't seen before.

"You have the touch." Betty nodded emphatically at Zara. "You weren't born with it like pretty little prince pasty over there, but you got it now, even if you don't got the same parts. A human body shared with one of our kind. You don't hum the same tune he does, but you definitely got the right stuff. And that look in your eye..." Betty cackled wetly. "You know what you want. Show me your conviction, girly. Show me your will."

Zara turned the hilt in her hand, looking at Oscar.

The blade is missing and cannot be reforged. But that doesn't mean you can't stab people with it. You just need to really want to do it.

Oscar swallowed.

You're not much the type for that, though, are you, Cricket?

"Do it," Oscar said softly.

Zara blinked, her eyes travelling back to the hilt.

"Focus your mind on what you must do," Betty croaked. "Have no doubt. No doubt in yourself, and no doubt that you will be the one to do it."

For a moment, nothing happened. And then a blade made of pure light burst forth.

The blade Oscar made that night in the cemetery was barely longer than his thumb. Faint and flickering. *This* was a sword. As long as an arm, clear and smooth, it pulsed in the hilt in Zara's hand so bright it hurt Oscar's eyes. Motes of dust swirled around it as it chased the darkness away.

"Holy shit," Paige whispered.

"Whoa," Zara breathed. "By the power of Gay-Skull."

Amazement and envy wrestled viciously inside Oscar's chest. This had been the only thing he had. The one thing only *he* could do. Zara could fight, Dmitri could fight, and now even Marcus could fight. They were all so strong. And now he was being left behind again. Just when he'd thought he was starting to catch up.

Taking a deep breath, Oscar forced a smile to his face and pushed all those feelings away. "That's amazing, Zara."

"How do I switch it off?" she asked numbly.

Betty shrugged. "What am I? The instruction manual?" she barked. "When you wanna cut, it wants to cut. When you don't..."

Zara frowned, narrowing her eyes, and just like that, the light went out, dropping the room into dank, miserable darkness again. The halo of the blade still stood in Oscar's vision when he blinked.

"Why? Why did you do all this? You were never going to take it from us, and you knew Oscar had it in his bag when you touched him."

Betty smirked. "You met the Bean-Nighe. There're ways and means, sweetheart. Hers may be fancier, but mine are more reliable. All it takes is one little touch from yours truly, and I can see where you been, what you got, and what you want." She shrugged. "Sometimes it's better to know what someone's done rather than what they're gonna do."

Oscar frowned, remembering the night in the cemetery. The

Bean-Nighe had read Marcus just by touching his hands. Those tentacles of Betty's must have had a similar effect.

Betty grinned broadly, raising her palms. "I just wanna say. I've been alive a long time kid, seen and done some good porkin', but that stuff you and the winged wolf get up to in the sack is a thing of beauty."

Oscar's cheeks burned.

"You can do all that?" Paige was still rubbing at her throat and dragged her scowl away from Vandle long enough to shoot Betty a look for disbelief. "But you're just..."

"Just what?" Betty gave a wide smile, showing those small, browning teeth. Light shone through the window from the head-lights of a passing car. As the room dimmed again, it fell beyond darkness, but only for a moment.

When the light returned, the room was *different*.

Gone were the mouldy peeling walls and dingy windowpanes. The broken boxes and rotted furniture. The room flickered in ethereal candlelight. Rich, opulent midnight and gold silks draped the walls, fine mahogany furniture cushioned with soft and plump pillows, the small table, ruined before, stood sturdy and filled with plates of the most delicious looking foods Oscar had ever seen. His eyes barely had time to take it all in before they found Betty. Vandle stood beside her, running her fingers through her slick white hair, a crooked smile on her face, unchanged. But beside her...

Betty was *beautiful*.

A lush mane of hair like spun gold towered on top of her head, statuesque features painted delicate and angular with immaculate makeup, blending to a sculpted jaw, and proud nose. She ran a midnight blue sequinned glove down the deep dip in the collar of her matching dress, from her Adam's apple to the toned crease in the centre of her lean, muscular chest, smattered with fine dark hair. Giggling, she swished her hips so her bulky skirts shimmered like shooting stars in the candlelight.

"What you see...isn't always the truth." Betty smiled beatifically. Her voice was still deep, but soft, rich, and melodic instead of rasping. "Sometimes, we must test the players to see whom we wish to back in the game. I've never been a fan of a blind bet."

"Jesus, that was a bit of a fucking glow-up. From bollock-chops to babestation in the blink of an eye." Paige stared around the room, mouth gaping in astonishment. "Can I get in on the action?" She looked down at the opening in her jacket where her wine-stained shirt peeked out.

Betty laughed softly, waving a gloved hand elegantly. The wine stain faded until the shirt was crisp and white once more. Paige grinned.

"There is nothing wrong with wishing for things to be as they were. Glamours are sometimes selfish, and not necessarily beautiful, but almost always useful." Betty smiled.

"Wait," Oscar said, confused. "So, which was the glamour...before or now?"

Betty chuckled, and Vandle smiled sharply behind her. "That would somewhat defeat the purpose, wouldn't it?" The drag queen smiled. "Maybe I do live in squalor, feasting on insects and sleeping on a pile of rotting rags in the corner. Or maybe I live in luxury. Perhaps I simply wished to have you drop your guard, to give and not just take information. Or maybe..."

She laughed again, this time the rattling empty drain of her former appearance. And then she spoke. The thick American accent was back. A car passed by, lights strobing through the windows, and in the blink of an eye, the room was its ugly former self. Creeping mildew and ruined contents. The Betty from before grinned, a thin line of spittle on her chin as she put her hands on the hips of her ugly dress once more. "Maybe I was just fuckin' with ya."

19

THE DOUBLED AGENT

Song's body shivered; their wide eyes turned on Marcus. Burnished gold alight and mouth open in a perfect 'o' of surprise, and then they were gone.

Their body broke apart and had vanished before it hit the ground, disappearing in wavering light like a sparkler being extinguished in the night. A million fireflies scattering and fading in an instant.

"No!" Marcus wailed.

No.

Dmitri felt the air chill. Every particle around him hummed. The earth groaned beneath his feet under the sheer pressure of the *wrongness* upon it.

Marcus moved to dash toward the spot where Song had fallen, but Dmitri grabbed his shoulder, holding him fast.

"Song!" Marcus cried.

"They will return." Dmitri's eyes traced the shadows, searching for the Umbran.

Marcus gasped a breath. His body quaked with fury and pain, voice distant. "I can still feel them. They feel far away, but they will come back to me."

"Marcus, Lyn," Dmitri growled. "It's here. Be ready."

Every instinct in him told him to change his form.

The beast within was practically trying to claw its way through his skin, but he held it back. It pressed harder against him, wanting to be released. He clenched his teeth, forcing the urge away, but in spite of himself, he felt his bones creak and muscles strain.

No.

I can't change.

Not again.

I might not be able to change back.

Dmitri snarled, and Marcus twisted out of his grasp, yowling at his crushing grip.

"I'm sorry—" he began.

Then, from between the twisted trees, stepped a man.

Or what had been a man, at least.

His face was sallow and bloated, skin like wet crepe paper with thick, black veins prominent beneath. A filthy trench coat hung from his shoulders, barely disguising the sickly bloat of his belly. His white T-shirt was smeared with dark brown dried blood, and his jeans filthy and stiff with faeces and urine.

He stank. So much so, it was like a dose of smelling salts that pulled Dmitri from the brink of shifting. A slap around the face with the stench of rot and death and that terrible wrongness.

Marcus stepped forward beside him, clenching his fists. Dmitri felt the air flex around him like a twitching muscle.

Good. He still has power. He can still fight.

"We have much in common, you and I," the thing rasped. It smiled, dark lips parting with open teeth, showing blackened gums and a swollen, dark tongue.

"Umbran." Dmitri's voice was hoarse.

The vile creature's smile faltered. "That is what they called me...as they called a fly a maggot." Dark blood trickled from the corner of its mouth. It looked too fresh to be the corpse's own.

"Why have you done this?" Dmitri gestured to the torn mound of tissue and flesh on the ground that had been the Gwyllgi.

The thing regarded the ruined guardian, breathing slow, wet, bubbling breaths. When it responded, it did not respond to Dmitri, but to Ocampo, who still stood by the thing, poised like a serpent ready to strike with eyes narrowed. "You," it said. "You hate this place. These people. I can feel it." It looked around, lifting a hand. Dmitri noticed there were fingers missing, raw nubs and bone visible.

"Absolutely." Ocampo smiled.

Dmitri's lip curled in a snarl.

"We could be allies," the Umbran gurgled.

Ocampo's dark eyes darted to Dmitri and Marcus almost unnoticeably fast. Her body was stiff, and her face a mask of indifference. "Why? What is your goal?"

The Umbran cackled, and more dark blood ran down its chin. The corpse the creature drove seemed somehow familiar, but Dmitri couldn't place him.

"The Gate," the Umbran said. "I need to open the gate."

Marcus flexed his fingers. "No more gates."

Ocampo took one step closer to the thing.

"You're talking about a world parallax?" Ocampo asked stiffly.

The Umbran nodded once, fixing her with its cloudy, dead gaze.

"And what do you need of me?" Ocampo's eyes shifted to the remains of the Gwyllgi. "Nothing that leaves me in such a state, I should hope."

The Umbran cackled softly. Its chest heaved. It seemed the thing could only force the corpse to speak in short bursts. "I almost have enough strength. Yours will not be needed. But I do have need of a new vessel."

Ocampo's pale hand touched her chest. "Me?" she asked, with thinly veiled disgust.

The Umbran shook its head carefully as though shaking more vigorously may cause it to come apart. "This shell liquifies and rots as we speak. It is bound together with my strength and its own bitter hate. I need one born of this world but with the touch of our own."

"No," Dmitri snarled immediately. The monster inside him roared.

No.

"And what is in it for me?" Ocampo mused, placing a delicate hand on her hip.

"The end," the Umbran rasped. "The end of all of this."

Ocampo stiffened. "You do not mean to merge the worlds?"

"I mean to end them." The Umbran's voice was thick with wretched hate. "I cannot take any more. I need to end them."

Stiff silence hung between them.

Ocampo shot Dmitri a twisted smile. "I think I should take you up on this offer."

Dmitri growled. "No. You can't."

Ocampo waved a dismissive hand, strutting over to the Umbran with a muffled clopping of heels. She stopped a healthy distance away, her eyes travelling up his rotting shell with disgust. "Though we should find your new body quickly. I'm not sure if I can bear this one long."

The Umbran cackled wetly again.

"And these?" Ocampo asked, a malicious smile spreading across her face as she gestured toward Marcus and Dmitri.

No. No. No.

This was bad.

Fighting Ocampo had taken Dmitri, Zara, and the Gwyllgi the first time. Now, against her and the Umbran, there was no chance. No chance without shifting. No chance without never coming back.

"Song is close," Marcus breathed.

Dmitri growled and allowed a little bit of the pounding

strength inside him free. Stopping it was like trying to plug a cannon hole in the side of a ship with his thumb to stop the crushing ocean from flooding in. But he managed it. He felt his jacket tighten at the shoulders and arms. His joints screamed as they began to stretch.

"We will kill them if it pleases you." The Umbran bared the corpse's teeth in a grizzly grin.

"Oh, it pleases me." Ocampo smiled slyly.

The Umbran took a slow step forward and raised its arms. The night flooded to it from the sky and shadows, cloaking its arms, curling and rolling around them like living oil. It tensed, and the blackness hardened into twin blades of the darkest shadow reaching almost to the ground.

And then Ocampo attacked.

She struck viciously, a crushing blow to the back of the head.

The back of the Umbran's head.

There was a wet crunch, and the thing collapsed, falling to the ground. An expression of violent victory appeared on Ocampo's face, and she raised a leg, ready to drive a foot through the thing's decaying shell.

Only the Umbran never hit the ground.

It went through the ground.

Sinking straight through like it was nothing, into the earth.

Into the dark.

It was gone.

"Did this bitch just save us?" Marcus crowed in surprise.

"Quickly," Dmitri snapped, raising a hand to Ocampo.

The Umbran stepped out of the night beside her as though darkness were an open door, its face twisted in a rotting mask of malice.

Ocampo lashed out with a fist, but the thing was quicker. It swung one oily bladed limb, severing her arm entirely at the elbow. Ocampo let out a ragged scream even as the Umbran twisted. Pivoting its body, it thrust one of its blades through her chest. Blood sprayed as it pulled loose. It spun, a ragged, soiled corpse puppet, swinging its other bladed arm and cut her across the middle. A spray of hot blood showered across Dmitri's face as the two parts of her fell—the upper half tumbling beside Marcus, the lower pitching forward where she had stood. One high heel fell loose from a pale, still twitching, foot.

Dmitri roared.

The Umbran was already stepping toward them, dark blood trailing from its split-lipped smile.

"No!" Marcus moaned desperately.

The Umbran raised a bladed arm, and Dmitri lunged forward.

"No!" Marcus screamed again, raising both hands and closing them in fists. He tensed his body, squeezing his eyes shut.

Dmitri hit first, but not against the Umbran.

The air was thick and dense, like he'd run into a huge cushion, the full weight of his body pummelling into it and springing him back, jarring him to his bones and almost causing him to fall over.

"Whoa there, big guy," Marcus said hoarsely. "I felt that."

Dmitri turned, his bones still humming like a tuning fork.

Marcus stood, hands raised and teeth bared, both fists clutched before him and a look of concentration on his face. "I don't want anyone else getting split in half tonight, especially not you. Oscar would be—" His body jolted as the Umbran struck, a wave of oily darkness thrashing against the shield and dissipating into the night.

For a moment, Dmitri thought he might fall, but instead, Marcus widened his stance and looked up at the thing, eyes flashing, and shot a feral grin. "Is that all you've got? It barely fucking tickled."

The beads of sweat forming on his brow said otherwise.

The next crushing blow almost forced him to his knees, and he let out a cry. Dmitri felt the hair lift on his arms, on the back of his neck. But the shield held. Dmitri's heart thundered in his chest.

This power...

"Marcus," Dmitri began gruffly.

"It's strong, but I don't have to hold out long." A bright trickle of blood ran from his nostril. "Song is close. Their sending is stronger now. It's harder to transfer energy when they're discorporate but possible."

Dmitri swallowed as he looked back to the Umbran, to the corpse puppet whose strings it pulled. One jagged, dark-bladed arm ground against the shield, twisting and scraping. The thing sneered.

"If you flee now, you can save yourself whilst I feed on these fools," The Umbran's voice rasped, its milky eyes boring into Marcus. "How long do you think you can hold me back?"

A chill ran through Dmitri's veins. *Feed on? So that was how it had grown so strong.*

Marcus ground his teeth. "Fuck around and find out," he spat. Blood leaked from his nostril into his dark moustache.

Dmitri prepared himself to fight.

INTERLUDE THE THIRD: THE
SHADOWS THAT BIND

The Umbran thrashed against the thickened wall of solid magick.

It could see the fear in the human's eyes. Sweat running down his dark skin.

Once the Unforgiven had been purged from this plane, even if it were fleeting, its bonded was weak. Besides him, the Theian and the darkborn were easily managed.

Still, it filled the Umbran with so much fury to be impeded by one human.

It roared as it put forth its full power, the power of the darkborn it had consumed—a rattling shriek of death and blood and bones. But it was a torrent of oil against water, its shadows spilling around the unseen barrier.

The corpse the Umbran wore shook under the pressure of its assault. The dead man's memories bubbled to the surface once more. It had known the dark-skinned man in life. Perhaps liked him, even. The Umbran grinned, dark blood running down its chin. Even *that* affection was deeply threaded with spite and confusion.

The human was growing weaker. The Umbran could smell it.

"Soon, your body will fail. What power the Unforgiven has gifted shall be spent. Then, I shall tear you to shreds."

"I'm not the only one running on borrowed juice," the boy had the nerve to shout back. "Guess we just have to see who runs out first."

The Umbran cackled. "You would compare a drop to an ocean?"

The darkborn, Tza, was bristling. Preparing to release. To fight. The Umbran could feel his power building. It was not insignificant, perhaps close to the beast it had slaughtered behind them. He would be easily dispatched, though.

The Umbran smiled again, ready to resume its assault, ready to bleed the boy dry of every spot of magick he wielded, and then his blood too...and that interesting jelly humans seemed to have around some of their inside parts. The Umbran liked that.

But then...it felt *something*.

Like the shifting of tension on a spider's web.

Something powerful and delicious.

Magick.

A greater well than this boy borrowed. Old magick as deep as bones. One of the two great powers it had felt in this place had unveiled itself, and it was close.

Without speaking, the Umbran sunk into the shadows, allowing itself to be taken by the darkness, like a rushing river, pulling it towards its destination. The last thing it saw before it did, was the wide, surprised eyes of the human.

The Umbran followed the fading scent of magick, shooting through the darkness like a signal through a fired nerve, unerringly seeking its destination.

It wasn't ripe and flowing any longer, but it could still sense the faint, irresistible residue of the magick's flow. It was different from the delicious and rancid stink of hate—sharp, sweet, and light, like a stinging cut in the fabric of this world, rather than a festering gouge. With even one less darkborn consumed, it may not have had the ability to trace it, but the Theian gatekeeper had been powerful. Its blood had flooded the corpse with new strength.

In moments, it found it, pulsing through the walls of a building like a fragile heartbeat. Magick so deeply stitched and ingrained, it would have been impossible to find from afar. And in it, the source.

The Umbran stepped from the darkness, snapping through wards that were flimsy against its new strength, and found itself in a filthy room riddled with power. A squat Theian stood before it, eyes widening as she realised her error.

"Vandle!" the Theian cried, and there was a flash of pale movement. The Umbran traced it, flitting between shining surfaces above.

Ah.

A light dancer.

The Umbran smiled even as the creature flashed out of the closest mirror, hands raised to attack.

With a flick of a wrist, it pierced her.

A single spear of shadow from the ground through the belly.

Her crimson eyes widened, and she fell to the floor.

Such a weak light could never stand against the deepest of shadows.

The powerful one staggered back, spluttering, saliva dripping from her thin lips. "You shouldn't be here. You shouldn't be able to find me."

The Umbran breathed in. Tasting the scent of the Theian on the air. Identifying her flavour.

Oh.

"Hello, Truthspeaker," the Umbran's voice rattled wetly.

The Theian quailed.

"I want you to know that you are the final piece. Your power will give me enough to end this. Your sacrifice is appreciated."

Yes. This power would be enough to crack the wards on the house like nothing, and pluck the touched one like a juicy berry.

"I ain't gonna sacrifice nothin'!" the Theian cried, and let out a whip crack of power, pushing herself forth on translucent tentacles from beneath her attire.

The Umbran snarled, lashing to one side to avoid the Truthspeaker, but she would never have struck anyway. The Truthspeaker sailed across the room, wide from where the Umbran had stood. "Vandle, get me outta here!" she cried.

The pale one pushed up from the floor, leaping for the tall glass panel in the corner, pressing her fingertips against it. Her other hand stretched toward the squat one.

The Umbran roared, throwing its full force into its arms, pulling on the shadows in the room. The walls groaned as magick tore. They bled darkness and light. Tendrils of black tore through the air and snatched at the Truthspeaker, grabbing her in their clutches.

"Go!" the Truthspeaker howled, even as the Umbran squeezed. Even as the darkness began to split her flesh and crush her bones. "Warn them!"

The pale one looked aghast.

Warn them? Yes. The Umbran could taste him on the air now, only faintly under the cloying sweet magic that filled this place. The human touched by Theia had been here recently. The key to the locked door of eternal peace. The Umbran smiled. *So close now.*

The Umbran squeezed again, and the Truthspeaker shivered. Flickered. At once, a squat, bedraggled thing and a sinewy, elegant creature. "GO!"

And then she burst apart like a smashed fruit.

A shockwave of dying magick burst loose, and several of the mirrors placed above and around the room shattered. Sparkling reflective glass showered in fragments and motes as the meat of her pulped between the Umbran's inky tendrils.

The Umbran prepared its strength to lash out at the light-dancer next, but it was too late. Her body was already moving, diving into the unbroken mirror she was beside. She slipped into the nothing between spaces, where shadows could not touch.

Roaring in fury and victory, the Umbran lashed out at the mirror, shattering it too into pieces.

The walls bled of their colour and dingy, mottled stains. They might have been grand and opulent, but were instead splattered with dark blood and tissue.

"It's over," the Umbran snarled, letting the shadows retreat as it moved to feed upon the mashed remains. "It's finally going to be over."

And it began to laugh.

20

BAD NEWS TRAVELS FAST

O scar was glad to find the lights on back at the house.
Glad because the glowing eyes of the house meant
someone was home, which usually meant Dmitri. His excitement
soured when he walked into the living room and found no sign of
him, only Tildy sitting on the chair, a small book pinched
between her fingers. Oscar recognised the book. It was a worn,
old thing written in Romanian. Dmitri said it was the closest to
truth humans had gotten down in writing about him and his past.
It was kept in the office.

That meant Tildy had been snooping around.

Oscar's jaw clenched, but he fought off the scowl as Ed let out
a low *bork* and head-butted his leg in the form of what Oscar
thought might be a pit bull. Oscar reached down and rubbed a
surprisingly silky spot behind one flopping ear as he heard Zara
and Paige arguing their way through the front door behind him
about which Betty Blumpkin had been the glamour.

Tildy smirked, raising one eyebrow and putting the small book
down. "Nice evening? You've been quite the busy little bees,
haven't you?"

"Very. Have you been okay whilst we were gone?" Oscar forced a smile. He felt a flash of victory at how successfully he masked any irritation in his voice.

Tildy huffed like a snuffed candle; he almost expected to see a little bit of smoke come off the top of her head. "Had fun with dear Betty?"

Oscar remembered that translucent tentacle pinching him. "Tildy, what kind of mon—" He caught himself. "What kind of Theian is she?"

Tildy smiled. "She, like many of us, has been called many things, none of them quite the truth. Melusine. Cecaelia. For all we know, she could be the Lady of the Lake."

Oscar opened his mouth to reply, but his jaw just hung open wordlessly instead.

Well, she did give Zara the sword.

"So, what did dear Betty say?" Tildy asked.

"Don't tell her!" Paige belted out, barging into the doorway beside him, excited. "Not until she tells us if ugly Betty is the real one!"

Oscar cast a glance behind him, finding Zara in the hallway. She still held the rusted hilt in her hand.

"Oh, darling, of course I know." She waved a hand. "The question is what makes you so sure both aren't the truth."

Oscar thought for a moment. "Wait, what?"

"For fuck's sake," Paige moaned, opening her jacket and scowling at the returned stain on her chest.

There was a bang as the front door burst open behind them, and Zara cried out in horror.

DMITRI'S JACKET was split at the shoulders and across the back. The pungent odour of char and almost feral musk told Oscar he'd come very close to transforming fully. Other than that, he seemed unharmed. With one arm he supported Marcus, his face weary and blood streaked across his cheek. He could barely stand.

"What happened?" Oscar asked, forcing his way past Paige.

"The Umbran." Dmitri staggered forward. He was carrying something under his other arm, a mess of hair and—

"Will you please be careful?" Ocampo snapped. "I am not a cheap suitcase, you ridiculous fool."

Oscar's stomach lurched up into his throat. She was...*in half.*

Ocampo's slopping entrails smeared against the wall as Dmitri struggled to close the door behind them, leaving a gelatinous streak across the pristine white.

"You're getting me everywhere!" she snarled. "I'm not paying for that."

"Shut up," Dmitri growled.

"Just put me down. I can move quite adequately myself."

"I don't want you ruining the floors."

"You can walk on your guts?" Marcus interjected, sounding drunk.

"I am not a pitiful human. I have control of my entire body," Ocampo snapped back.

"Where's Song?" Zara asked.

Marcus' head lolled back, and he moaned loudly.

Oh, no.

Zara thrust out the hilt to Oscar as she moved to help Dmitri with his burdens. He took it clumsily, and she reached for Ocampo.

"No!" Ocampo snapped. Her voice had lost none of its usual command. "I do not wish for you to see me like this. I will not be handled like some mewling babe."

"Enough, Lyn. Now is not the time for pride," Zara scolded.

Dmitri hefted the woman's torso into Zara's arms. She lifted Ocampo under her arms gently, so they were face to face.

"Do not," Ocampo snarled, batting her away with one arm. It looked weak, pink, and raw. Far frailer than her other arm.

Had she just grown that?

Zara kissed her on the cheek, her face awash with relief.

Ocampo...is blushing?

"Put. Me. Down. This. Instant." Ocampo bit off her words, quelling Oscar's momentary surge of empathy.

"Let me get you some towels to stop you from getting everywhere, and then we can figure this out," Zara said gently.

"Towels are in the—" Dmitri began hoarsely.

"I know," Zara yelled back, already on her way to the laundry room. "I had months to do snooping, remember?"

Oscar rushed to Dmitri and Marcus, pushing the hilt in its old familiar place at his waistband as he slipped Marcus' other arm over his shoulder. "Are you okay? What happened to Song?"

"They'll be back," Marcus said weakly. "It just...takes time."

"He stopped the Umbran. Single-handedly held it at bay with his power. It was incredible." Dmitri's brow furrowed as Marcus' tiptoes dragged on the floor through the hall and into the living room.

"Used up what I borrowed. Nothin' left but dregs," Marcus said in a sing-song voice.

Oscar's eyes widened in shock. "You used it all up?"

Marcus grinned. "Yup!"

"What's wrong with him?" Oscar frowned.

"He's drunk on magick. It will pass, but he will be this way for a few hours."

Dmitri set Marcus down on the couch. His head rolled weakly. Oscar looked at him for a moment and then scooped up a scattered cushion and propped it under his neck. That looked better.

"The Umbran has slaughtered the Gwyllgi." Dmitri's voice was ragged. "We have no idea what happened to the Bean-Nighe still, but we know the Umbran has gotten stronger. It seems to be using the creatures it has killed. Making itself stronger by feeding on their flesh. Even among the most depraved of our kind, that is something of a taboo. It grants incredible power but reduces us to our primal urges. It must have been doing this since it came through the parallax, growing more powerful over the months." His eyes shone with concern.

"What happens if humans eat monster meat?" Marcus slurred. "Asking for an Oscar."

Dmitri's face darkened. "It does not bear speaking of. The result of that is where many of the myths of demons come from. Not all monsters of this realm have been Theian in origin."

"It's okay, we can figure it out. Betty Blumpkin told us what to do," Oscar said, shaking off his horror. *The Gwyllgi? How is that possible? That thing was something out of legend, literally.*

Dmitri stared at him, wrestling with something.

"We just use the sword. I had it all along, and Zara can use it now. Her blade is way bigger than mine was," Oscar babbled, "and she can cut the Umbran like night and day, and—"

"Oscar, it wants you," Dmitri cut in.

Tildy straightened up on the chair behind him.

"What?" Oscar frowned.

"The Umbran. It wants you. To use you as a vessel. The one it's in is not strong enough. It needs someone who has the touch of both worlds."

"What about me?" Paige asked sharply from her seat beside the door. "Is it after me too?"

Dmitri shook his head roughly. "It's not the same. You carry the aura, but your blood does not sing the same way. You are more resonant with the veil than most other humans, but I do not think the link is strong enough to satisfy the Umbran's need."

"Always the bridesmaid." Paige rolled her eyes.

"And Zara?" Oscar asked.

"I...don't think so. She is already—"

"Ocupado," Marcus supplied, grinning dopily.

Dmitri nodded.

"What will it do?" Oscar's mouth was suddenly very dry. "If it gets me."

"It will use you like a puppet. A costume for its grim parade to meet its terrible ends. I cannot let that happen." His hands cupped Oscar's face, and he kissed him gently.

"INSTEAD OF A DARK LORD, IT WOULD HAVE A QUEEN!" Marcus' magick drunk voice crowed.

"Give him up." Tildy was on her feet. "If the boy is what he wants, then give him up." Her earrings tinkled as she shook her head furiously. "Or we will all be slaughtered before he is taken."

"I will not," Dmitri growled.

"This is pitiful, Dmitri," Tildy spat. "You are immortal. To think you would be tamed by this whining twit is absurd! Give him up, or we will be torn apart like Vander and Alouicious! I didn't want to leave them either, but it was them or me! I had to let it take them, I—"

Dmitri rounded on her. "I should have guessed you had some hand in their deaths. Allies for centuries, yet you surrendered them the first chance you got to save your own skin."

"He is NOTHING," Tildy roared, her eyes lit with blue fire. The hairs on Oscar's arms lifted, and the air seemed to crackle around her. "Give the Umbran this foolish boy, or I will hand him over myself."

Dmitri threw a punch, but Tildy caught his fist in the air and twisted his arm. She hissed, releasing his hand, and with a flash of limbs, snatched him by the throat. Dmitri's eyes bulged in her powerful grip. Oscar saw his gaze fix on the crescent moon axe he'd left uselessly by the fireplace.

"This human is nothing. Not deserving of the energy it cost his mother to push him out. Less than—"

Paige moved across the room before Oscar even saw her. Her hand whipped out in a flash, and there was a crack as her palm struck Tildy full force across her snarling face. "Don't you ever talk about our mother." Her voice was ice and steel.

Tildy's blue, glowing eyes shifted to Paige, and she flicked a strand of blonde hair from her eyes the slap had set loose. When she spoke, blue flame licked from her lips. Scales were beginning to form up her neck and around her ears. Oscar's whole body buzzed with fear and horror.

"I will slaughter you all and feed the boy to the Umbran myself. Then it shall let me live freely." She raised a hand at Paige, her fingers a dusky blue now, tipped in long sharp claws. She was changing.

Paige staggered back, eyes wide and mouth flapping. Dmitri twisted and choked in her grasp, veins prominent in his temple and eyes wide, waking with burning embers.

"Stop!" Oscar's voice tore out of him, hard in his throat. Hard enough to make her freeze, those glowing eyes shifting to him. "Let him go, and don't you lay a finger on her."

"Oscar," Paige breathed, stepping back, eyes on his hands.

"I said, let him go!" Oscar screamed.

Tildy hissed, and then her eyes too fixed on Oscar, flickering flames dulling as they bulged. Her fingers loosened around Dmitri's throat, and he stepped away with a splutter. Tildy was still staring at Oscar in amazement. No, not quite him, just his hands. Oscar looked down.

He'd been so panicked he hadn't even realised he had pulled out the rusted hilt. Now, it was clutched in his fists and pointing right at Tildy, only it wasn't just a hilt anymore.

But that doesn't mean you can't stab people with it. You just need to really want to.

The blade that burst forth was not as big as Zara's had been, as long as his forearm perhaps, but it shone almost as bright.

"Well, isn't that something," Tildy whispered, stepping back. The blue of her eyes was still fading, and the scales retreated back down her neck. "Looks like the kitten has teeth." She gave a sickly smile. "Well, one at least."

"I only need one," Oscar said flatly, not quite believing what he saw.

I tried to do this for months. Hadn't the first time been Marcus?

Anxious not to take his eyes off Tildy, Oscar flashed a glance at his friend behind him. Marcus was seemingly unconscious on the couch, head back and mouth open.

It was me. I did it.

"As I was about to say, Tildy," Dmitri snarled. "The Umbran is seeking to end everything. This world and Theia. I am not sure how yet, but it seems it wishes to use Oscar to that end. You may be like a cockroach, but I doubt even you could survive the obliteration it plans."

Tildy smiled awkwardly. "Oh. Well, you might have led with that, darling."

"Get out," Dmitri spat.

"No," Oscar said firmly. Dmitri's eyes flashed to his in surprise. "We don't know everything yet. We can't send her away. Tildy, why don't you go and make yourself comfortable in one of the guest rooms. The smallest one should do well."

Tildy jolted like she'd been slapped again but then plastered that simpering smile back on her face. "Why, how gracious. Truly, I was mistaken which of you was the real host here."

"Oh, just fuck off and away upstairs to your room, and don't come down for supper, bitch. I'm pretty sure you just got grounded," Paige managed, though she still looked pale and shaken.

Tildy stormed through the living room door, narrowly missing a collision with Zara.

"Everything okay?" Zara asked. She was still holding Ocampo.

"I heard everything. She wanted to kill them and deliver Oscar to the Umbran," Ocampo said archly. Where she ended was swaddled with towels.

"Careful, darling. Don't get worked up, or your nappy might leak," Tildy snarled from the stairs.

Ocampo's smile was murder. "Thank you, Tildy. In return for your kindness, I won't share that you pissed yourself a little bit when the boy pulled out that sword."

The only response was Tildy's loudly stamping feet on the stairs.

Oscar looked down at the glowing blade in his hand.

"Good work, Booboo." Zara smiled, setting Ocampo down on the couch beside Marcus. He lolled slightly, his head falling onto her shoulder. Ocampo looked flabbergasted and tried to dislodge him but was unable to without losing her balance.

Zara placed one hand on Oscar's shoulder and held out her other. "Oh. Right." Oscar stared at the blade.

Just want it to stop.

The blade winked out.

Swallowing, he placed the hilt in Zara's open hand.

"Well, that was fun!" Marcus smacked his lips groggily.

"You're awake!" Oscar felt a wash of relief.

"What is she again? The Princess Snide, I mean," Paige asked, walking unsteadily to the other couch and dropping down limply.

"Uh, some kind of ancient water dragon," Oscar said.

Paige looked like she might throw up.

Oscar smiled.

Had Paige really slapped an ancient, powerful monster just to defend him and their mother?

"What happened to Marcus exactly?" Zara asked, passing the hilt between her hands. "From what Lyn tells me, it sounds like the Umbran had you on the ropes. Why did it leave you?"

"I'm not sure." Dmitri scowled at the ceiling as though he could hear that Tildy was up to something on the floor above. "It just stopped. Like it sensed something, and then, it was gone."

Zara grunted thoughtfully in reply.

"It went swimmingly otherwise, of course," Ocampo said dourly. "Barring the loss of the ethernal and my other half."

"Not your better half, but still pretty good," Zara shot back.

Ocampo's scowl deepened in a way that was dangerously close to pouting.

"Did Betty tell you anything of use?" Dmitri asked.

Oscar frowned. *Did she?* It was difficult. Like the Bean-Nighe, he got the feeling he understood less than half of what she'd said, but it was just less delightfully whimsical.

"I don't think so," Zara admitted. "Though the glamour was quite amazing either way."

"Many of our kind use glamours, but Betty has some of the strongest magick we know of," Dmitri agreed.

There was a knock at the door, and the room stilled.

"Who could that be?" Marcus said thickly. "Everyone we know is already here."

The knock came again.

It wasn't the door at all.

"There!" Paige shouted, pointing at the large square mirror above the fireplace.

In it was a familiar face, pale and long with slicked-back white hair. Only now, it was covered in blood as red as her eyes.

Vandle.

Screaming.

"What on earth?" Ocampo muttered.

"She's trapped," Zara said, stepping forward and raising her hand to smash the mirror.

Vandle shook her head desperately, waving her arms.

"No!" Paige shouted, jumping up and grabbing Zara's arm. "Look, she doesn't want you to break it!"

Dmitri stormed to the mirror and tore off the bundle of dill above.

The alabaster woman still thrashed against the inside helplessly.

"Then what—" Zara began.

Paige looked straight at the mirror. "Vandle, Vandle, Vandle!" she shouted.

The mirror quivered.

All seven feet of Vandle's slim body collapsed through the mirror, panting raggedly and covered with blood.

"How did you know to do that?" Marcus mumbled, dazed and blinking.

"It's just like the myth." Paige shrugged, eyes wide and body stiff. "Maybe she needs it as permission or something?"

"Some do." Dmitri's eyes were still fixed on the mirror.

Vandle gasped on the floor. Zara was beside her, pressing her hands to a gushing wound at her side that was quickly soaking the rug with claret. "What happened?"

Vandle's dark eyes searched around the room desperately. "Betty's dead," she gasped. "Betty's dead, and it's coming."

"What's coming?" Marcus replied dopily.

Then, there was a great shuddering groan.

The bay window shattered. Splinters of wood and glass showered the room, and Oscar raised his hands, desperately guarding his face.

Brick and wood crumbled away as the debris cleared, parted by the night itself.

There, standing before them, was a man.

Less a man than a corpse overflowing with darkness.

"It is time."

It smiled.

21

WHAT GOOD CAN IT DO?

D mitri was the first to move.

Oscar had barely lifted his hands away from shielding his face, and Dmitri was running. His eyes glowed in the night as his shirt tore, flesh stretching as his muscles grew, arms and hands rapidly elongating to unnatural proportions.

He leapt with uncanny grace, one large, clawed hand snatching his axe from where it lay by the upended chair beside Vandle's still, debris-covered body.

Oscar heard him growl something unfamiliar.

"Nenorocitul Dracului!"

The curved blade of the axe sparked into searing blue flames, and Dmitri sprang at the Umbran with inhuman speed and power.

The burning blade screamed through the air.

And stopped.

A dark tendril lunged from the shadows of night like a striking snake and coiled around his wrist, suspending him in the air.

The Umbran raised a hand, three fingers missing, festering meat and bone visible. It did not even deign to turn its head as darkness lanced from the earth. A large pike speared Dmitri's gut, piercing him front to back. His glowing eyes bulged, and the axe

191

slipped from his fingers, clattering uselessly to the ground, its burning edge snuffing out. Blood poured from Dmitri's open mouth.

"Dmitri!" Oscar screamed.

As though Oscar's cry had rekindled something within, Dmitri roared, his eyes burning like furnaces. A torrent of searing flames burst from his mouth toward the Umbran.

A swelling cloud of shadows engulfed the flame and poured like liquid night to cover Dmitri's mouth like a muzzle.

Darkness prevailed.

Paige fled, running toward the door to the hallway. The Umbran flicked its head, and a tendril of dark thrashed out, narrowly missing her and crashing into the doorway, half collapsing it in a shower of plaster and brick as she tumbled from view with a scream.

"Paige!" Oscar cried.

"Oscar, go," Zara barked. "Take Marcus and get as far as you can!"

She was moving now. The hilt burst to life in her hands, spitting out her broad glowing blade of will.

Oscar stared at Dmitri numbly as he writhed on the spike, his shirt hanging off him in tatters. His stretching limbs returned to more human forms as his body tried to heal.

Ocampo was off the couch. What was left of her body had swollen and grown, skin mottled and leathery. Her eyes shone as she used her arms to drag herself, the bulging towels covering her bisected waist coming free. Her guts undulated beneath her, propelling her behind Zara and leaving a thick trail of blood and mucus on the floor.

Our floor.

This is our home.

We are happy here, and this thing has come to take that all away.

Oscar stared numbly.

"OSCAR! GO!" Zara shouted over her shoulder again, bursting forward.

"I can fight too!" Marcus was staggering to his feet, face a grim mask of determination. "Let me help."

Oscar caught him as he almost fell.

"Help me," Marcus groaned to the space around him. "Give me more. I need more."

Confused, Oscar stared. The air beside Marcus seemed to shimmer.

Was that Song?

Oscar caught the edge of a faint wave of denial and sadness.

Refusing to give Marcus more?

No. Refusal to take more.

Ocampo heaved off the ground, fingers lengthened into claws. She'd barely gotten into the air when the Umbran snatched out. A massive hand of darkness grabbed her, closing around her torso and one arm with crushing force. She shrieked in agony.

Oscar dragged Marcus toward the half-collapsed door but was unable to look away.

They were losing. They were losing this fight so fast.

Zara ducked under the dark fist clutching Ocampo, swinging the willblade and slicing through its thick, oily wrist. The rest of the arm broke apart in the moonlight, and Ocampo's crushed body fell limp on the gravelled drive with a sickening thud.

Zara rolled as a wave of blackness lashed out, cutting through the air above her as she ducked. A burst of light carried her off the earth as huge dark spikes erupted from the ground where she'd stood but a moment ago. The Umbran, or the rotting man containing it, snarled, dark blood and spittle foaming at its mouth.

"You," it spat, in a bubbling voice, pointing at Oscar through the shattered front of the house.

Oscar froze, pulling Marcus closer to him.

Zara leapt, and the Umbran thrust its arm, sending forth

another giant fist of darkness. It clutched around her in the night, and the willblade fell to the ground with a clatter, its blade blinking out of existence.

"No," Oscar gasped.

Zara snarled and flexed. Ethereal light bulged from her body, and the fist of darkness shook and broke apart, unable to contain her. When Zara landed on the floor, she was...different. Before, he'd seen the spiritual energy leave her body as a fist or even as a burst beneath her feet to increase her speed or make her jump further. But this...this was armour. An entire body of ghostly energy swirled around Zara, making her appear twice as big. An exoskeleton of raw spirit energy.

She raised her fists, and the ghostly figure did too.

Oscar remembered what she had said when he asked if she'd gotten stronger.

Learned a few new tricks?

Well, no shit.

"Zara can do it," Marcus breathed. "Song won't give me more strength, but Zara can do this."

The Umbran roared, thrusting both hands toward Zara. Twin columns of pitch swirling night, each as tall as Zara's ghostly armour, exploded out of the shadows and struck at her with colossal force. Zara didn't try to move or dodge...she simply raised her hands, and the spirit's arms caught the descending darkness in the air. Oscar felt the earth shake beneath his feet with the impact, and the house groaned.

As the dust cleared, Oscar saw she was still standing. Her ghostly arms shook, her face twisted with exertion, but she held the darkness at bay. More, she was pushing it away.

"She's doing it!" Oscar breathed.

Then, a single spear of dark burst from the ground and drove through her belly. It punctured the ghostly armour smoothly and slid through her like butter. Zara's eyes bulged.

Screaming with audible agony and fury, she squeezed her fists, and the darkness burst apart between her ghostly hands. The Umbran watched calmly, cracked lips smiling murder.

With shaking hands, Zara reached down to the spike lodged in her belly. Bright red blood was spreading on her shirt, spilling down her front. Her mirroring aura crushed it with one glowing fist, and it shattered into nothingness, like a deadly spear of glass.

"Relent, and you shall live a little longer. It will be more painless than this. You can have the pleasure of witnessing the end," the Umbran croaked.

Zara panted heavily, a thin line of blood leaking from the corner of her mouth. The ghostly armour flickered weakly around her. Her eyes met Oscar's, large and afraid.

"Come here," the Umbran said to Oscar. "World walker. Child of the veil. Come here, and I shall give thy friends a painless end."

Zara moved, jumping in a flash and swinging her arm, one massive spiritual fist slamming through the air with force. The Umbran snarled, waving down his hand. The darkness from the very sky poured loose, driving Zara into the earth with a crash. The slick night spread across her like oil, pinning her as her armour faded. She coughed as more blood leaked from her mouth and nose.

"Come, child. Let us end this." The Umbran raised a hand toward Oscar.

Oscar felt tears running down his cheeks freely now. His body was shaking. He looked at Dmitri, still clinging to the dark spike through his body, desperately twisting and trying to get free. Ocampo was barely twitching on the ground.

And Zara. Zara waved a hand weakly beside her. The willblade. It was so close, barely a finger away.

Maybe she could...

Their eyes met for a moment, and she focused on him fiercely and nodded. Oscar's mouth went dry.

Does she mean...

Oscar swallowed.

"There is no sense in fighting," the Umbran drooled. The darkness-infested corpse stumbled forward.

Oscar's stomach turned. Threads of shadow seemed to be the only thing stitching the parts of its rotting form together. *How was such a frail-looking being so strong?*

"Marcus, wait here." Oscar moved carefully, turning and guiding his friend back to the couch.

"Oscar, no. You can't," Marcus sobbed, tears running down his cheeks. "You can't give up."

Oscar swallowed. "I love you," he whispered, squeezing his hand.

Marcus let out a wail, trying to hold onto him, but he was too weak. Oscar was already pulling away and turning his back on him.

He stepped slowly around Vandle's pale, still body in the centre of the room...over the broken bricks and wood.

"Oscar, please. Don't do this," Dmitri moaned, suspended in the darkness by his puncturing wound. The muzzle of shadow had ebbed from his jaw, perhaps weakened by the Umbran's preoccupation with Zara, but its remnants lingered at his throat.

"I love you, Dmitri." Oscar smiled through his tears.

Dmitri twisted desperately, letting out a futile cry.

"This is the right choice." The Umbran sounded...exhausted. "We must end these worlds. End all this hate. We cannot let them suffer any longer."

Oscar blinked, looking at Zara. "I love you."

Zara smiled tearfully. "I love you too, Booboo."

Oscar took one more step forward, so he stood mere feet from the Umbran.

"It is time," the Umbran breathed, relief thick in its voice.

It closed its eyes, raising a hand toward Oscar's chest.

"Now," Zara cried.

She thrust her hand, and a faint, ghostly light burst forth, connecting with the willblade. The rusted hilt flicked from the earth, sailing through the air toward Oscar.

This is it.

We have one more chance.

And it's me.

Heart pounding with adrenaline, Oscar snatched the spinning hilt from the air and—

The rusted metal slipped through his fingers, bouncing painfully off his chest with a *bonk* and clattered uselessly to the floor by his feet. Oscar stared numbly.

The Umbran let out a low, long, wet cackle.

And then, the darkness began dripping from the corpse's eyes, its nose, and ears. The missing meaty, swollen wounds of its absent fingers and nails and the broken splits in its torn belly were pouring darkness. A black darker than the deepest shadow, vast and terrifying, was twisting through the air, cocooning Oscar.

The last thing he heard was Dmitri screaming his name.

22

BRING ME A HERO

Darkness slammed around Oscar.

Again, and again.

He cringed and cowered, expecting to feel it driving into his body. Taking him. Claiming him like it had the man's corpse before him. But it didn't. Instead, it was rebuffed. Like a wave crashing against the hull of an impenetrable ship. A bucket of inky water on a windshield.

Oscar relaxed his arms a little, peering out and standing straight. The dark retracted. He saw the broken house around him again, Dmitri struggling desperately on the spear that held him. Zara panting on the ground. The darkness pulled back—not all the way, but enough. The body it had spewed from stumbled, a sagging, rotting puppet falling apart as the dark strings holding it together broke one by one.

"Why?" the Umbran croaked, a haggard whisper. "This cannot be."

Oscar swallowed, standing straight. "Why didn't you take me?"

The darkness swirled, the body pulled taut. One arm broke

free and fell with a dead thump to the ground. It bubbled in the shadows, fizzling into nothingness.

"Why didn't you take me?" Oscar asked again, louder now. He wiped his tears away with the back of his hand.

"I...cannot," the darkness groaned through the body. "Why? Why can I not?"

Oscar frowned. *What?*

There was a slow, drawling laughter from the floor. Ocampo lay limply, her frail new arm twisted at an awkward angle, the other propping her up. "It seems the boy has everything you want...but not what you need. He is a fool who does not hold on to hate."

The darkness hissed and boiled. "Impossible!"

Oscar swallowed. He crouched and picked up the willblade.

"Hate!" the Umbran screamed so forcefully, the body it rode's jaw fell, slack and broken. "Hate me!" it burbled, dark congealed blood running down the corpse's throat. "Hate me, or I will kill them all. I will make them suffer!"

Oscar shook his head, holding the willblade in front of him. "I don't hate you. I feel sorry for you. I understand. You can't take any more. You want it to end. I...I can help you with that."

The Umbran howled. Every remaining whisper of shadow poured from the broken corpse and rushed at Oscar all at once.

"Do it, Oscar!" Marcus shouted.

Oscar focused his will.

I have to do this.

Light burst forth from the hilt, piercing through the swelling darkness that rushed toward him with a resounding crack. Oscar felt the force of it through his arms.

"HATE ME!" the Umbran screamed.

"Finish it!" Zara cried.

Oscar felt the hilt hum in his hands. The light grew brighter. Longer. As long as Oscar was tall, but somehow it weighed nothing at all. It pierced through the Umbran's misting shadow and into the rotting corpse that barely even resembled a man anymore.

I have to do this for them. I have to save my friends.

The Umbran and everything it held shuddered. The inky sap pinning Zara melted away. The spike piercing Dmitri sunk back into the ground, his body landing with a thud.

Oscar saw Ocampo watching him. Watching him fight. She smiled and nodded.

"Oscar!" Dmitri moaned, pushing himself up, clutching his stomach. "You can do this. You could always do this. This is you. It was always you."

Tears ran down Oscar's face again.

I have to do this for Dmitri.

The blade grew again, bigger, thicker, brighter—as though it were cutting the very night in two. The Umbran screamed, renewing its struggle, a tornado of darkness thrashing against him, the light.

"Come on!" he heard Zara cry.

"You can do it!" Marcus was chanting.

"Oscar." Dmitri's grey eyes fixed on him, full of love.

"Finish it," Ocampo laughed.

And then he heard one more voice.

"Oscar?"

He turned his head. Standing in the broken doorway to the living room was Paige. A scratch above her eye leaked blood down her face and onto her wine-covered shirt. He stared at her as the tornado of darkness fought back, as he held his will against it.

Paige smiled. "Fuck him up, bro."

Oscar laughed, tears flowing down his face.

I have to do this for my family.

Brightness, like he had never seen, burst from the hilt. Light so bright he couldn't see anything anymore.

For a moment, there was nothing.

Only light.

His body was gone. No hilt in his hands, no earth beneath his feet. There was nothing.

This was what he needed to do.

This was the willblade.

Total conviction.

Total truth.

But...

A flicker of darkness.

A wisp of shadow in the light coiled toward his chest.

It wasn't total truth, was it?

He'd thought it as he walked toward the Umbran. Walked toward his likely end. He didn't want to give up. Not like he had before. He didn't want to give up. Not this time.

The flicker of darkness curled, searching the space before his chest, searching for its way in, for something it knew was there but couldn't quite reach.

They can never know.

But this...I need to do this.

And just like that, he was back inside himself, the hilt back in his hands, shaking with the force as he split the darkness with its blade. The blade of his will.

I have to do this...for myself.

Oscar screamed. The willblade burned in his hands, and the night exploded with brightness.

The Umbran shattered into a million shooting stars, and the rotting body that had held it slumped to the ground with a thud, bubbling into a dark pool of wet nothingness.

THE BRAG

(EQUUS SYCOPHANTAM))

23

THE BEST OF TIMES

While Oscar was helping the others back inside, Tildy reappeared, unscathed, skin pale, and blue eyes wide. Her pink lips pursed as she watched him from the hallway.

Oscar opened his mouth to ask her to help. Dmitri was so heavy, and he couldn't move much whilst the large wound on his abdomen was rapidly healing. To make things worse, Oscar's palms were sore and angry where the hilt of the willblade had scorched them, and he could barely grip anything at all.

Tildy's eyes sparkled, and she smiled.

Oscar froze.

This would be a perfect time for her to attack.

Everyone was weak and vulnerable. She could kill him or any of them as she pleased. Oscar's eyes searched desperately for the willblade. It lay on the floor where he'd dropped it when the hilt had become hot. Strangely, the hilt itself shone now. Much of the rust seemed to have burned away, leaving it a shining gold. Oscar looked back to Tildy, who licked her lips nervously.

"It's gone," Oscar managed, forcing the strength to speak into his chest. "The Umbran is dead. Help me get the others inside. You're safe now."

Tildy's body quaked strangely. For a moment, he thought she might transform, but then a delighted smile lit up her face, and she sprang into action, delicately walking through debris in her green pumps to lift Ocampo and set her on one of the now dusty couches.

Oscar quickly moved to retrieve the hilt. He dropped to his knees beside the slick black mark on the earth, all that remained of the Umbran, and reached tentatively toward the willblade. He jolted in surprise when he found it no longer burning hot but cool against his fingertips. Carefully, he moved to lift it, hissing at his stinging hands as he did. It felt heavier now. As he tucked it into the crook of his arm, Oscar spotted something else.

A coin.

Frowning, Oscar reached out and picked it up.

It wasn't like any coin he'd ever seen before. It was large and unfamiliar, thicker than most modern currency. It felt strangely old, but it was not faded or rusted; instead, it was a dark shining black. Something about it seemed important.

There was a groan from the middle of the room, and Oscar turned in surprise, tucking the coin awkwardly into his pocket with another gasp of pain. He rushed back through the debris and was surprised to find Vandle moving. Zara was leaning limply, one shoulder against the wall that had a huge crack down the middle. Her eyes met Oscar's, still wet and shining, and she smiled.

THREE WEEKS LATER, the house was still a wreck. Though the living room had taken most of the damage from the Umbran's attack, the effect that it had on the structure of the house made the damage from the gaeants look like scuffed paintwork in comparison.

The master bedroom wall was half caved in, with broken furniture and smashed bannisters on the landing. The torn bay had set a deep crack along the inner wall and left the floor of the front bedroom—where Tildy had hidden for the entirety of the attack—unsupported and dangerously sagging.

Dmitri had used some of his contacts to quickly get builders in place, no questions asked. Now, most of the front of the house was out of bounds, covered in scaffolding and sheets.

Zara sat at the breakfast bar in the kitchen, wearing her favourite dungarees. Every time Oscar looked at her, she was grinning over the large bowl of cereal in front of her.

"Hey." Marcus was slathering more jam on his barely golden toast, until it finally crossed the point of being more jam than bread. "Hey, look at us. All superpowered and living in one house like a big happy family. Who woulda thought? Not me!"

Oscar grinned, and the air beside Marcus emanated a warm feeling of amusement. Song was almost visible sometimes now, but most of the time, they were a thickening blur in the air, like the sun beating off a car bonnet.

"Don't say things like that." Zara swallowed a mouthful. "You'll wear out our welcome."

Oscar wasn't sure that was true.

"With the champ?" Marcus squeezed Oscar's arm affectionately. "Last man standing versus the strongest thing we've ever met? I don't think so."

Oscar blushed.

"I can't believe you've been so chill about the house getting trashed." Zara shook her head. "You guys had just gotten it so nice."

Oscar shrugged, grabbing a slice of toast. The skin on his palms hadn't been burnt too badly. Zara and Dmitri had dressed it in some strange lotioned bandages until just a couple of days ago. It looked good, if a little pink, but felt tight. "It's just stuff. I'm just glad no one got hurt too badly."

"No one but Doctor Bitchcraft upstairs," Marcus said brightly and then bit into his toast.

Oscar grimaced. Ocampo was upstairs and had been sharing a room with Zara. She seemed to be avoiding him still, but he heard her moving around sometimes and almost caught her voice once or twice from the landing. Zara said she was almost done regrowing. Oscar wasn't sure if she stayed out of the way because she disliked him in general or because of what had happened.

After the fight with the Umbran, she'd been on the sofa watching him cautiously. He'd felt the need to say what needed to be said. "Thank you for fighting for us, Lyn. Thank you for being on our side." She'd blinked at him, dazed, and what he did next still haunted him. Unsure what to do, he moved to the sofa and hugged her. She'd gone as rigid as a board. Shortly after that, she said something quietly to Zara and was helped up into one of the rooms. He hadn't seen her since. Zara thought the whole thing was hilarious.

Oscar was enjoying having Marcus and Zara close. Marcus was regaining his strength quickly, and Oscar sensed he wanted to be here more because he was lonely without Song. Every day, he told them they were closer to being reformed. The ethernal kept giving Oscar affectionate nudges; they had seen how he had protected Marcus.

Lyn Ocampo being a houseguest wasn't even the strangest thing about their lives now.

After the Umbran had been defeated, Tildy had been anxious to leave. But then Oscar had found her standing on the porch, staring out at the night.

"You talked about your friends before," Oscar had said. "And you had Dmitri before. You haven't been alone for a long time, have you, Tildy?"

Tildy recoiled like he'd slapped her.

Then she'd given him *that* look. The one like she might tear off his head and wear it like a hat for high tea. "What?"

Oscar had filled the staggered silence; he could barely believe his own words. "You can stay a little longer. Until you're ready to move on."

There was a flash of emotion in her eyes, and she reached out to pat his shoulder with her soft lily-white fingers.

Since then, she too had ventured out of her room rarely, seeming quiet and withdrawn. She did come out to collect and return books from the office, which she devoured at an alarming pace. Oscar suspected she may not stay much longer.

Vandle and Paige had gone.

He'd thought Vandle wasn't going to make it, but she healed even quicker than Dmitri. By the time everyone had struggled inside, she was propped against the fireplace. She accepted the offer of a cigarette from Paige and watched as Oscar finally found his exhausted way into Dmitri's arms to be showered with kisses and whispers of love. Oscar could have fallen asleep right then, but Vandle was standing not long after. She said she needed to make sure Betty had a proper send-off. Oscar wasn't sure what that meant, but the strikingly tall, red-eyed woman left, back through the mirror, which somehow remained intact despite everything else being damaged. Oscar was left with the prickling concern that after Paige said her name three times, Vandle could just come back whenever she pleased. He spent some time searching for that bundle of dill in the debris and hanging it in its place once more.

Paige had sparked up a cigarette and sat on the floor. Oscar didn't have the heart to ask her to help. She looked pale and shaken, eyes glassy with shock.

"Can I go now?" she finally asked, in a puff of smoke, when everyone was in one room and definitely breathing.

Oscar had sat on the floor beside her, his body protesting at the effort, and looked out the gaping face of the house at the surrounding trees and stars. "Maybe you should stay one night? To keep an eye on me?"

Paige snorted a short laugh and jabbed his arm with her

knuckles. "Maybe I can. But I think you can take care of yourself now, you little spunk-muppet." She ruffled his hair. She hadn't done that since he was little.

He still hated it.

The next morning, she'd left, bright and early. She said she might track down that leprechaun. Well, either that or go stay with her friends 'to get away from this freakshow' for a while.

Other than the ruined house and their unusual guests, it was almost like none of it had ever happened. That was part of the reason Oscar kept the black coin in his pocket now. He'd wondered about the man whose body the Umbran had destroyed. Who had he been? It didn't seem right for him to have no one know what happened to him or remember his loss. He felt like he needed to keep the coin. Someone needed to remember what had happened to the man, even if they may never know his name. He hadn't shown it to Dmitri for fear he would want to take it away.

Oscar was just pouring himself a bowl of cereal when Dmitri came downstairs. He'd been busy in the attic, having finally gotten around to emptying the rest of the luggage from their travels.

He was more casually attired than he usually liked to be, dark navy jeans and a white T-shirt snug around his muscles in a way that made Oscar nearly overfill his bowl with cereal and cover the countertop. The corner of Dmitri's mouth lifted as though he could sense Oscar's thoughts. He'd fully recovered, though the pink puckered scar on his abdomen seemed to be fading slower than his wounds usually did. Dmitri thought that was because the Umbran had been a pure Theian. Fortunately, the insides it had skewered seemed to have healed better.

"All done?" Oscar asked, curious.

Dmitri nodded, walking behind him and wrapping one arm around him, kissing his cheek. Oscar breathed him in. Whatever he'd been doing in the attic had made him sweat, and the deep, smoky scent made Oscar feel a little dizzy.

He was long past suspecting Dmitri of using any kind of pheromone on him. He knew now that his natural scent just did things to him.

"It is finished," Dmitri said. "I am going to meet with the builders. There seems to be some problem with getting the glass."

"Can you give me a lift?" Zara asked. "Lyn is still sulking, and I haven't been to see Nani in a couple of weeks."

"Of course." Dmitri nodded. "I can bring you back too if you like. I should not be long; the contractors seem to be trying to scam us for materials, so I just need to do some convincing."

Oscar smiled. Dmitri's pheromonal abilities had such practical uses sometimes.

"Shouldn't be much trouble," Marcus mumbled. "We know how good you are at that. Heard you convincing Oscar a lot last night. I don't know why you had to keep going, though; he was saying 'yes' for ages."

Oscar felt his cheeks burn.

Maybe we were a little overenthusiastic last night.

Also, maybe it is actually time for everyone to go home soon.

"Don't worry, Os." Marcus nudged him. "I know you gotta put the work in. It's not just about him hitting your bitch switch; you gotta put the mix in the oven if you wanna bake them buns."

Zara snorted milk. "No thanks, Marcus!"

"What?" Dmitri asked, curious.

"Nothing," Oscar cut in quickly.

"Dmitri." Marcus' face was serious. "I need to ask—"

"No!" Oscar cried.

Marcus tilted his head. "Um, why can't I ask Dmitri about his cool axe?"

"Oh." Oscar's cheeks flooded with colour. "Sorry, go ahead."

"I'm guessing it's some kind of enchantment? Ethereal fire bound into the metals?"

Dmitri nodded warily. "Yes, it is."

"And the activation," Marcus said. "I heard it, something about...Necrototal Dracula?"

Dmitri looked a little uncomfortable at that. "It is a dangerous weapon. It was designed with the purpose of killing only. I do not wish to encourage your interest."

"You know I'm going to figure it out, so just tell me."

Dmitri sighed. "Fine. It is the axe's name. 'Nenorocitul Dracu-lui.' Please, do not speak it in its presence, or you may burn down the house."

"Nenorocitul Dracului," Marcus repeated. "Romanian? What does it mean? Dragon of death or something?"

A shadow of amusement passed over Dmitri's face. "No. It actually translates closer to something like...'Fucking Bastard.'"

Marcus' eyes widened in shock.

Zara laughed. "That's its name?"

Dmitri smiled. "The story is that it was not intended to be named so. The craftsman named it by mistake, cursing after acci-dentally burning himself on it during its enchantment."

"Still a funny name for an axe." Oscar smiled.

"One more question." Marcus grinned. "Dmitri, is there any chance you could get Oscar pregnant?"

24

THE WORST OF TIMES

Oscar, still smiling from Dmitri's last kiss, waved back at Zara in the passenger side of Dmitri's car as it rounded the corner before he closed the front door.

Sometimes he was so happy, he thought he might just start crying the minute he was left alone and it started to sink in.

He could hear Marcus speaking from the kitchen, voice low and intense. He realised he must be speaking to Song. Shifting on his feet awkwardly, Oscar wondered if he should give them a minute. It seemed rude to interrupt his friend and their...Song. Then something caught his eye. Something unusual at the top of the stairs.

Quietly, Oscar made his way up.

The ladder to the loft was still down. Had Dmitri forgotten to put it back to its normal place? Oscar was just setting his hands on it, to push it back up, when a face appeared in the gap above him, pale and beautiful, a tumble of blonde hair atop her head.

"Tildy? What are you...you shouldn't be up there."

"Come, Oscar. I owe you the truth." Her blue eyes flashed mysteriously.

"Dmitri said—" Oscar began.

"Are you forbidden passage in your own home?" She arched an eyebrow, and before he could answer, disappeared from view.

I owe you the truth?

What is she talking about?

Chewing his lip, Oscar wondered whether he should call for Dmitri. Maybe he should just walk away or ask Marcus to come with him. But Tildy hadn't caused them any trouble in a while. The niggling curiosity was already pulling at him.

He heard a clatter from above and worried what she may be doing. Dmitri had said there were dangerous artefacts up there.

Oscar checked at his hip, finding the willblade securely tucked in his belt, then gripped the ladder and began to climb.

THE ATTIC WAS dark and held a deep musty smell that reminded Oscar of the house the first time he'd been here: damp, stale, and empty.

The space had been organised adeptly. Various boxes and chests were arranged at the edges where the roof tapered the height of the ceiling. Pieces of old and unused furniture filled with trinkets and sealed bottles sat around. He had to walk around an old dresser and bureau before he found Tildy. The old wood laid on the beams beneath him creaked softly. She sat on a small threadbare stool, a box open before her, papers scattered on the floor. Her broad, aqua trousers were bunched around her legs, and her white ruffled blouse was rolled up at the sleeves. A large opal sat at her throat among the froth of her collar.

"You have been the most gracious host, Oscar Tundale, and I would be remiss if I held the truth from you any longer."

"What are you talking about?" Oscar asked.

Tildy waved him delicately to the tall-backed chair beside her. Oscar moved the box from atop it, eyes briefly scanning for spiders before he sat down.

"I have known dear Dmitri for many years, as you are aware. But what he did not know is, even after our paths diverged, I kept my eye on him from afar. Not only were we husband and wife, but we were allies for a time. I felt a responsibility for his actions, being his elder."

"You didn't like that he was hunting other monsters? Theians hurting people, I mean," Oscar asked.

Tildy spared him a sharp, brief smile. "There is much I did not like, but that was a factor, yes."

Oscar frowned, trying to peer at the open package she held in her hands. She tilted it aside absently, obscuring his view.

"During that time, some things came to my attention. Some unusual dealings. I would not have shared them with you, but as you have been so kind to me, I felt I must."

Oscar shook his head, confused.

Ever so slowly, Tildy handed him the package.

Oscar's heart lurched strangely in anticipation as he took it in his hands.

Slowly, he slid out the contents, bundled together and secured with string.

He looked at Tildy as she watched him with a patient gaze.

"What is this?" he asked, peering at the bundle. "Old photographs?"

Tildy simply nodded at the bundle.

The knot was only loosely tied. Oscar only needed to pull one end of the string for it to open up. The first picture was Dmitri.

It was a faded sepia. His hair was shorter, slicked back behind his ears. He wore some kind of military uniform. It must have been a hundred years old, yet he barely looked any different.

Oscar smiled.

So handsome.

He wondered if the uniform might be in one of the boxes up here. That might be fun.

"Keep going," Tildy urged.

He did, moving through images of people he didn't know, several of Dmitri, in different clothes, with different hair. Face always sculpted and handsome, untouched by the years.

"Stop," Tildy snapped suddenly.

Oscar froze.

"What?"

Tildy nodded again at the photo in his hands.

It took Oscar a moment to recognise Dmitri. He wore a bright patterned shirt Oscar was unaccustomed to seeing on him. His hair hung in thick, greasy-looking curtains, a trimmed moustache on his lip. They were in a kitchen. Some kind of party. The wall was covered in ugly wallpaper, a faded teal adorned with little bunches of flowers with pink roses. So many things looked familiar.

Oscar saw the fridge.

He remembered it. The same humming fridge he had imagined filled with body parts as he searched for Marcus.

"That's here." Oscar ran his thumb across the photograph.

His eyes travelled back to the other people. One man had reddish-brown hair, an unruly mop, and blue eyes that sparkled. He wore a dark suit and had one arm around Dmitri. *Who had he been to Dmitri? He looked just like...*

And the woman.

Gaunt cheeks at odds with the swell of her belly. Her dark hair was coiffed neatly, and she smiled like someone with a secret. She looked just like Paige.

But it couldn't be.

"Who is that?" Oscar breathed, but he knew the answer. His heart pounded in his chest.

Tildy watched him patiently.

Oscar's heart beat faster.

The man. The man Dmitri had his arm around...

Oscar swallowed, feeling bile burning in his throat. "That's—"

"Your parents," Tildy said. "And your sister, not long before her birth." A lacquered nail tapped his mum's round belly in the photograph.

Oscar felt tears stinging his eyes.

What?

Why?

No more secrets, Dmitri had said.

No.

No, he hadn't.

He'd said no secrets from now on...

A tear ran down Oscar's cheek, and he stared at the picture like its inhabitants might begin to speak and explain their story—explain why Dmitri hadn't told him about this...to make it okay.

But it wasn't going to be okay. How could this be okay?

"Why would he—" Oscar swallowed a sob.

"I suspected he had never told you," Tildy said. "I thought you deserved to know." Her voice was shaking slightly.

Oscar looked at her. Was she crying too?

No.

She was laughing.

Her eyes crinkled, and she wore a wide satisfied smile. The cat that got the cream.

"Why?" Oscar swallowed the lump in his throat. "You...you didn't do this to help me. You didn't do this because you thought I deserved it." Anger at Dmitri bubbled in his chest. Snakes of betrayal twisted in his stomach. "You did this just to hurt me."

Tildy laughed softly like tinkling bells. "All the greatest things in life serve more than one purpose. Truly, this has served many."

Oscar swallowed again and couldn't bite back a sob. He dropped the picture on the floor and stood. "Get out," he snapped.

Tildy smiled. "With pleasure. I suspect my business is finally done here."

Oscar's hands were shaking.

His legs felt weak, like his whole body was pulling him downward. Not just that, but his whole body felt heavy. Dragged down. Like something in his pocket weighed far too much.

"And Oscar, darling," Tildy said smugly.

He froze, anger simmering.

"Next time you want to challenge someone, you had best make sure that they are in your league. Frankly, you're lucky I just didn't tear you to shreds."

Something inside of him gave way. A wall to a dam, releasing a flood of fury. He turned on her. "Shut up, Tildy. Just *get out*."

And in that moment, he hated her.

25

THIS IS HOW IT ENDS

O pening the door to her parent's house always felt strange to Zara. One, they left it unlocked despite living in one of the less desirable areas of Hackney. Mum said she would never have her door locked when her family might want to come in. Two, as much as her memories tried to impress on her that this was 'home,' it wasn't. It was just where she grew up.

Closing the UPVC door behind her and pulling up the handle, so it was at least on the latch, Zara trod on her heel and pulled off one boot. The house was a little too warm, as usual—she wouldn't be surprised if the heating was on despite the weather—and the smell of food was heavy in the air.

"Mum?" Zara kicked off her other boot and paced down the hall through the kitchen door, only to find...well, not the last person she would ever want to see, but close.

"What's up, cuz?" Rami said through an irritatingly handsome face full of food. He sat at the table, spoon in one hand and elbows propped on the table's edge, in a state of perpetual flex. Everything Rami did was an excuse to flex. He wasn't in his police uniform today, instead wearing pale denim jeans and a white T-shirt a size too small for him that strained around his chest.

"Hey. Is Mum in?"

Rami swallowed, dropping his spoon in the bowl. He leaned back and stretched. Zara rolled her eyes as the veins in his biceps and neck bulged. *How had Oscar ever dated this asshole?* Zara didn't have an out since they were cousins, but anyone who wasn't blood-related needed to stay far away from this.

"Upstairs with Nani," Rami said. "She's having a good day today. That's why I came over."

"Oh, really?" Zara eyed the bowl heaped with rice and meat. "You didn't just come over to eat all our food?"

Rami smirked and eyed her up and down.

Damn.

Irritation lit up in her like a spark to a puddle of petrol.

Rami had always made fun of her for being fat when they were younger, and now here she was, commenting on his jumped-up, muscle-Mary dietary intake. And she'd said 'our.' This wasn't Zara's home anymore. Her father had made that very clear when she came out. Even if things were better now, she could still never forget those words.

Swallowing her anger at herself, Zara forced a nonchalant shrug. "I'm heading up then."

Rami nodded, still smirking.

She was just turning when he spoke again.

"How's it going with the Ghato?" Rami asked. Cocky as he was, even he couldn't make that sound like a casual question.

"It's going," Zara shot back, sparing him a wary glance over her shoulder.

The spirit inside her, the Ghatokacha that Nani said she'd carried for almost three hundred and fifteen years, had been promised to Rami. But that was before Zara had been at death's door, and transferring it had been the only way to save her.

"Not too much of a burden?" Rami pressed, picking up his spoon again, dark eyes fixed on her.

"Not at all. You know me, getting my fight on. Dealing with

monsters powered up by eating the flesh of other monsters. Getting the work done."

Rami's eyes flashed curiously.

Zara waited.

She knew it was coming.

It was always coming.

"Well, just let me know when you want me to take over." He gave a tense approximation of nonchalance. "I've been training my whole life to bear it. Imagine what good it could do if it were wielded by someone like me instead of..." His eyes travelled over her again, and he sneered.

The flame that had been burning in Zara amped up to a bonfire.

She put her hands on her wide hips, turning to face him. She knew her eyes were glowing. Rami's eyes widened, and his mouth hung open, full spoon halfway to his face.

"Yeah, I can imagine. Maybe when there's not so much to do anymore, and the world can handle a little boy trying to play as one of its protectors, I'll hand it over. Until then, *cuz*, don't trouble yourself. I've got it."

The food on Rami's spoon slid free, sauce and meat and rice falling onto his crisp, white—too small—t-shirt.

"Fuck," Rami growled, quickly brushing it off himself, snatching for the kitchen towel beside him. In doing so, his beefy arm clumsily knocked his glass of water, sending it over the edge of the table.

Zara had already turned and was smiling when she heard it shatter. "Try not to make too much of a mess." She grinned and made her way upstairs.

～

"I THOUGHT I HEARD YOU." Zara's mother smiled. She was just closing Nani's door as Zara reached the top of the stairs.

"Hey, Mum. I think somehow a pig got loose from a farm and is in the kitchen eating all your food and making a mess." Zara reached out for a quick hug.

"I'll call the RSPCA." Her mother's eyes twinkled before embracing her. She smelled of clean laundry and just a little of the sweet floral perfume she'd used since forever. It made something inside Zara's chest feel warm.

"How is she?" Zara asked.

"Tired." Her mother sighed and suddenly looked just that. "She is having a good day, but you know how that burns out her energy. I worry she doesn't have many good days left; they get fewer and further between."

The warmth that had been inside Zara's chest froze, and she forced a stiff smile.

"It's hard to be sad when someone so amazing has been part of our family for generations, but I just don't know what we will do without her." Her mother's eyes shone, and she dabbed their corners.

"It's like the moon just disappearing from the sky one day," Zara agreed.

Her mother hugged her again.

She didn't let go as quickly this time.

"Don't tire her out. I know what you two are like when you get together. I'm so proud the family has another strong woman to protect it for my lifetime, and who knows how many beyond it." Her mother's voice was muffled in her shoulder.

Something about those words set an uncomfortable prickle across Zara's skin.

How many people's lifetimes would she live if she kept the Ghatokacha?

How many friends will I have to say goodbye to?

THE SMELL of dying was not just blood and rot.

Zara had been around dead and dying people before.

She'd washed and wrapped children who didn't have the strength to carry on.

She'd pushed on chests and held hands in the resuscitation room.

More recently, she'd found mangled limbs in hedge bottoms.

But dying smelled like this, too.

Like the crisp smell of clean linens mixed with sour milk. Stale breath, and body that no matter how many times you cleaned it, was soiled again by the time you covered it with fresh sheets.

She left the door open.

She hated the idea of associating this smell with Nani. Nani, whose smell was sweets and nuts.

Nani Anjali's eyes were closed, and they stayed that way as Zara quietly took the seat beside the bed. Her skin was blotchy now, paper-thin. Wrinkles like cracks breaking apart the woman Zara had grown up staring at as she read her stories. White hair cut short to her jaw, dry and fluffy. Nothing like the snowy sheet it had been all the years Zara had known her.

Since Nani had given up the Ghatokacha, she had aged rapidly.

Before, she looked the hale eighty-something she had claimed to be, but now she looked ancient. Like she might jolt to life and spit out a mouthful of dust and sand any minute, a mummy buried for centuries. The centuries she'd actually been alive.

"Hello, my girl." Nani's eyes did not open. Her voice was barely above a whisper.

Zara smiled. "Hi, Nani." She reached out and took her hand. Light and frail, skin warm and hanging on the knobbly bones of her knuckles.

Nani let out a long sigh in response.

"How are you?" Zara asked softly.

For a silent few moments, Zara wondered if she'd fallen asleep again, but then the crinkles in her face deepened in amusement, and she replied, "Tired and old."

Zara laughed. "You've always been old, but the tired is new."

Nani chuckled, a sound that filled Zara with joy. When had she last heard that?

Nani's face relaxed, and she opened her eyes.

Zara winced at their pale cloudy shine, not clear as they had always been.

Tired and hazed as they were, they narrowed, a shadow of their former razor-sharp wit within them. Her frail voice shook. "You. You have touched darkness."

Zara froze.

"The deepest shadow. It is here?" Nani's voice rose, cracking as her body stiffened.

"What?" Zara moved to comfort her, but Nani pushed her away with a strength belying her twisted form. "You mean the Umbran? It's gone. We killed it. "

Zara's phone buzzed in her pocket.

"The darkness. The darkness is here. It isn't gone. When it's gone, its touch will fade, but it is here. IT IS HERE," Nani wailed. Her body was twisting and thrashing, then her voice shifted, deepening slightly, and her shrivelled hands gripped Zara's wrists painfully. She spoke firm and low in a language Zara did not recognise. Not Hindi, something harsher, her voice rasping as she chanted.

"Nani, stop." Zara tried to gently release her hands where yellowing nails dug into her skin.

"Zara, what's happening?" She heard her mother's voice behind her, worried and frantic.

The hum of Zara's phone continued, but she ignored it.

"I don't know," Zara breathed, staring into Nani's rheumy eyes.

"You don't know," Nani rasped sharply, back in English once more. "You don't know what it is you bear. What it is you must do."

"Zara, come away." Her mother was moving in, trying to pull Nani back, to lay her back down.

"You must unlock the path. You must find who it is you are, or all is lost," Nani cried, her pale eyes rolling. She spasmed and then fell back limply.

Zara's mother cradled her sagging form, easing her onto the bed.

Zara's heart hammered in her chest.

You must find who it is you are?

The shadow remains?

What is she talking about?

Zara's phone buzzed insistently against her thigh. "Mum, I'm sorry."

Her mother shook her head sadly, eyes shining with tears as she stroked Nani's hair away from her face. Nani's breath was low and steady. "It's not your fault, she gets like this. Don't worry."

Zara swallowed.

She pulled out her phone.

Eight missed calls?

Marcus.

It buzzed again in her hand.

Turning from the room, from her mother and Nani, she pressed 'accept' and held it to her ear. "Marcus, now isn't a good time," she hissed.

"Zara."

She froze.

Something about his voice was stiff. Hollow. Not Marcus.

"What is it?"

"You need to come back to the house now. As soon as you can. It's urgent. Dmitri is already on his way to collect you." He sounded toneless, like he was reading the words from a shopping list.

"Marcus, what's going on?" Zara's blood chilled.

"As soon as you can," Marcus repeated.

The line went dead.

Zara turned back to her mother and Nani, eyes wide. "I have to go."

A horn honked from outside.

"Is everything okay, love?" Her mother looked at her with concern, still stroking Nani's hair.

Zara shook her head, the uneasy feeling settling in her bones. "No. I don't think it is."

THEY DIDN'T SPEAK the whole drive back.

Twenty minutes felt like an hour.

Something passed between Dmitri and her when she got in the car.

A look.

His pale eyes, like storm clouds hanging in an afternoon sky, were alive with panic.

Panic.

When had she seen him panic?

His grip on the steering wheel left his knuckles white. At any moment, she expected it to shatter in his hands.

She focused instead on trying to still the bubbling nerves within her. She didn't call Marcus to ask what was going on. He said they needed to be there, and that's what they needed to be. She knew it to her core. So instead, she focused ahead, her entire body as still as she could keep it, and willed the car to move faster.

MARCUS SAT on the porch steps when they arrived.

He looked younger than she'd ever seen him look, his curled posture, knees to his chest. Almost childlike.

Ed was next to him, a golden retriever, about as close as he could manage without being on his lap, one of Marcus' arms around him. For taking the form of a large dog, Ed looked to be making himself just about as small as he could manage, and Zara had the strange thought that perhaps he was in this form for Marcus rather than himself. Song's disembodied shimmer was all around them.

Zara was already running toward the house when she heard Dmitri slamming the driver's side door behind him.

"What happened?" She was somehow breathless despite the mere feet of distance.

Dmitri stormed past them, up the steps, and into the house.

Marcus' russet eyes fixed on her, wide and listless. "I did it."

Was he in shock?

"Did what?" Zara demanded.

"I remember you telling me not to tell people it had happened. Because if they know before they set off, it makes them more likely to have an accident on the road. So, I told you to come back as soon as possible rather than what had happened."

A tear rolled down his cheek, but his features did not change.

Zara's breath came in short, ragged gasps. A crushing force was pressing on her chest from somewhere.

"What you're saying is what we do when someone at the hospital has died, Marcus." Zara swallowed, panic threatening to consume her. "When we want the family to come into the hospital but not know they're too late."

Marcus nodded weakly. More tears came streaming down his face, and his lips quivered.

"Marcus, what happened? Is it Lyn?" Zara's voice broke, frantic.

She knew it wasn't even before Marcus shook his head, his body starting to shake as more tears came.

"It's Oscar. Oscar's dead."

From inside the house, she heard Dmitri's roar.

❧ IV ❧

IN THE ABSENCE OF
LIGHT

26

THE COOLING REMAINS

Zara had been in more high-pressure situations than she could remember, and witnessed more life-or-death moments than she could count. She'd sat and listened to families afterward who told her that for them, it was like things went into slow motion, or fast motion, or some other way to describe the world around them just being wrong.

But this was the first time it had actually happened to her, and it was like being underwater.

She couldn't breathe. When she tried, it was like the air wasn't right; it was thick and hostile, and her body couldn't handle it. Her ears roared like the ocean of the world around her was pressing in on her with crushing force. Marcus' voice sounded faint and tinny as he continued to speak at her. Her limbs felt weak and clumsy as she staggered up the steps and into the house.

Lyn was there, standing in the doorway to the living room.

Her dark eyes were unfathomable, face a mask of control. But control over what?

She stepped forward smoothly. It hadn't been long since she'd become steady on her newly regenerated legs again, but she already moved with the grace of a dancer. She reached out with those pale and delicate fingers.

Zara stepped away from her touch.

"Lyn." Zara's every breath felt like a gasp. Her head swam. "What happened?"

Lyn retracted her hand carefully, her dark eyes flooding with concern. "I'm sorry. I'm not sure. I believe he and Tildy were in the attic. I was resting. When I awoke...Zara, I didn't go up there. I didn't want to disturb anything."

Zara staggered toward the stairs and slumped against the wall, fighting to get her breath under control, willing it to steady.

"Zara, you need to sit down," Lyn said softly.

"No," Zara barked and took a lurching stride up three steps, then another three, using her hands against the wall to steady herself.

As Zara reached the top of the stairs, a metallic and sulphurous stink grew heavy from above.

Something dripped on her forearm. Instinctively, she tried to wipe it off, and it smeared across her golden-brown skin.

Blood.

Zara looked up.

The ceiling was weeping with blood.

Oscar's blood?

Dark patches of it soaked through from above, so much, it was beginning to drip down in beads.

A thick droplet landed on her cheek, and she allowed it to run down her jaw like a crimson tear.

"Zara, I don't think—" Lyn began. She had followed her up the stairs, Zara realised. *To make sure I don't fall?*

"Stop," Zara snapped, her eyes still fixed on the spreading stains above. Something hardened in her, like the sight had pushed her from a ledge, and the liberating free-fall of horror had her in its grasp. She forced her breath into a controlled rhythm and gripped the closest rung of the ladder. "I need to see."

Lyn stepped back, but those dark eyes did not leave her.

Zara climbed.

The top three rungs were slick with blood, and her hands almost slipped. The stink grew stronger when she entered the loft. Stale and sharp with a sour edge of rotten eggs in the darkness. She flicked the switch beside the hatch, and nothing happened.

Clambering onto the panelled floor, she took one step forward, and something crunched under her heel.

Glass?

The lightbulbs have shattered?

Zara thrust her hand—still sticky with blood—into her pocket, finding the familiar shape of her phone and thumbing on the flashlight, leaving a smear of crimson on her screen.

Her heart crumbled inside her chest.

So much blood.

And not just that.

Macerated skin and tissue and the remnants of organs. Everywhere.

A tangled mess of intestines draped from the dresser beside her, touching her elbow when she took a step forward, causing her to flinch away.

"Oscar." Her voice came out small, choked.

What did she do?

What did Tildy do to Oscar?

Zara's shoes squelched. She wasn't sure if it was blood on the floor or if it had just soaked into her socks. She brushed something aside with her foot.

An eyeball.

Oscar's eyeball.

The ladder creaked behind her, and Zara turned her head, expecting to find Lyn following. Instead, Marcus' face appeared, eyes wide and dark skin almost grey.

"Marcus, you don't have to come up here."

Marcus shook his head quickly, large eyes scanning the gory decorations in sight and the sickly tinge to his complexion deepening. "I want to be together."

Zara nodded once with understanding, and he scrambled up as she ventured further forward into the gruesome grotto decorated with her best friend. Her family.

Her Oscar.

"Dmitri, are you up here?" Zara shone her light around. There was no one. Nowhere for them to hide. Nothing but death.

Then it occurred to her that Tildy may still be here. Not in the attic, but somewhere in the house or nearby. For the first time in what felt like an eternity, the Ghatokacha sparked inside her, its energy burning away a little of the grief and horror with a desperate thirst for a fight.

No, it wouldn't be a fight.

Tildy would be obliterated.

Zara rounded the dresser and spotted a scattered bundle of pictures on the ground. Half the stack was already saturated, and the few left that were unspoiled had edges curling with blood.

Crouching, she picked up the picture on top. It was stained, but she immediately recognised Dmitri in a rather unflattering seventies get up. Two people were with him. Looking at their faces, she knew almost instantly who they were.

Oscar's parents.

What was this?

And where was Dmitri?

"Zara." Marcus' voice from behind her jolted her out of her numb shock. "What should we do?"

"We find Tildy." Zara swallowed. Her voice sounded cold and unfamiliar even to her. "And we make her pay."

And then we get answers from Dmitri about whatever he was keeping from us. From Oscar.

There was a shuffling noise behind her as Zara carefully wiped the excess blood from the photo on her dungarees.

"Uhhh, Zara?" Marcus said softly.

"Yeah." Zara sniffed, willing herself not to come apart. *Not yet.*

"I think we already found Tildy. I mean...I think we're standing in her."

Zara twisted around. Behind her, Marcus was holding up an ear, torn free with one ragged edge soaked in blood.

Hanging from the lobe was a beautiful, ice blue gem.

EVEN WITH THE door under the stairs open, the heavy thumping sound from below was barely audible. It took Zara a moment to realise that it must be the mini-gaeants they'd locked up in the basement. That felt like years ago, but it had only been a couple of weeks.

Marcus sat at the foot of the stairs, his head between his knees, still recovering from the horrors he'd seen above. Ed was curled beside the doormat nearby as a corgi.

Dmitri closed the door to the basement behind him. The black rucksack slung over his shoulder looked full and heavy.

His face was severe, pale skin practically white, eyes shining with fervour.

"Dmitri, what's going on? Where is he?" Zara said, trying to control her voice as though that may control what was happening inside her too.

"It's not him," Dmitri growled. "It's all Tildy. There is nothing of Oscar left in that room."

"I suspected as much," Lyn said through the open door from where she sat at the kitchen counter.

Zara shot her a look.

"I tried to tell you. You wouldn't have believed me until you saw for yourself anyway."

Zara grunted. *That was true.*

"You," Dmitri spat. "You were here. You must have heard everything." Dmitri stalked past Zara and into the kitchen.

Zara followed.

"Tell me what you heard." Dmitri dumped the rucksack onto the ground. It struck with a metallic sound and such weighty force, Zara almost expected it to go through the floorboards. He turned on Lyn, the veins on his arms and neck bulging, and his eyes shining with an inhuman glow.

"She must have coaxed him into the attic. I have no idea what happened after that." Lyn checked her nails idly.

Dmitri snarled. "You let this happen. You could have stopped this."

Zara moved and stood between them, holding up the photograph. Its edges were curled with Tildy's blood. Oscar's parents stared back at Dmitri. He froze.

The glow from Dmitri's eyes faded, and his jaw dropped, showing his pointed teeth. His eyes met Zara's with regret.

"I didn't let her do anything," Lyn said crisply, oblivious that Dmitri had already been stayed. "Tildy was her own creature and stronger than I at present in any case. I could not have stopped her even had I known what she was up to. Though I cannot say I would have if I could. It seems she got her just desserts."

"What have you been keeping from us, Dmitri?" Zara asked flatly.

Dmitri's shoulders sagged. "I can explain. It's just...it's..."

Zara sighed. "Complicated," she finished for him.

Dmitri's eyes fixed on hers, desperate and lost. "Zara. I...I don't know what to do."

"We need to find Oscar." She could offer him no more comfort, or else the brittle seams that held her together may give way. Any rage she held for Dmitri cooled, shrunk away and packed up easily to be dealt with later.

"I think...I think it's taken him." Dmitri's voice shook.

"What?" Zara frowned. "What do you mean?"

"It just doesn't make any sense," Marcus said from the bottom of the stairs. His voice sounded distant. "Oscar wouldn't do that. Couldn't. It's almost like something we've seen before. Almost like—"

"The Umbran," Lyn finished crisply.

"But he killed it," Zara growled. "We all saw."

There was a crisp, loud knock.

Zara looked at the front door in confusion. It hadn't come from that direction at all.

Lyn stood smoothly, looking ready to fight.

For a moment, Zara wondered if it was Vandle again, at the mirror in the living room.

But then, the knock came again. Three times.

Marcus staggered in unsteadily from the hallway. Zara took his arm in hers and led the way into the kitchen. The shimmering air trailing closely to Marcus seemed to be vibrating excitedly, and Ed padded cautiously behind.

"There." Lyn pointed one pale imperious finger toward the corner.

The fridge?

Zara looked at Marcus in confusion. He was smiling.

Stepping forward, Dmitri opened the fridge door. When he did, what was inside wasn't the bright shelves filled with condiments or anything else Zara might have expected.

It was dark.

Darker than the night.

A pale face edged out of the black, a face with large round eyes, bereft of both pupils and iris—long orange hair the colour of moulding fruit.

The Bean-Nighe smiled.

27

LEFT BEHIND

Everything was darkness.

Darkness, in a way, that Oscar felt was almost familiar.

It wasn't like the nothingness he'd been in when he travelled to the Bean-Nighe's realm. This was different. There was was white light around him for a little more than an arm's length. Beyond that was ever-shifting swirling shades of black in every direction he could see. The light around him flickered, like he was a final failing light-bulb, alone, in the abandoned dark.

Slowly, he lifted his hand, expecting to see nothing as he had that night in the cemetery—when he had travelled to the between.

Perhaps more frighteningly, this time, he was not met with infinite consuming darkness.

His hand was there, every finger, nobble, and hair...only it was strangely translucent. It flickered and returned, faint and pale like someone had attached some terrible filter to him. He looked down at his body. All of it was the same. Not only that, but he felt just how he looked. Thin. Faded. Like he'd been rinsed too many times, and everything that made him *Oscar* was washing out.

He swallowed and looked around. The more he became aware of this strange place, the more he could feel it.

The gnawing shadows around him. The ominously swirling void felt threatening, like it might collapse in on him at any moment and swallow him up.

Where am I?

He vaguely remembered being in the attic with someone.

Tildy?

She'd shown him something. Something that had shocked him. Hurt him. But what—

Oh.

Dmitri and his parents.

Stark misery pulsed within him, and for a moment, the darkness around him seemed to inch in. Oscar felt the nothingness pulling on his edges, as if he were the last dregs of murky bathwater, and it was trying to drag what was left of him down the plughole.

Where am I?

Almost immediately, he knew.

He had hated Tildy.

Hated her so much for trying to come between him and Dmitri. It was an invigorating feeling for all of a second...until he felt something pushing into him. Something piercing him into his core from within. The same thing that was swelling around him now.

Hate.

Crushing, pointless, spiteful hate.

The Umbran.

Panic blossomed in Oscar.

He'd failed.

Somehow, some part of him knew he would. The moment he had been holding the willblade, piercing its body, that single doubt had come upon him. The doubt he'd kept giving up a secret. The doubt people wouldn't want him anymore if they knew he'd given up on them. On himself.

And now, that doubt had ruined everything.

Oscar cowered, sliding down and curling his body in on itself, afraid.

It was over...

No.

It **wasn't** over.

He remembered the way Dmitri had smiled at him that morning as he turned before he got into his car.

He remembered he loved him—and he was loved.

He remembered Zara and Marcus at each arm. Laughing and teasing—and he was loved.

He remembered everything.

He remembered being afraid.

He remembered Tildy. Her smirking face. The bubbling hate inside his chest.

The memory of her flesh tearing and blood spattering.

A raw flash of guilt seared through him.

No. That wasn't me. It was the Umbran.

Any hate Oscar held for her evaporated, replaced by pity.

He felt as though the dark pressure around him quivered. Something far away screamed.

She hadn't deserved that. She hadn't. Even if...

Dmitri. Dmitri had known his parents. He'd never told him. What did it mean? He felt himself flickering, weakening as the darkness inched closer once more.

No.

He remembered laughter.

He remembered the smell of Zara's hair when she pulled him into her arms and squeezed him. He remembered the way Marcus' eyes lit up when he smiled.

He remembered Dmitri's lips on his.

His voice.

If anyone ever tries to keep us apart, I will pull the moon from the sky to guide my way back to you. I would tear the earth in two to find you.

Oscar forced strength into his arms and legs, and he felt his whole body. Weak and cold. Shivering. Fragile. But there. Alive.

He was still here, and this time, he wasn't giving up.

JENNY GREENTEETH

(FLUMEN PYTHONISSAM)

28

THAT'S THE GREAT PUZZLE

"What the fuck?" Zara breathed.

The Bean-Nighe tilted her head, lank auburn hair swinging free of the door to the fridge and cascading onto the tile floor.

"How—" Dmitri began under his breath, then his back stiffened, and his voice grew bolder. "Please, help us find Oscar. That is why you're here, isn't it?"

The Bean-Nighe sighed softly, one of her hands emerging from the pitch, and brushing the hair back out of her face with long pale fingers. "Come. Quickly. We mustn't be felt like poor Betty was."

Dmitri grunted and darted into the hall, grabbing his rucksack.

"What's in there?" Zara frowned.

"Chains. In case we need to restrain..." Dmitri's voice trailed off, and he looked troubled.

"Wow." Marcus smirked, stepping toward the open fridge door. "I had no idea you were so kinky, Big D."

The Bean-Nighe's hand raised in warning. "Not you, little brother. Not with your special friend."

Marcus' jaw dropped, and he looked at the mist beside him.

"They cannot come here," the Bean-Nighe said sadly before her voice brightened. "But one day, we will see each other for true once more."

Then, abruptly, she disappeared back into the dark mouth of the fridge.

"She expects us to just wander into a refrigerator?" Lyn scowled.

"Like a delicious Narnia." Marcus sighed.

"No time to talk. Let's go," Zara said. "I hate to think of that thing using Oscar's body like it did that other guy."

Marcus whistled through his teeth. "Well, shit. Who had dark-Oscar on their apocalypse bingo card?"

"I'm coming," Lyn said firmly, rising to her feet.

Zara shook her head. "Lyn, you should stay here with Marcus."

"You don't tell me what to do." Lyn's words were crisp, but her tone gentle, concern flickering in her eyes.

Concern for me or for Oscar?

"Fine." Zara nodded. "Marcus, will you be alright here alone?"

Dmitri was already disappearing into the fridge.

Marcus nodded at the heavy air beside him, and Ed pawed the tiles nearby. "I'm not alone."

Lyn moved smoothly past her and ducked into the darkness. Zara turned to follow.

"Zara," Marcus said quickly.

Zara turned, one leg already into the void, which tingled strangely.

Marcus took a shuddering breath, his eyes shining. "Just...save him, okay?"

Zara nodded. "I promise."

ZARA BLINKED.

She'd been expecting to find herself in the Bean-Nighe's cave, its cold stone walls lined with shelves filled with fateful oddments and trinkets.

Instead, it seemed as though they were in some kind of nursery.

Unlike the cool air she had been expecting, it was damp and close, warm as breath. Horizontal wooden slats crossed the walls, and a thick plush rug took up most of the floor, though strangely, what wasn't covered was raw mulch. A long millipede ran over Zara's boot, and she shook it loose, scanning the room for the others.

The walls, as before, were littered with shelves crowded with seemingly useless and unrelated items and jars, though far less than on their previous visit. The handle of a broken spade. A golden goblet trimmed with various jewels. An antler of a stag, each curved spike with a cork on it and a label hanging from it in an untidy scrawled hand. Across the middle of the room were two thin threaded wires with old and dirty clothing decorating them like bunting. A tired crib sat to one side, covered in cobwebs.

Zara only saw one thing she remembered from last time. A bone. Almost as long as she was tall. Since their previous visit, it seemed the Bean-Nighe had been whittling it. One of its ends now finished in a massive spike.

"How charming." Lyn's voice from close behind startled her.

Zara turned angrily. "Don't do that!"

Lyn's lips curled, amused, the way that usually sent shivers—the good kind—up Zara's spine.

"Tell me. Tell me where to find him." Zara heard Dmitri, his voice low and earnest.

Lyn moved ahead.

The fact she'd regrown her lower half in less than a week should have amazed Zara, but given she'd seen her incinerated, eaten, torn limb from limb, and come back just as good, it had simply impressed her. She might have walked like Bambi on ice for a few days, but she was pretty much as good as new after lots of rest. It surely didn't help she insisted on wearing those heels. Zara remembered Lyn's disgust when she'd suggested she wore trainers. She would rather walk barefoot, she'd claimed. Zara had to remember to ask her about the heels one day.

Lyn shifted a particularly grubby-looking dress hanging in the way aside and rounded a corner that had barely been visible before. Zara followed closely behind, finding the Bean-Nighe fussing over a pot on a small rusty stove on one side of the room. Her cream dress flowed around her seemingly wafting in all the wrong directions as she moved, and turned to snatch something off one of the shelves and drop it in the pot with a *plop*.

Dmitri stood beside her, his fists clenched and back ramrod stiff.

"Please, just say something." His voice shook.

"Bubbles," the Bean-Nighe absently replied.

Dmitri's face sagged, his mouth flapping. "Does that...mean something?"

The Bean-Nighe shrugged, poking a decapitated pink teddy bear's head beside the stove thoughtfully before picking it up and dropping it into the pot.

"Not very nice, is it." Zara stepped beside Dmitri. "Imagine someone just dropping you off here to have your fortune told to see if you're going to live a normal life or die on the way out."

Dmitri's face was full of despair, a look she'd not seen from him before, and Zara felt a deep stab of guilt followed by a cool spread of dread across her skin.

Oscar. We're here for Oscar. We can do this.

"The Damsel!" the Bean-Nighe cooed excitedly. She spun around, one long-fingered hand snatching towards Zara's own. Zara danced back, evading her touch.

"No, thanks," Zara said firmly. "No predictions for me today."

The Bean-Nighe stuck out her bottom lip like a child that hadn't gotten its own way. "Spoilsport."

"Want to tell us why you came out of the fridge?" Zara asked bluntly, folding her arms.

The Bean-Nighe's frown slipped away, and she giggled. "She's learned to ask better questions now. Where else was I supposed to be?"

"The cemetery," Dmitri said roughly. "We looked for you there."

The Bean-Nighe tutted, picking up a coppery spoon as long as her forearm and stirring the contents of the pot. Zara stood on her tiptoes and saw the concoction was a sickly muddy brown. "The between is closer to both edges now. I can open the curtain wherever I want to peep for the show. It was looking for me there. Wanted my bones."

The Umbran wanted her bones?

Zara's mind raced back to the mess in the attic. Had she seen any bones there? From what Marcus had said about Gax and the Gwyllgi, those deaths sounded much the same.

"Why did it want your bones?" Zara asked.

The Bean-Nighe's orb-like eyes fixed on her. "To kill us all." She leaned forward, very slowly, and pointed beside Zara. "Pass me that."

Zara turned, finding only a small jar that looked empty. "This?"

"Yes," the Bean-Nighe snapped. "Quickly, it's important."

Zara snatched up the jar and handed it over. The Bean-Nighe popped off its lid and tipped it with delicate grace, though Zara saw nothing come out before she pushed the lid on again.

"Bones are important. Bones of friends and bones of old, they hold a power so far untold." She sighed, stirring her pot once more.

"Bones of Theians," Lyn said darkly. "They were used in the rituals of old. The rituals to make parallaxes and to seal them."

"Where is Oscar?" Dmitri growled, shifting on his feet impatiently. "We don't have time for games. Just tell me where he is."

The Bean-Nighe frowned. "No games to play today. Cricket's gone."

Dmitri swallowed. "Gone?"

She waved a pale, delicate hand in the air vaguely. "To the away."

"Where?" Dmitri asked.

"In himself," the Bean-Nighe said softly. "Though it's not really him anymore. It's *Him*."

"Who?" Dmitri snapped desperately.

"The Hate Eater," the Bean-Nighe whispered.

Zara shook her head. "The Umbran?"

"'Orrid thing it is an' all," a voice ribbited from beside them.

Zara jolted in surprise.

It can't be.

"Gax?" Dmitri sounded both shocked and relieved.

"In the flesh." The Bugge, not much taller than her knees, stepped from a recess Zara hadn't seen before, beside the crib, almost completely hidden in the earthen wall. Did that lead to another room?

What kind of peculiar warren has the Bean-Nighe brought us to? Some kind of supernatural safe house?

"Though not if the Umbran 'ad its way," Gax grumbled. "I imagine it would much like to 'ave used me, bones an' all."

"We thought you were dead," Zara breathed.

The Bean-Nighe giggled and sighed. "Just because something is gone doesn't mean it's dead. Sometimes it's just really hard to find again. But that doesn't always mean you should stop looking."

The Bugge scowled, and brushed his mossy beard with stubby, green mottled fingers. He grimaced with a show of square yellow teeth. "I imagine you found what was left of me lady fren', Dandeli. Nice lass. We'd bin 'avin a fair old time of it 'fore that 'orrid thing ripped 'er up. Would've 'ad me an' all if I 'ant rushed to old Beanie 'ere an' 'er whisked us off."

"I'm glad you're safe old friend, and I am sorry about Dandeli," Dmitri said gruffly.

Gax growled, a sound like a large toad croaking. "Don' be sorry; you 'int the one that killed 'er. Do us a favour, though, and blast that lump of no-good nothin' darkness off the face of the planet?"

"We'll do what we can," Zara promised.

"Focus," the Bean-Nighe trilled. In a flash of movement, the Bean-Nighe thrust out her spoon, and Dmitri accepted it clumsily. The waif skipped by him and off around the room, over to the cobwebbed crib. "It's all over for today and forever. It's all over from now until never," she sung sadly.

Zara cleared her throat. "The Umbran...we thought he killed it."

The Bean-Nighe peered into the crib at nothing, shaking her head. "Lies."

"It was destroyed. We all saw it," Dmitri insisted.

"Will only works if you tell yourself the truth, silly bean." The Bean-Nighe laughed. "Cracks are made to be broken, and broken is made to be dead dead dead. Everyone dead. Just like Betty." She shook her head sadly.

"How is this inane drivel supposed to help?" Lyn scowled.

"What did Betty have to do with this?" Zara persevered.

"She still does." The Bean-Nighe cocked her head. "She's a part of it all. Well, some parts of her are. That's why I wasn't needed in the end."

"The Umbran, it...has Oscar?" Dmitri's voice was hoarse.

The Bean-Nighe paced slowly back across the room. "Oscar has it, and it has him. They're a snake eating its own tail now. But they want to end that and bite it right off. Only they need to open or close the right door to do it."

Dmitri frowned, his eyes shifting to Zara's in confusion.

"Did this babbling witch ever actually help you?" Lyn was tapping one heeled foot impatiently.

"I couldn't do anything." The Bean-Nighe's pale orbs of eyes slid over Lyn with disinterest. "I have too much to do to disappear yet. If I get too close, I can't see. There's too many stories still to tell and not enough time to tell them." She snatched her spoon back from Dmitri possessively and rapped him firmly on the forehead with it.

He wiped the sticky residue away with the back of one hand.

"So, are you helping us or not?" Zara asked. "Can you lead us to Oscar?"

The Bean-Nighe smiled. "No. But I can put you where he's at before he comes where you're to."

"Fine," Zara said.

"And the Umbran, how can we stop it? Is what you're making? Something to help?" Dmitri asked, gesturing to the pot of murky fluid.

The Bean-Nighe continued idly stirring, face severe. "If Cricket can't stop it, then you have to stop it for him, just like he'd want to stop it too. Best if he's the one to do it, though." She banged the spoon on the edge of the pot, flicking free the gloopy contents. "If you're wearing armour that you can't take off, it's not really armour but a cage. Better to break out of a cage like that than try and break in."

"I think...that means there's still time," Zara said cautiously.

"Only if you try," the Bean-Nighe agreed softly.

"You 'ad bloody well better try," Gax grumbled.

Dmitri nodded, still peering into the pot hopefully. "And this?"

The Bean-Nighe smiled proudly. "Soup."

With that, she clapped her hands, and they were gone.

❧ 29 ❧

STRANGERS IN THE DARK

Oscar's fading legs shook beneath him, but he locked his knees and moved on.

Despite the fact that he could not see much at all, he could at least feel himself now, even if what he felt was mostly just cold. The shifting void centred him in the eye of its storm even as the swelling clouds of shadow threatened to drown him. As he walked, they moved. Parted around him to welcome him to more identical space.

All he could see was endless swirling. Nothing with a side of nothing.

But he could feel a faint trace of something other than the ominous void. A flash of alien fear, almost like one of Song's sendings. It disappeared several times, and it might have taken him hours to retrace his steps and find it, but eventually, he did.

It was weak, but it was still there. Someone else. Someone like him, alone and afraid. He could feel them, cowering and small. They were close.

"Hello?" Oscar's voice sounded barely like a whisper.

He tried to take a breath and shout, but the sound of his voice was still a muffled squeak.

I have to. I have to do this.

Oscar straightened his spine and puffed out his chest.

"Hello?" This time his voice came out louder, echoing into the dark. The sound bounced back at him, rattling in the void. Then a few moments later...

Stay away.

It was not his own thought, more like someone else's pressed onto him. It was weak, flickering, and filled with doubt and fear.

"Who's there?" Oscar said.

Don't you talk to me.
You're disgusting.

Oscar swallowed, and took a step forward.

Someone else's thoughts in my own head? What's happening?

"I know you're there, and we need to get out. It might be easier if we do it together."

There was a long pause, then.

Why?

Oscar frowned. "Because...something bad is happening. I'm pretty sure it's the end of the world, so we have to get out and stop it. We can't just...give up."

There was a long pause once more, and then for the first time, Oscar caught a flicker of movement in the darkness.

Faint and barely there, the slightest shimmer of a man, like a presence on a double-exposed photo. He was far fainter than Oscar himself—so much so, that he could barely even make out his features.

The man was sitting on the floor, one hand open and palm up.

In his faint palm, he held something round and as dark as the void. It was like a black hole in the centre of the man's hand. Oscar immediately recognised it as the coin he'd picked up. Instinctively, his hand reached for his pocket as though to try and find the coin there. His barely-there fingers brushed against his barely-there leg, neither with enough substance for such an action.

The faded man sitting on the ground looked up at him, then his fist closed around the coin, which stayed just as visible for a moment, and then disappeared.

Then Oscar realised. He *had* seen this man before. "You...who are you?"

The faded man scowled. He was handsome in a typical sort of way, but his features were marred by disdain. "My name is Harry Barlow."

30

A BURDEN SHARED

O scar led the way.

Walking in the darkness was like walking nowhere. He still couldn't be sure whether he was even getting anywhere, or simply walking on the spot whilst the inky clouds billowed around him. The faded figure of Harry Barlow followed behind him. He seemed to be trying hard not to look directly at Oscar, lip curled in permanent disdain.

"There's nowhere to go." Harry's voice was a faint, distorted rasp, like the hiss of an old radio.

He was older, Oscar realised, after scrutinising his translucent form. It had been hard to tell from his rotting corpse, but judging from his appearance here, Oscar guessed he was close to forty.

"Walking is doing something, at least," Oscar said. "We can't just do nothing."

We can't just give up.

"It won't let you out. It will never let you out."

Oscar frowned. "What do you mean? Do you know where we are?"

Harry's faint form stopped. "Are you stupid or something? I

was watching. I saw you fighting it." His face twisted in disgust. "I saw everything."

Oscar chewed on his lip; he couldn't quite feel the scrape of his teeth there like he usually could, more like the dull memory of it—like in a dream. "What do you mean?" he asked finally.

"The Dark." Harry's eyes flashed to meet Oscar's for the first time. "I've been inside it all this time."

All this time?

Since that night with Ocampo in the cemetery? How is he still here?

"You and your friends are a real freak show, huh?" Harry hissed.

Is it because the Umbran needs hate to take hold? This man does seem to have a lot of that to hold on to...

Oscar looked at him and forced a smile. "Well, we're definitely extraordinary, I guess."

Harry spat, though nothing came from his mouth with the action. "I don't know who's worse. The monsters or the ones like *you*. Not only have you gotta be..." his muffled voice trailed off, "but with monsters?"

Oscar bristled. "I don't think that's the biggest problem we've got right now. If we're stuck inside the Umbran, then we need to get out. Dmitri said—"

Harry barked a laugh that might have been harsh if he had a full voice. "I don't care what Spring-Heeled Jack says, asshole. Do you think I'm stupid? I'm already dead. I'm never getting out of here."

Oscar frowned, remembering the man's rotting body falling apart and dissolving before him. "Maybe there's some way to bring you back?" He failed to sound hopeful.

"Even if I wasn't dead, what makes you think I'd help you?" Harry growled, turning his back. "Maybe the world needs to end. Who wants freaks like you just strutting around, thinking you can do whatever you want, fuck whoever you want, and be whoever you want?"

Oscar tilted his head. "But...we can, can't we?"

Harry spun back around, eyes full of fury. "That's the problem. You've got no values. It just isn't right; the whole world is falling apart. Even without monsters, you and your little friends would just fuck everything up."

"You don't like that I'm—"

"Queer?" Harry's voice was louder this time, not the rasp from before.

Oscar flinched. He was used to the word; he liked it, but not the way Harry said it. Something about the way it fired from his mouth made it feel wrong. Like a dirty weapon.

"Well, I'm sorry you don't like it," Oscar said. "But it's who I am."

Harry laughed cruelly. "Whatever, freak. I'll leave you to it. Die alone."

He turned away, his faded form flickering as he moved toward the darkness.

Despite his distaste for him, the sight of him leaving made panic flood Oscar's chest.

He wasn't sure if it was because he didn't want to be alone, or if it was because he didn't know what it would mean for Harry if he left him here.

Would he disappear? Would he just stay inside forever?

"Wait!" Oscar blurted out, snatching out with his hand.

To Oscar's surprise, despite his touch on his own body feeling like grasping smoke, it collided with the other man's hand solidly.

He saw Harry turn, his eyes widen in surprise, and then he wasn't there at all.

OSCAR WAS LOOKING *out over a dark river. Streetlights and buildings reflected in its shifting surface, and the dull sound of cars and voices hummed on his periphery.*

He heard a soft sobbing.

Startled, Oscar spun, his feet digging into the sand beneath him. There, in the darkness was a boy. A boy huddled with a woman, her hair a loose mess, and front stained with dark spilled wetness. Her bulging eyes streamed with tears as she panted desperately.

The boy looked at him. He cradled one of his hands to his chest, and even in the darkness, Oscar could see it was curled into a charred claw. Then, the boy screamed.

~

OSCAR STAGGERED BACK, blinking and dazed. His whole body stung like his bare skin had been beaten with nettles. It eased to a tingling sensation humming inside him.

He was in the nowhere again.

Harry stood before him, his eyes wide. He raised a hand to his chest, and Oscar could see the flesh on the back of it was thick with scar tissue.

"It was you," Oscar breathed.

Was the Harry here clearer now? He didn't seem quite so faded anymore. Now, Oscar could see the sapphire blue of his eyes, the rough, unshaven line of his jaw, and the stains where his white T-shirt stretched around his gut.

"What did you just do?" Harry snarled, stepping back. His voice was louder than before. He looked down at his hand as if he were as surprised as Oscar to find himself more solid now.

"I'm sorry, I was just trying to stop you from leaving, but—" Oscar swallowed. "That was you, wasn't it? The little boy with his mother by the river." His eyes wandered back to the scars on his hand.

Harry's face slackened in shock. "What did you just say?"

"Didn't you see something?"

"I did," Harry said. "A stupid kid, crying and crying. Looking out the window, thinking every car was his parents coming home."

He shook his head sadly, his eyes dropping to his feet. "It was…" He stiffened, realising whose memory he'd seen. "Pathetic," he finished venomously.

Oscar frowned. He'd seen *him*. Waiting for Mum and Dad. He barely remembered that himself, though he did remember crying a lot. He remembered Paige telling him tears wouldn't fix anything.

"Did you see anything else?" Oscar asked, hopeful. If memories of his parents were within him, maybe that meant he could see more. Maybe he could finally know more about them.

"No," Harry snapped. "And don't you touch me again, freak." He was admiring the more corporeal shape of his hand. The sneer on his face softened, and his eyes shifted to Oscar again thoughtfully. "Uh, whatever. Let's just get this over with. I don't want you pushing any more of your queer little thoughts into my head."

Oscar rolled his eyes. "It's too late. I'm sure you've caught the gay now."

He meant it as a joke, but Harry's eyes widened.

Sighing, Oscar turned back to the nothing and started walking.

31

WHERE EVERYTHING UNHAPPENS

Zara opened her eyes, and bright light bore into them.

For a moment, no breath came to her, like the shift in reality had knocked the wind from her lungs. Then, she dragged in a gasping breath as if she'd just surfaced from the depths of the ocean. A freezing cold ocean.

She moved her hands frantically, colliding with something.

A wall? No, glass.

She pushed, and the chilled glass resisted for a moment, but then with a pop, sprang away from her palms.

The boxes beneath her crunched, their contents mashing and breaking as she shifted and sat up.

Zara blinked, icy wetness wicking into the seat of her jeans from beneath, and looked around the dim, empty room.

"Really? Two for two. You'd better fucking send me to a better place next time, you spooky bitch," Zara grumbled, climbing out of the chest freezer. *What even was that?* She rubbed a hand down her back where something wet was still spreading.

She licked it.

Ice cream.

Could be worse.

The light from the freezer was near enough the only light in the room, or as Zara quickly realised, the shop. Stacked shelves of crisps and a whole rack of tacky paraphernalia told her where exactly she was.

Stonehenge.

There was a creaking in the ceiling above her. The thin polycarbonate squares bowed.

Before Zara could think on it further, with a loud crunch, they tore open. A dark figure fell through with a cry, landing in a heap that upended a tower of sweets and nuts, scattering them everywhere.

Lyn sat up quickly, her angular face livid with shock and eyes wide. She looked up at the split in the ceiling and then at Zara, astonished. "I just appeared up there."

"Yeah, I'm starting to get the impression she likes to mess with us when she's putting us back. You probably shouldn't have been so sassy," Zara grumbled, holding out a hand to help her up.

Lyn took it, struggling to her feet, and dusted herself off the powdered flavourings from some of the burst bags of snacks. Sharp disdain returned to her face, somewhat spoiled by the petulant edge to her voice. "I am not *sassy*. I am just generally tired of everyone's nonsense."

Zara smiled, and the corner of Lyn's mouth quirked.

"How can it be that was even less fun than I imagined, and I imagined it as no fun at all?" Lyn tugged on the bottom of her blouse.

"Sounds about right for one of our usual adventures." Zara shrugged.

"And Dmitri? Where did she put our hound?" Lyn's dark eyes scanned their surroundings.

"Who knows?" Zara replied. "Maybe we should stay put for now. He'll find us."

Lyn grunted thoughtfully. "Her riddles...did you get anything from them?"

"Maybe," Zara said. "It's hard to tell. Irritatingly, the things she says usually become clear after they actually happen."

Lyn's delicate features twisted in confusion. "Then what exactly is the point?"

Zara shook her head, moving forward to wrap her arms around Lyn's waist, and Lyn's pale hands rested upon her shoulders. It felt good to stop for a moment. To be on pause and not feel like they were wasting time. Dmitri would find them soon. He had to.

"I don't know...foreshadowing?" Zara chuckled drily. "I think maybe I understood enough to know that we still have a shot at saving Oscar. Even if she said we couldn't, I don't think it would have changed anything. We're doing this."

Lyn folded her arms, her face becoming severe. "Zara, I think I understood one thing. Perhaps the most important one, though I didn't need that ghostly waif to hint it."

Zara's jaw clenched. The weight that had been looming over her, that she'd been trying to ignore, pressed down.

"The Umbran is trying to end everything. Obliterate reality. It is using Oscar as its vessel and key, so the simplest way to remove the threat is to remove—"

"I know." Zara's voice grated her throat. She stepped back, away from Lyn.

"It is one thing to know and another to do." Lyn's dark eyes wandered away from Zara's. "If the moment comes, I will do it for you."

Molten fire and ice pumped from Zara's core. The spirit within her bubbled.

"You want to kill Oscar." Zara's voice was barely a croak.

"I don't." Lyn's eyes flashed back to Zara's own and drove into them. "I want to save you. Save you from doing it if it needs to be done."

"It won't come to that." The boiling energy inside her agreed.

"It might," Lyn said sadly. "If it comes down to choosing

between one human and the existence of more realities and souls than we can imagine—"

"No, it won't. We'll stop him, and Oscar will fight it off. The Bean-Nighe said—"

"That if he could not stop it, we must stop it for him. Just like he'd want us to," Lyn cut in.

Zara huffed, heat flushing through her skin.

"Do you think Oscar would not choose to end himself, rather than countless lives be lost?" Lyn took a step forward, tilting her head. She reached out with one pale, delicate hand. "Zara, I have threatened that boy. Threatened him with ending even one life other than his own. He would do it in a heartbeat."

"You don't even like him," Zara snarled, batting her hand away. "Don't talk to me like you know him."

Lyn sighed, her dark eyes shining sadly. "Actually, I think I might."

"Like him?" Zara snorted a derisive laugh. "I don't think you get it, Lyn. We're not just friends; we're family. Family is more than blood. It's laughter and tears and needing to be together even when you want to be alone. Him and Marcus...they're everything to me."

Lyn's tone was uncharacteristically gentle. "I think I like him and know him. I put him through misery and fear and saw the threads keeping him together. Your threads, Zara. All of you. Humans are a fragile thing; it only takes a tap in the right place to shatter most of them apart. Oscar makes me think he was never a complete thing to shatter in the first place. Or maybe he was, and now his pieces are just stuck together harder than they were before. He is a stubborn mosaic of who he loves and who loves him. Between him and you, and the loud one, of course, you make me wonder if I may have been wrong about humans all along. Be that as it may, we must be prepared for the reality that he cannot be saved. If that is the case, Dmitri could not bring himself to hurt the boy. That I know too now, in a way I didn't before. I could..." She cleared her throat awkwardly. "I do not think I could bring myself to do the same to you if the situations were reversed."

Zara blinked, taken aback.

The sentiment settled onto her uncomfortably.

Am I ready for this?

"What needs to be done is not always the easiest thing to do, Zara. Sometimes it even feels wrong. So, I offer this as a kindness. To Dmitri, to you, and to Oscar as well as everyone else," Lyn finished. She swallowed and adjusted her blouse.

"Well, don't." The heat within Zara was cooling now, the weight of the truth she knew but didn't want to allow settling heavier upon her. "We're going to save him."

Lyn nodded sadly. "I hope so."

There was a gentle tap on the window. Zara turned and saw Dmitri peering in at them from the night.

"One second." Zara rushed to the door.

"Wait!" Lyn snapped, just as her hand reached for the handle.

Zara turned to see her striding to the counter, where a burglar alarm with a flashing light was on the wall.

Oh.

"But we don't know the code..." Zara knew if the alarm sounded, they'd have to either move very quickly or start coming up with a damn good story.

Lyn shrugged tiredly and snatched out with a clawed hand, tearing the whole box from the wall. It let out a sad bleep and died. "I figured it out."

Zara grinned, turned, and pulled on the door. After a little spiritual boost gave it some convincing, it popped loose on its hinges with a brief screech of protest, and the cool night welcomed them into its embrace.

"Where did she put you?" Zara mumbled.

"It doesn't matter," Dmitri said quickly, turning away.

Zara grimaced, catching a distinctly public bathroom-like whiff about him.

"He's here then," Lyn said darkly. "Stonehenge."

"So it would seem." Dmitri's eyes were already scanning the night.

"I always wanted to come here. Not exactly the right circumstances." Zara squared her shoulders.

"This is where it happened," Lyn said. "It makes sense that this is where it should unhappen."

"What happened?" Zara frowned.

Dmitri grunted. "The sealing. This is where the druids created the seal between Earth and Theia."

"Oh." Zara swallowed, her skin prickling unpleasantly, as if in warning. "Well, let's go save Oscar."

32

WANTS AND NEEDS

They had been walking forever.

Oscar's brain told him his feet should hurt, but his faded limbs didn't ache at all. Instead, his brain gave him a dull, unpleasant hum below his knees.

"You can walk for as long as you want. We're not going anywhere," Harry grumbled from behind him.

Oscar ignored it. It was one of the less colourful and less offensive complaints he'd made. Not that he'd responded to any of those either, but he wasn't particularly sure what to say to the man in any case.

I'm sorry you died?

I'm sorry you hate me?

"You're already dead. You just don't know it yet," Harry said flatly.

Oscar froze.

It was the first time he'd said *that*.

"You don't know that." Swallowing, Oscar turned around. The man was watching him, eyes full of hate.

"I know it as well as I knew I was dead the second this thing got in me," Harry snarled. "You don't think I know what this thing is? I've been inside it, watching everything it's done. Everything it's destroyed."

Oscar frowned. *Watching.* He'd said that earlier too. "How were you doing that?"

Harry's face shifted, a mask of indifference covering spite a little too late. "What?"

"You could see what it was doing when it was in your body? How did you do that?"

Harry stared back at him.

"Tell me," Oscar pleaded.

"I just wanted to. I wanted to see what it was doing, and I thought about it really hard, and it was like falling asleep, but waking up. I couldn't do anything, but I could see what was happening. I haven't been able to do it since..."

Since your body is gone, Oscar thought darkly. He swallowed. "You meditated?"

Harry sneered. "Nothing fruity. I just wanted it enough. Maybe only people strong enough can break through. Someone like you probably doesn't have a chance."

Oscar nodded, dropping down to the floor and crossing his legs.

"What are you doing? It's not like it will make any difference," Harry grumbled.

"It might, and maybe that's enough."

Oscar closed his eyes.

Nothing happened.

Oscar's eyes being closed gave him the uneasy feeling that the swirling shadows might be creeping closer, wisping tendrils reaching out to wrap around him and tear apart this echo of himself.

Unable to fight the urge, he opened one eye slightly.

Harry was watching him. He shook his head, curling his lip and turning to walk away, and mumbled, "Prick."

Oscar squeezed his eyes shut again.

Please.

I want to see.

I want to see.

I want to...

He swallowed, fighting that uneasy feeling again.

No. I don't want to see.

I need to.

He pushed.

What if the Umbran was doing something terrible?

To my friends?

To Dmitri?

I need to see.

He pushed harder.

He ignored the chill spreading across his skin.

He ignored the fear the shadows would claim him.

He pushed, and something gave way. It was like opening a door you had expected to be locked, and stumbling through.

Oscar knew he was still in the nothing, surrounded by the swirling darkness.

But now, he could see and hear.

It was still dark but not the same unearthly pit of shadows. Instead, it was night. Tunnelled vision moving too fast, blurry. It wasn't quite right, like he had his face too close to a television screen. It didn't mean he was *in* the picture, just closer to it. An impenetrable shield between him and his self.

Oscar blinked, his eyes sliding over the rapidly moving scenery, trying to recognise something, anything.

But it was all unfamiliar. Some fields? Crisp, dark night sky, darker than the city. They were somewhere different. The countryside maybe? He knew the Umbran could travel at will, seemingly sliding through the shadows, but it felt strange to imagine it riding his body like a fleshy skateboard to do it.

Then, Oscar saw a flash of something pale. A hand dark with gore.

My hand.

A raw numbness yawned inside him, a familiar feeling of help-lessness swelling in his heart.

His hand was taking something a startling white but streaked in blood. It was pushing it into place amongst other things that looked alike, like a grizzly 3d jigsaw. Oscar saw a skull, its jawbone too long to be human. Another, small as a child's, but with teeth like daggers.

Disgusted, Oscar *stepped* back, and the vision was gone. He opened his eyes and blinked up at Harry, who was watching him sourly. "What did you see?"

Oscar blinked. "Bones. It's making something with bones."

33

SCARS UNHEALED

The damp earth squelched beneath Zara's boots, and she cringed, looking back to Lyn, who trailed behind.

Lyn refused to meet her eyes, instead focusing on her own feet, pale, bare, and streaked with mud.

She'd been unable to walk on the loose earth in her heels. Rather than carry them, she tossed them into the nearest bin. Zara was careful to make no comment about the cost—she knew Lyn's tastes in shoes were decadent. Dmitri clearly didn't care, but even he knew better than to poke the bear.

"Head for the main monument. No doubt whatever it's planning to use is related to the veil there." Lyn's voice was ice.

Dmitri grunted in agreement.

"Is it a closed parallax?" Zara asked.

"Of a kind," Dmitri said. "Older, though. This place is one of a handful on Earth where the planes between worlds match precisely. A point of dimensional planetary alignment. It used to be elsewhere—Wales, I believe—but when the gate was sealed, it disrupted the alignment and caused a shift in reality. As Lyn said before, it used to be that beings could move freely between Earth and Theia. Some things that began as Theian joined your evolutionary chain in the centuries before. I suspect that is why some dispute the plausibility of your terrible lizards of the past."

Terrible lizards?

Dinosaurs were Theian?

Fuck. Marcus is going to be pissed he missed this.

"Just how many things from Earth are Theian?"

"A fair few. Possibly the most notable being cats," Dmitri replied darkly.

"Cats?" Zara said blankly. "Weirdly, that makes a lot of sense."

"For centuries, this place was used for communication between Earth and Theia. Theians and humans had a functioning agreement of sorts. That was until a group of Theians took it upon themselves to breach Earth and try to cause as much havoc as they could. It was then, a group of powerful druids sealed it."

"But it left a scar," Lyn said sourly.

"So?" Zara said. "Didn't the world parallax do that in the cemetery?"

"Not all scars heal as well. You know this. It is the same with the veil. The world parallax was a clean cut, sealed tight. Here, this was a tear of full-thickness. It healed poorly in ugly ridges and pockets of festering magick."

"And that's why the Umbran is here?"

Dmitri and Lyn exchanged a glance.

"I have a suspicion," Lyn said. "The Umbran somehow plans to re-open that wound and bring the worlds crashing back together, ending them both."

Zara's mouth was suddenly very dry. "How? When you opened the world parallax, that didn't happen."

"No," Lyn agreed simply. "I tried to use a surgical blade to graft our worlds together. To tear open a full breach without the aid of a parallax would be the equivalent of trying to mash them together by using a five thousand megaton mallet. It would essentially create the energy of multiple black holes instantaneously, and obliterate existence."

"That sounds bad."

"We wouldn't have much time to find out," Dmitri said.

Zara narrowed her eyes as they crested the hill.

The squat structures of the obelisks were in view. Each iconic pair with a third propped over their top. Weird...she had expected them to be bigger.

She scanned the shapes, looking for some kind of clue.

"There." Dmitri pointed into the darkness.

"I see it," Lyn agreed.

Zara followed, wishing her night vision was as good as theirs. "What is it?"

Dmitri shook his head, his voice grim. "Bad."

ZARA FOUND the first body not far from where they had stood.

The state it was left in wasn't what sickened her. Not after the things she'd seen—or done—to other living things.

Not after Tildy.

What sickened her is that it was a normal person. The man had a kind face, even in death, which hadn't come recently. His dusky skin was puffy, bloated, and boggy, and something had been chewing at his fingers. His face had gnawed holes, and she could see things moving inside, but had no desire to learn what insects had made the dead man their home. He wore a dark security uniform.

They found a car and two more corpses not long after. Those were fresher. The dark blood staining their uniforms and the seat was dry and almost black. Their faces were slack, lips blue. Perhaps they had come looking for the first man.

"Why aren't there more?" Zara looked around, worried that there might be. "Why are they still here?"

"The site has been closed for weeks for restoration," Dmitri said. "There was a sign on the shop window. This must have been the patrol to check everything was okay."

Zara grunted. "It definitely wasn't okay. These people haven't been dead long. I'm pretty sure more will be looking for them."

"Then we must be quick," Dmitri replied.

Beside her, Lyn tensed.

"What?" Zara felt her muscles follow suit reflexively.

"Over there. Movement," Lyn hissed. Zara could see her eyes had turned golden yellow as she focused in the dark.

"Just don't hurt him," Dmitri pleaded. He hefted the heavy backpack on his shoulder. "Hold him down, and I will chain him up."

"Maybe you should be the one to grab him, Dmitri," Zara suggested.

"I cannot."

Zara looked at him. The vulnerability in his eyes startled her.

Lyn's face held an echo of sympathy but only for a moment. "Dmitri. He is infested—filled with the Umbran—he could destroy everything."

"We have to find a way, Lyn. The Bean-Nighe said—" Zara began.

"That silly moon drunk bint isn't here." Lyn's voice was a whipcrack, and she raised her chin stubbornly. "She said there may be a way, but if it comes down to letting the worlds be destroyed or killing Oscar Tundale, there is only one clear decision we can make. I do not expect either of you to be the one to make it, but I will do what needs to be done out of mercy."

"If anything happens to him..." Zara began darkly, but she didn't know how to finish. Fire pumped into her limbs, and Dmitri let out a low growl. Zara didn't know what made her angrier—that Lyn wanted to kill Oscar or that she might be right.

"You lay a hand on him, and I won't leave your head intact this time," Dmitri snarled.

Lyn shrugged her narrow shoulders, turning her nose up at

him. "I may have wished to end the world before. How was I to know Theia was gone? But better this foul world than none at all. Do what you will, *dog*, but you are not so bereft of wisdom that you would let the world burn."

"We will do everything we can," Zara said roughly.

Dmitri's eyes burned in the night. His voice shook. "We will save him. We have to."

Zara nodded slowly. "We have to."

SURVIVAL OF THE FITTEST

"Aren't you tired?" Harry grumbled, traipsing behind. "Aren't you sick of doing this? What makes you think you're not already dead? You can't stop it, and you know what it wants, don't you? It's all over."

Oscar carried on walking. "Do you think we'd still be here if it was already over? I mean, I don't know, but I don't think so. It wanted to end its suffering, but it seems like we're still in it. As long as we're here, it isn't over."

Harry chewed on that sullenly for a while. Oscar took respite in the peace; he wasn't particularly happy the older man had decided to get chattier all of a sudden.

"I know you haven't got a chance," Harry finally replied.

"We don't know anything." Oscar's voice, thin as it was here, rose. "We don't even know where we are. I assume I'm some-where inside it. Inside me inside it. But we don't know why you're still here, given you're—" Oscar stopped, closing his mouth so quickly the memory of his teeth clicked.

"Dead," Harry finished bitterly. "It's okay. I know what I am. It was worth it if I could take a few of those bastards down with me."

Bastards? The monsters the Umbran had killed?

"Why?" Oscar remembered the boy and the sobbing woman beside the river. "Why do you hate them so much? What happened at the river?"

Harry's face froze, his eyes shining with rage. "One of them took my father. Killed him in front of me. Tried to kill me too. After that...after that, my mum was gone too. She was still there, but something inside her snapped. She wasn't herself anymore."

Oscar shook his head sadly. "I'm sorry that happened to you. I lost my parents too. They just never came home one day."

"I DON'T CARE!" Harry roared suddenly. "I don't know why I'm here, but it's sure as shit not to share sad life stories with you, you little freak."

"I'm sorry, I just——"

"Your little boyfriend saved me as if that made things better. Like it meant people weren't being killed everywhere by his kind. Unnatural. Disgusting," Harry spat.

Oscar's eyes widened. "Dmitri saved you?"

"Spring-Heeled Jack," Harry snarled. "I learned all about him after that night. Do you know how many people he's murdered? Do you know who it is you give yourself to? You're the fucking devil's whore."

Oscar met the man's eyes. He felt many things inside himself, first and perhaps worst, an echo of shame he hadn't felt for years. Anger swallowed that shame quickly, followed by a cold and certain calm. "I know Dmitri did some bad things, and I don't know how bad or what things, but he's doing his best now. He tries to help people."

"If you want to help people, you should all just die." Harry turned on him, his body was practically vibrating with rage. "People like you are what is wrong with the world. Maybe *you* are the reason your parents never came back. Did you ever think of that? Maybe they wanted to get rid of you."

Oscar felt the words slide into his heart. An old wound, familiar but forgotten. He let them pass through him.

"Yes, I did. All the time, actually."

Harry laughed cruelly.

"And if they did, then that's on them. I can't change the choices they made, and I can't judge them because I don't know what happened."

But maybe Dmitri does.

The thought bit into him. A new blade. Sharper and deeper. He forced himself to keep speaking, though his voice shook. "I just have to do whatever I can. To live a good life and be happy."

Harry turned around, his face a twisted mask of fury. He took a step closer.

"I think sometimes, would they be proud of who I am? What I've done? Do you ever think about that?" Oscar asked, taking a step back.

"My dad's dead and my mum's in a nuthouse," Harry spat. "Who cares what they would think?"

Oscar stepped back again, cautiously. "I think as long as you are proud of yourself, then—"

Harry lurched forward suddenly, his hands grasping out at Oscar. Oscar tried to get away but tripped over his own feet and stumbled back.

He felt whatever counted as ground in the nothing hit his back. Not as painful as it should have been, more like a memory of what it might have felt like. A buzz of past pains.

But then Harry was upon him.

"What are you doing?!" Oscar cried out, throwing up his arms.

Harry snatched at him. One of his hands, the unscarred one, closed around Oscar's throat.

OSCAR WAS STANDING on the stairs. Someone was screaming. Not in pain or fear, but rage. He looked beside him, and there was a girl. She clutched a teddy bear to her chest. She wasn't crying; she looked like she was waiting for something to end. Something that happened all the time.

A pretty woman with blonde, frazzled hair stormed into the hall, throwing a carrier bag full and spilling with clothes.

"Just go. I don't want you here anymore. You can't keep a job, and you can't help me out. You can't even care for your daughter. We're better off without you," she shrieked. Her eye makeup was smudged, tears drying on her cheeks.

The man that followed was Harry.

His hair was shorter, neatly trimmed around the ears, and his waist was a little slimmer. He looked younger. His eyes were still haunted but had fewer lines around them, and there was no salt and pepper in his hair.

"You don't understand, Elaine. You never listen. I have important work to do. I can't just forget my duty to deal with normal shit." Harry spoke like the woman was being unreasonable. Like he was sick of her silly game.

"Oh, sure. The whole mysterious spy job." The woman, Elaine, laughed.

"I'm hunting," Harry growled.

"I don't want to hear it," Elaine snapped. "Take your shit and get out."

Harry looked at the bag of clothes on the floor.

"You don't own a fucking thing here, Harry. It's all from me. All from my parents. Maybe if you managed to finish a week's work, you might get a paycheque. Well, guess what? Now you'll have to work, or your sorry arse will be out on the street," Elaine snarled.

"Laney, I…" Harry raised his hands, his eyes searching her face, not pleading but searching for weakness. For a way to convince her.

"I don't want to hear it. Get the fuck out." She raised her chin.

Harry's brows downturned, angry. His eyes travelled to the girl on the stairs.

"Don't even think about it," Elaine snapped. "I want you out. You're *bad for her, Harry. Bad for everyone around you. I don't want you near her again. You're sick, just like your mother."*

~

OSCAR GASPED, thrashing weakly.

Harry's weight tumbled off him, but the larger, older man twisted on the floor, and staggered to his feet.

What was that? It was horrible.

"Get back here," Harry roared, grabbing Oscar's leg. His voice was so loud, and his body was much more substantial than it had been before. He looked almost fully formed now. He was strong, too. Much stronger than Oscar. Much stronger than he had been just moments before.

Oscar grabbed at the floor, seeing his own hands were fainter now. Barely even there.

What's happening? What is he doing to me?

Harry spun Oscar around, snarling in his face as he did.

He was definitely more solid now. Oscar looked up at him, panic paralysing his body.

"You don't get it, do you, freak? I figured out how it works after the first time you grabbed me, and it happened by accident. It's survival of the fittest here. I've lasted this long, and now, I'm going to take everything you have," Harry spat. Saliva flecked on Oscar's face mixing with futile tears that were starting to flow. "That way, even if there is some way to get out, it won't be you that does."

His scarred hand closed over Oscar's face.

WHAT BRINGS SHADOWS TO LIGHT

Zara tried to breathe naturally.

She knew the Umbran must sense her.

It just didn't care she was there.

Spots of rain fell from above, cool droplets kissing her skin in the mild night. The moon and stars barely cast enough light that the monument itself was visible. Three or four times her own height, the structures were impossible for the time they were built, but still relatively unspectacular compared to the thing she saw as she edged closer—the abomination standing at the heart of the stone circle.

Everything was so much closer together than she imagined, the standing sarsen stones interspersed by large rocks. At the centre of them was a new and hideous monument. It was almost the same shape as the others, but instead of the smooth stone edges worn by time, jagged ridges of deformed ribs and twisted skulls lined its edges. Long bones were bound together by sinew, occasional scraps of stray flesh and hair hung in tatters, and the whole thing was streaked with blood. It stunk with the sour, cloying stench of rotten meat and sulphur.

A shape moved around it quickly, slim and long-limbed. Its

hands pressed and adjusted the various bones and skulls delicately, ensuring they were fixed and secure.

"Oscar," Zara said softly.

He turned.

It was Oscar, but it wasn't.

Everything looked the same—his long face and narrow nose, his pale, freckled skin. His unruly hair curled under his ears in the wind. *That* was Oscar.

He smiled, secretive and self-assured. His stance, limbs firm and certain. His posture, straight-backed and confident. None of that was Oscar at all.

And then there were his eyes.

Not the bright blue they had always been. Not the colour of the ocean on a sunny day. Now, they were black as oil slicks, infinitely swirling.

Zara had heard about eyes you could fall into, and these were eyes you didn't want to get near for fear of plummeting for eternity.

Eyes that would drown you with spite.

The Umbran—wearing Oscar—tilted its head in an almost familiar way. In his hand, he held a skull, still slick with gore, bone stark white. Its teeth looked human at the front, but at the back, they were jagged barbs.

Was this the skull of a more human monster or just one that had begun to change?

Tildy? Or...someone else?

Oscar's arms were covered in blood and shreds of meat. Dark stains were splashed on his shirt, his neck, and face. He smiled, a cruel and patient smile shaped by centuries his body hadn't seen.

Zara swallowed bile.

"Hey, Booboo. What you doin' there?" she tried to sound flippant.

The Umbran turned, hefting the skull and pushing it into a gap between the other bones. It slotted in easily, as if this were its true place, not atop someone's shoulders, but wedged neatly between a pelvis too large to be from anything human-sized and some spiny skulls that looked to be attached to one another.

Zara's eyes travelled over the structure the Umbran had built. What it must been preparing for since that night in the cemetery. Bones of all kinds meshed together, becoming one. One skull appeared to have an additional face on the back, with teeth like knives, still intact. The skeletons of several small sheep-like creatures made up the base of the pillars. From there, twisted femurs, jointed spines, and long, jagged fingers all melded into one, forming twin towering obelisks of bone. The third sat across the top, propped between the two great ossified columns, just like the other structures around them. Those others had been there for centuries, longer than anyone knew. This one was new but made of things that may have been even older.

"It is almost complete." The Umbran used Oscar's voice like it didn't quite know how. It was him, but a rasping, hissing version of him.

Zara's heart wrenched.

Still, it was not like the broken, mangled vocal cords of the corpse it drove before. This was still Oscar's voice, even if it was filled with something that wasn't Oscar at all. It was laced with hate, like deadly snakes slithering through grass.

"I can see that." Zara eyed the bizarre structure.

No, she knew what it was. A gate to the end of all things.

She swallowed. "So, I know you're in there, Os. It might be hard to hear me, and I know it must be scary. But I need you to fight. There's so much here for you. Me, Marcus, Dmitri...we all need you."

The Umbran reached for another bone on the small pile on the ground. A short rib, Zara realised.

A tendril of shadow pushed from the ground to hand it to him. As he took it, the Umbran spoke softly through him again.

"Your friend is gone. His suffering is ended. As yours soon will be."

Zara's jaw clenched.

Liar.

Oscar's flesh was just as pale as it had been since she'd met him. Well, other than that one time he got sunburned in the park. She could see the way his chest still rose and fell. The way his limbs moved.

He was still alive.

He has to be.

The Umbran pushed the rib into its place, and something changed. Zara felt a humming in the earth beneath her. The column sang with energy, spreading through the bones and growing ominously.

The Umbran smiled. "It is done."

"Oscar. Please, do this for us. I know you can do this. Please fight," Zara said, desperation growing in her voice.

The Umbran turned. "Do not despair. It will be over soon. You will all rest soon. Finally." Its foul voice held something she'd not heard before.

Pity.

Zara took a deep breath and raised her fist in the air.

That was the signal.

The darkness burst into light.

The lamps buried in the earth were almost blinding. Zara would have been stunned if she weren't expecting it. As it was, she narrowed her eyes and moved in a burst of speed as the Umbran hissed and raised Oscar's hands to shield its eyes. Zara dragged on the well of power within her, feeling it fill her, allowing the fury and joy of the Ghatokacha to pulse through her veins as she focused it into her right arm. Twisting to move beside the Umbran, she pistoned her fist, not at the monster wearing her best friend, but at the monument of death it had built.

Before the light that had burst out around her knuckles could connect with a satisfying crunch to the gate of bones, something caught her arm.

Zara blinked.

Oscar's hand clutched around her wrist.

Despite the bright lights, darkness like tendrils of ink wove their way up his arm, strengthening his grip.

The bottomless black eyes of the Umbran regarded her impatiently. "You could have chosen to live a little longer. To see the end."

"Oscar," Zara snarled, her voice harsh in her throat. "Get your arse out here right now."

Oscar's fingers squeezed around her wrist; she felt the bones grating together painfully.

The Umbran reached to Oscar's side. Zara's eyes followed his hand, as he closed pale, bloody fingers around the hilt of...

The willblade?

He had it with him.

Zara's heart beat a dreadful beat. *At least that means it's here.*

"I might have used your bones if I knew you were so desperate to be involved," the Umbran hissed.

She had to get the willblade off him, just in case. Besides, it was a blade of light, it wasn't like the Umbran would be able to...

The Umbran's fingers closed around the hilt and pulled it loose. The space around them *throbbed*, and a blade burst out. It was not like the blade she nor Oscar had ever summoned.

This blade was blacker than night, hungrily devouring any light around it, edges ragged and bleeding. Where the blade of light was full and overflowing, this blade only wanted to take. It seemed to sap the very warmth from the air around them.

Zara used the opportunity and the swell of panic in her chest to unload a pulse of energy that tore from her core, battering at the wall that kept her and the Ghatokacha separate.

The fingers around her wrist loosened enough for her to slip free, dancing back around the rocks at her feet.

Sneering with Oscar's mouth, the Umbran raised the blade of darkness and pointed it at her. Zara felt the malice and spite screaming from it.

That was the Umbran's will incarnate. Every rippling, hateful edge of it.

"Oh." She swallowed. "So, this is going to be a little tricky, huh?"

The blade of darkness hummed through the air where Zara had stood a moment before, biting deeply into the earth. She was very careful not to let it touch her, panic pounding in her chest.

With a burst of light beneath her feet, she bounced back several feet, her boots sliding on the wet earth beneath her as she landed. The Umbran stalked toward her, black eyes swirling angrily.

The rain fell heavier now. A sad drizzle misted the lamps in the ground, dampening her.

"Come on, Os. This shadow guy is a right wanker. You can totally beat him." Zara grunted as she danced away once more.

The Umbran twisted Oscar's arm, flourishing the dark blade and grinning savagely. His messy, curling hair was wet and starting to stick to his head.

From outside of the lamp's light, she saw movement.

She knew it was Lyn.

Lyn was watching, waiting, chains in hand, ready to pounce when the moment was right. Dmitri would be back in seconds, too; he'd needed to switch on the lamps from the control station nearby.

"You keep speaking to your friend, but he is gone," the Umbran hissed, black eyes narrowing.

Zara felt the ground churn beneath her feet, and on instinct, she jumped aside.

Despite the light where she stood, shadows were writhing like snakes, curling and seeking her ankles to bite and latch on to. "Tricky tricky," she murmured.

He wasn't as strong as before. Nowhere near. Perhaps it was because the corpse it had used at the house had been feasting on monster flesh, or perhaps being beaten once had taken some of its strength.

Oscar's body might be the home it needed to finish its business here, but whatever it had done to its previous body, whatever strength it had taken by eating the other creatures it killed, was diminished.

I can do this.

I have to.

The Umbran's arm lunged despite them being several feet apart, and it released its grip on the hilt.

The black, burning sword hummed through the air. Zara desperately dodged to the side to avoid it. The air screamed around her as it soared past, and her shoulder connected painfully with the ground.

Twisting, she saw the blade lodge into the earth just for a moment, darkening it slightly before the swirling blackness blinked out, and the hilt fell to the ground with a thud.

She met eyes with the Umbran for a moment and then leapt, snatching out for the shining hilt.

Her fingertips touched it.

A shadow slipped beside her, pushing the willblade away and sending it skittering across the ground to Oscar's feet. He leaned down and picked it up slowly.

Zara moved to get up, but the shadow coiled around her wrist.

The black blade burst to life in the Umbran's hands once more as it stepped toward her, raising the blade above its head.

Zara pushed, forcing that energy within her to break the shadow's grip. She turned to roll, but more shadows were grasping at her now, pulling at her ankles and waist. She gasped.

Too slow.

With a rattling of chains, a figure barrelled into Oscar's side with such terrifying force that Zara cried out. Mottled leathery skin and glowing yellow eyes. Lyn's hair flowed wild around her transformed face. The Umbran skidded across the floor, rolling to his knees with a grace that seemed strange on Oscar. He righted himself, his face showing no pain or fear. Simply anger.

"Lyn!" Zara cried. "Don't hurt him!"

Lyn gnashed her pointed teeth angrily, hefting the coiled chains she had looped around her shoulder. Her clothes hung from her in tatters, exposing her glorious and monstrous form as she stalked around the Umbran's much smaller vessel. Her long, dark claws raked the air menacingly. "You will kill us all with your kindness," she growled from between her jagged teeth.

The Umbran spun, the blade of darkness slashing out. Lyn swayed to one side, rearing back with almighty force, her clawed hand raising to strike him down.

Shadows shifted around his feet, dragging Oscar to the side.

"Whatever it's trying to do only works if his body is alive," Lyn growled, yanking the chains from around her shoulder and lashing out with them, trying to swing them around Oscar's body.

The Umbran slashed with the blade of darkness, cutting cleanly through the chains, severing them in half and leaving Lyn with a short handful of links. The rest of the chain rattled against one of the stones and fell.

So much for chaining him up.

But Lyn was quick.

She cast the useless handful of links at Oscar.

He slashed again, and as he did, she stepped inside his guard, one long hand grasping around his wrist, preventing him from stabbing at her.

Her claws bit into his shoulder, and blood blossomed on Oscar's white T-shirt.

Zara wanted to scream, wanted to tell her to stop. But she couldn't.

Lyn rose one clawed hand into the air for a smiting blow.

"Lyn!" Zara choked.

Lyn froze, her claw shaking in the air above. She let out a snarl of frustration.

The Umbran took advantage of the moment, kicking her in the midsection viciously. Dark energy swirled around his leg and foot, blasting her back several feet into one of the monuments with a horrific crash. Zara expected it to sway or topple, but it stood impossibly firm in the earth, solid and unmoving.

Come on, Dmitri.

Zara struggled to her feet. The Umbran turned, vicious smile already melting from Oscar's face.

Zara heard screeching tyres, then saw a flash of headlights.

Shit.

Was it more security? The police or the army? She didn't have time to look. Her eyes were on Oscar's body as he swung the will-blade again, this time launching it at Lyn's recovering form. The dark blade arced through the air with terrifying force and precision, straight at her head.

"Lyn!" Zara cried.

The blade stopped. Inches from her face, stuck in the air. Lyn froze. Then the black blade winked out, just shy of splitting her skull in two.

At that same moment, something collided with Oscar's body, something squat and sturdy.

Shadows, stone, and flesh rolled, briefly thrashing on the ground.

Is that one of the gaeants?

"That wasn't very kind, Oscar!" Marcus hollered, climbing out of the passenger seat of the newly arrived car.

"Yeah, don't be a dick," Paige shouted from the driver's seat as she pulled on the handbrake. Ed bounded over her knee, spilling out of the car door, shifting from corgi to German shepherd as he did.

Zara's heart soared.

A gaeant.

Marcus had released one of the small earth monsters broken off from its cumulative body and used it to track Oscar.

"Marcus, you're a genius." Zara beamed.

"I know." Marcus shrugged.

The shimmering mist that followed Marcus was shaped almost like a person now. For a moment, Zara thought she saw the burnished gold eyes of Song within.

"Took you long enough, though." Zara grinned.

"It was a long drive." Marcus arched an eyebrow, nodding his head back toward the car. "Besides, that one is a nightmare behind the wheel. Honestly, I thought I might have been better off with the Umbran driving at one point."

"Oi, how was I supposed to drive well with dog-thing whinnying like Seabiscuit in heat in the back?" Paige snarked while she kept her distance by the open car door. "Now, less bitching and more saving my little brother."

"Deal," Marcus and Zara agreed at the same moment, flashing another grin at each other.

Dmitri emerged from the darkness, his eyes taking in Marcus and Paige, shining with something close to relief.

Marcus waved his hands, and the willblade's hilt sailed through the air.

Zara's reached out and snatched it as it flew toward her, clean, glittering metal slapping pleasingly against her palm.

The Umbran roared, and there was a smash. The gaeant was catapulted back in the direction it had come from, colliding with the newly arrived car and shattering its side and windows. Paige almost fell, trying to get as far from the car as possible whilst also reaching toward it protectively. Zara thought she might never have seen a move more Oscar-like in her life.

"JESUS, OSCAR, THIS IS A RENTAL!" Paige screamed, eyes bulging.

Ed barked at the broken pieces of earthen monster but kept his distance, pacing defensively in front of Paige.

Zara held out the hilt, and it hummed in her hands.

For a moment, nothing happened. Then, a blade burst forth, but it was weaker and duller than it had been at Betty's. And then it flickered out.

"Not the time for performance anxiety, Zara," Marcus mumbled.

The Umbran smiled with Oscar's mouth, turning his gentle features cruel. Blood ran from his temple and a small cut on his lip.

"Hello darkness, my old friend," Marcus sang.

The Umbran's smile only lasted a moment until Lyn barrelled into him again, sending the pair rolling on the ground in a jumble of limbs and snarls as she tried to pin him down.

"I will destroy your paltry world!" the monster roared from Oscar's mouth.

"I don't know what you think you know, buddy." Marcus stepped forward, hands dancing before him, trying to get a hold of Oscar. "But we have a perfectly normal number of chickens on this planet."

Zara shook her head in disbelief.

Marcus narrowed his eyes, his voice strained. "I don't have much. Song is holding out...they'd only let me trade my seasickness. Don't make this too hard."

Dmitri was shifting through the night beside Zara. "Restrain him. I will try and destroy the gate."

"No," Zara said stiffly. "You need to try and get that thing out of him."

Dmitri shook his head. "How?"

Zara reached out and took his hand in hers just for a moment; it was large and warm. She squeezed it, then let go. "Talk to him. Tell him everything. Make him remember."

THE POWER WITHIN

O scar's breath barely came, and what little he could muster
was lost to sobs. He could barely move. Any strength he'd
ever had was gone. His frayed edges threatened to come undone,
unspooling him into nothingness. It felt as if there were hardly
any of him left, like spilled water on the ground almost all dried
up by the sun.

Harry Barlow had touched him three more times, each
draining more of him away. Taking parts of Oscar to strengthen
himself.

With each touch, Oscar was overwhelmed with a horrid
memory belonging to the other man. Watching the girl who had
sat on the stairs, his daughter, leaving school from a car down the
street, crying. A group of people in an office laughing at him. A
woman who was all skin and bones staring absently, with haunted
eyes, as he promised her that he would prove what they'd seen at
the river that night had been real. Oscar knew she was Harry's
mother. He knew because every time Harry touched him, he
forced more of himself onto him, washing away Oscar's own
truths.

He was taking over.

He was claiming whatever last part of Oscar remained inside the Umbran, and now he was feeding on his dregs until Oscar was all gone.

"I'm stronger. So, it's only right I'm the one to move forward." Harry dropped his hand to his side. It was no longer scarred and burned. In fact, he no longer looked like Harry at all.

He's starting to look like...me.

"After you're gone, I'll find a way out and be on my way. Quite nice, actually, to have twenty years back. I won't be seeing your scummy little freak friends again, though, and I can promise Spring-Heel won't lay a hand on your scrawny little arse again," Harry chuckled darkly.

Oscar tried to get up, but found he couldn't. He was too weak now, and could barely move his limbs.

Oscar.

A flicker inside his chest.

Harry knelt beside him, a grim smile on his face.

My face.

He lowered his hand toward him.

Oscar. I need you to come back to me.

That voice...was that Dmitri?

Harry's hand connected with Oscar's face, and every part of him screamed.

∾

HE WAS IN A CAR. The dark night sky above.

An old car that stunk like burgers and stale air.

The wing mirror told him he wasn't just watching Harry now. He was him. *His eyes were tired and angry.*

Oscar recognised the street. This was Kinmount street. This was where Dmitri had lived. Where they had lived.

And then Marcus was there. He walked out onto the street smiling excitedly.

Oscar felt a deep pang of alien disgust. Harry's disgust. As he watched, Zara followed, as did...

Me.

Oscar felt Harry's thoughts, vile and noxious, swirling around in his being. Insults bubbled for Oscar's friends, vile slurs driving into Oscar's heart like nails.

Harry was watching us? All this time ago?

Oscar watched as Zara stared sullenly into the night. He remembered; they'd been fighting. Because of Dmitri. Because of everything.

Oscar felt himself flickering as Harry's thoughts drowned him in their noise. Through the din, he heard Dmitri's voice once more.

Oscar. Oscar, I love you. Please.

I love you.

Oscar felt himself flickering. He was disappearing.

I love you...

No.

Oscar pushed back.

He felt Harry's toxic pressure roiling around him like rank sewage.

I love them. I love these people.

He pushed harder.

They're my friends. My family.

Harry's suffocating energy thrashed around him, trying to submerge him. Trying to absorb him.

Something burned inside Oscar.

You want everything? You don't even know. Here. Take it. These are my memories. This is me, and you can't make that yours.

Oscar drove his memories back into Harry's smothering aura.

～

Tears rolled down Marcus' cheeks, and he laughed. He couldn't stop laughing.

He squeezed Oscar's hand.

The scars on his chest looked angry, but they were beautiful.

The doctor had said they'd get even better in the next few weeks.

The doctor had looked so happy for Marcus.

"It's me," Marcus sobbed, grinning from ear to ear. "I'm here."

Harry's energy recoiled, twisting around him. He forced disgust and shame on Oscar like a smothering blanket.

The fire in Oscar roared, searing through it and turning it to cinders.

～

The front door slammed. Zara's eyes were alive with fury.

"What happened?" Oscar asked.

She shook her head angrily.

Oscar waited. He didn't say anything, he just listened to her silence.

Finally, she spoke. "My Dad. I told him about me. He said—" A sob broke her voice, and she took a calming breath in and out. "He said if I was going to live in sin, I wouldn't do it under his roof."

Oscar listened. She didn't have anything else to say.

After a while, he put his hand on her arm. "What can I do to help?"

Zara grabbed hold of him and held on like he was the only thing keeping her afloat.

"NO," Harry roared, spikes of humiliation and fear driving into Oscar.

Oscar blazed. *This is me. They are me, and there isn't an end to that.*

Oscar.
Oscar, please come home.

Dmitri.
Oscar remembered.
His smile.
His rare laugh.
The way he looked at him when he didn't think Oscar was watching.
He remembered that first time, letting the memories burst out of him in a torrent.

DMITRI'S KISSES all over him. Everywhere. Taking his time, appreciating every inch. Coarse stubble scratching between Oscar's thighs. Then his heat pushing into him, slowly, painfully at first, but so right. He remembered the taste of the sweat pooling in the hollow of his throat, the crease of his chest. He remembered the feel of his lips on his as he wrapped his legs around him, Dmitri's tongue pushing into his mouth. His sharp teeth against his neck as he moaned, moving patiently, asking Oscar if he was okay, if this felt good...if he wanted more. Shared breath, dizzy and drunk on lust. Addicted to each other after just the first taste.

The barbed spite of Harry's thoughts jammed into Oscar's mind.

DISGUSTING. VILE. ABOMINATION.

Oscar smiled proudly.
*No. It's love. It's just **love**.*
Harry's energy shivered.
Stronger, Oscar pushed again at Harry, feeling him retreat

beneath his pressure, feeling him flee. The horror, the shame, the disgust all melted away. The hate cowered. Oscar felt something else, something deeper and stronger in Harry's mind.

Fear.

Fear for himself.

Fear that what he knew wasn't truth.

Jealousy.

Broken pieces of sorrow and loneliness.

They crumbled apart, brittle, fragile, and weak.

Then, Oscar was back. Back in the nothing.

The pale shadow of a boy fell away from Oscar, shaking and faint, frightened.

Oscar recognised the boy from the side of the Thames, where he'd held onto his mother and wept for his father.

Harry.

Oscar struggled to his feet, feeling his body far more solid than before, but so weak and tired.

The boy cowered, hardly daring to look up at Oscar.

Oscar took a breath, looking down at Harry. "I'm done."

The boy wiped tears away from his face, sniffling. He flickered, and for a moment, was not there. When he returned, he was even more faded, barely visible at all.

Oscar swallowed. "I don't know what's going to happen, but I won't be coming back here, Harry."

"Please, take me with you," Harry whined, his voice weak and high. "Don't leave me here." He flickered again.

Oscar shook his head sadly. "No."

Harry wailed, the shadow of his memory failing like sputtering flame.

"I'm sorry." Oscar felt a tear roll down his cheek. Maybe if things had been different for Harry, he might have been different too. But then again, maybe not. "I can't help you. I wish I could, but you would never have let me anyway. I don't think...I don't think you could have ever left here. You chose this, Harry. Over and over again, you chose this. I'm sorry for everything that happened to you, but I can't let you take everything away from me when you already gave up on yourself." Oscar swallowed. "I'm so sorry."

The boy screamed, scrambling to his feet and launching himself at Oscar.

His faded form vanished in the darkness, and he was gone.

The black coin fell from the space where he had been but winked out before it ever landed.

Oscar stood for a moment, watching the space where what was left of the boy, the man, had vanished into darkness.

Oscar let out a long breath.

I hope he has some peace now.

Then he heard Dmitri's voice again.

Come home, Oscar.

Oscar smiled.

He closed his eyes and concentrated.

He felt the fear of the shadows moving in on him, and he wasn't afraid anymore.

He pushed back as hard as he could.

And then he was gone.

37

I WILL FOLLOW YOU

Zara moved toward the gate of bones, clutching the hilt of the willblade in her hand.

Rain beat down now, plastering her hair to her head, soaking her clothes.

"Come home, Oscar." Dmitri's voice shook in a way that made Zara's heart tremble.

The Umbran thrashed, the force of its resistance knocking Marcus flat on his back, sending him sliding on the wet earth. Lyn snarled, her talons driving into the ground as she managed to pin one of Oscar's bloodied arms, struggling to hold him down.

"I didn't tell you the truth," Dmitri said. "I couldn't tell you, and I need you to come home so I can make it right. Oscar, I knew your parents."

The Umbran twisted, connecting both of Oscar's feet into Lyn. She sailed through the air, landing several feet away.

The Umbran was standing again, shaking its head as though to free itself from the hold of Dmitri's words. Snarling, it made toward Zara and the gate.

He's getting through.

I have to buy him time.

"It wasn't for long, just a few years. Your parents knew everything about Theia. About monsters. About me," Dmitri said.

The Umbran dashed at Zara. Oscar's body moved with startling rapidity and grace, sliding on the shadows like a champion skater. Zara roared and rushed at the Umbran. She didn't have to beat it, just buy time for Dmitri to talk.

"Your mother...your mother was like Marcus. She had a soul pact with an ethernal. She dedicated her life's work to studying samples from Theia. She had a greater sense of the veil than any human I've ever met. She was a formidable woman."

Zara swung a fist, the ethereal glow whistling past the Umbran's moving head. Oscar's swirling, unruly hair flicked beads of rain as he moved.

"When she was pregnant with you, the ethernal knew you would be the one—the one in which finally the Theian cells would sing."

The Umbran lashed out, shadows pulsing from Oscar's fingers in claws of darkness. Zara leapt back as they tore through her shirt, slashing the skin below. She gasped.

Just shallow cuts.

Blood flowed down her belly.

"She used the power of her soul pact to compel me. That should anything ever happen to them, I would protect you at all costs but never be able to tell you. Only now that you have learned of it yourself, I can speak." Dmitri's dark hair was slick to his skull, his stormy eyes fixed on Oscar and the thing using him. "I left them after that. I felt betrayed. Some years later, they were killed by a powerful monster. One that sensed what you would become. I understand that your mother finished it before she died. It wasn't until many years later when a threat arose again, the compulsion kicked in. That is why I came here, why I protected you. It tells me I must protect you. I cannot even lay a firm hand on you even whilst this darkness drives you. But I never..."

His voice cracked. "I never expected to love you. That was never part of the bargain. I thought I would hate you. Your parents and I, we didn't speak after your mother placed those magick's on me against my will. It was a violation." A tear rolled down his cheek. "But I love you in spite of all of that. I love you because of who you are. I cannot be without you, Oscar."

"I cannot be without you, Oscar."

Oscar could see Dmitri even as the thing controlling his body stamped the earth where Zara had lain a moment before. And even as Ocampo struck at the gate built from the monster's skeletons, her blows ineffective despite their force. It was more solid than stone.

The Umbran snatched her with a coil of darkness and sent her sailing through the air with vicious force.

"Dmitri," Oscar cried.

He'd heard everything.

He pressed himself against the image, willing himself through, but the impenetrable barrier remained.

"I'm sorry, Oscar. I never told you because I feared you would think I'd been compelled to be with you. That I loved you because of the touch of Theia in your blood, or your mother's casting. I love you in spite of those things. I love you because of you. Because of the way you make me feel."

Oscar pushed.

I need to be with him. I need to be with all of them.

He watched as Zara wrapped her arms around his body in a brutal hug, her ghostly armour flaring around her, pinning his arms to his side to stop the Umbran's attacks. "Come on, Oscar. You can do this," she panted. "Get this shady little bitch out of you."

He watched her eyes widen, and she staggered back. One of his fingers had driven into the flesh of her chest. He saw the spike of darkness he'd pushed through her. Blood pumped out of her body. She staggered back and fell to the ground.

No.

No.

His vision shook.

The Umbran twisted his gaze.

Marcus was up, hands clenched before him, his borrowed powers gripping the air around his body and thickening it like invisible cement. Oscar felt the Umbran stretch, like tensing a muscle, and Marcus wavered. Then like snapping elastic, the pressure gave out, and Marcus was flung back against the side of Paige's rental car, landing beside the remains of the crushed gaeant, with a crash of metal and tinkling of glass. Paige was running to him, screaming. "Stop it, Oscar. Stop it!"

Oscar pushed harder, and he hurt.

All of him hurt.

He felt the rain.

He tasted blood in his mouth.

"Oscar, if anyone can do this, I know it is you." The Umbran's gaze shifted to Dmitri, standing passively in the beating rain. He was holding out his hand and smiling. "You're the strongest person I've ever met, Oscar. No matter what happens, you always have *more*. I know you can do this."

Oscar pushed harder, and the vision bowed around him—concave, like a fish-eye lens.

I just need to push hard enough.

The vision faded to darkness.

An inky sea swallowed it up.

Despair rose in Oscar's chest.

No.

I need to do this.

He felt himself propelled backward, deeper into the pitch with insurmountable force.

He opened his eyes.

The darkness had changed around him. It no longer roiled like an endless ocean of night. It was swelling—amassing all in one point.

The Umbran had its turned its attention to him.

He felt its fury building like a vast tidal wave.

The darkness around him coiled, folding into itself, leaving the places it had been bare, stark light. It pushed him back, swirling. A monstrous, impossible vortex of hate.

"DMITRI, YOU NEED TO STOP HIM," Zara cried out, clutching the wound in her chest.

She was bleeding too much. She felt it bubbling in her throat, and her head swam. That last strike had hit something important, and her breath was becoming impossible to catch. If she stood and fought, she would die. Every part of the energy of the Ghatokacha was currently going toward trying to knit her tissue together to keep her alive.

She clutched onto the willblade's hilt.

She couldn't take another hit like that.

Zara pulled deep within herself, trying to drag out more of the Ghatokacha's power. The spirit screamed inside of her. Not in pain or in fury, but in joy. Liquid fire rushed through her veins, her chest expanded, and she felt herself *slipping*. She felt her grip on who she was escaping her as the pleasure and fury of the battle-spirit began to take over her body. The barrier separating them inside stretched impossibly, and she felt horribly overwhelmed by the spirit's power.

No.

Panic warred with the screaming fury inside of her. She forced the Ghatokacha away, drove it back down into the recesses of herself. Spite and irritation boiled from the spirit inside her, but it resumed using the energy she held to heal her wound.

I can't lose who I am. Not now. I have to save Oscar. I can't let the spirit take over. I have no idea what it would do. To me or to Oscar.

She hadn't even known she *could* let the spirit take over. Nani Anjali's rheumy eyes and panicked face flashed in her memory.

"You don't know what it is you bear."

Is that what she meant?

The Umbran strode toward the gate of bones.

"Oscar!" Dmitri cried, running toward it.

The Umbran stepped into the gate.

"Stop him!" Zara screamed, feeling blood bubbling in her throat. The willblade burst to life in her hand, a searing plume of light.

Dmitri fell to his knees before Oscar, before the Umbran, head bowed.

"I cannot hurt you, Oscar. I cannot. I will follow you anywhere."

Energy crackled around Oscar, red and angry...

Dancing from his body into the bones, lighting them with an eerie glow.

The gate burst to life.

38

OSCAR VERSUS THE END

The mass of endless death and darkness, larger than a house and filled with power older than time—the Umbran in its purest form—stared at Oscar with a million eyes. Faces shifted endlessly on its oily surface. Screaming, desperate faces. Skulls in shapes familiar and bizarre. Fear washed over Oscar like a wave of ice, and he let it. He let it flow through him.

"I know you're scared." Oscar's voice shook. "I know you can't take it anymore." He swallowed, straightening his back. "I'm scared too. I always have been. Scared I'm not enough, or I'll do the wrong thing. I'm sorry everything has been so hard for you, but I'm not going to let you take everything away. I'm not going to let you take everything away from me. From all of us. I didn't—"

Oscar choked, then forced himself to carry on, tears flowing. He felt his voice growing stronger. He felt *himself* growing stronger. "I didn't think I could ever be special, but I know I was wrong. I'm special because the people who love me make me that way, and the way I love them back makes it real. I'm not going to give up, no matter what. I'm never giving up because I need to go back and make them feel the same."

The surface of the darkness rippled, and then it released the full force of its hate upon Oscar.

Its inky mass moved in constant horrors, but an impossible monstrous maw opened from its middle, rows of teeth longer than Oscar was tall.

It screamed with the force of the hate of a planet. An endless howling cacophony of death.

The power of it tore at the threads that made Oscar, threatening to burst him apart and unmake him a million times over.

He held.

The particles that made him shivered under the pressure, breaking apart. He clung desperately to himself, to his precious memories. To his friends. His family. He felt himself come apart over and over again, buffeted by the endless foul torrent of hate.

Yet every time, he reformed.

Amazed, Oscar looked down.

Within him, inside his endlessly breaking and re-joining body, he saw thin lines of gold thread spreading from his core, clinging to every part of him and pulling him back together. Shimmering and unbreakable.

The Umbran howled in fury.

Oscar saw it then as his form rattled apart yet again.

Deep within himself, at the centre of the golden threads, right at his core. A shard of darkness.

The Umbran needs hate to take hold.

This part within him must have been what the faint wisp of darkness had been searching for before, when he drove the will-blade through Harry's body back at the house.

He had a splinter of hate buried deep inside of him that it had sought to take purchase, even before the flash he'd felt for Tildy. Now all he felt for Tildy was pity once more, nothing for the Umbran to hold onto. But inside him, tucked away, so deep he barely even knew it was there until every part of his being had been blasted away, was a dark nail of hate hammered into his heart. It could only be this that would allow the Umbran to hold on to him.

Oscar knew exactly what it was.

No matter what I did, how much I loved, deep down—I've always held a little hate for myself.

Oscar stood firm, staring into the darkness, his back straight, hair whipping around his ears. He let the hatred and fear rush over him.

At last, the shattering howl of the darkness subsided.

Oscar's ears still rung with the chaos and tragedy of it.

And then, Oscar opened his mouth and screamed back.

He pushed against the sliver of darkness, forcing it out of himself.

He screamed out everything he loved.

Everything he wanted for himself.

Everything he had denied himself.

The dark thorn shattered before him.

Oscar screamed for everything he couldn't stand to lose.

The massive, dark shape of the Umbran shook.

He screamed for everything he wanted to share.

He screamed until his voice cracked, and his knees shook.

Until tears streamed from his eyes.

The darkness shivered.

Then, a light split through the Umbran's middle.

A crack separated it in half.

It broke.

And everything was light.

39

ONE RAINY WISH

O scar blinked.

Rain spotted on his face.

Zara was standing right in front of him, face slack, her wide eyes the colour of freshly fallen autumn leaves. Blood darkened her shirt and ran from the corner of her mouth. Her arm reached toward him.

"Hi," Oscar said. His chest felt strange. Tight.

"Oscar?" Zara's voice was small and broken.

"I did it," Oscar panted. "I beat it, Zara. I saved myself."

A tear rolled down her cheek.

Oscar looked down at Zara's hand, her knuckles white, fist clenched around the hilt. A wide blade of light was driven through his chest.

Something shook deep inside him.

Zara sobbed.

Oh.

"It's okay," he said to Zara. "It's okay."

Burning, crackling energy from around him lit her face red.

So, the Umbran succeeded and opened the gate, but Zara saved everything.

He felt the gate pushing in with crushing force around him, a weight greater than worlds.

He smiled.

Maybe it would wait a moment longer.

"Oscar." Dmitri's voice tore from his throat. Oscar saw him kneeling only a stride away, his pale eyes staring, mouth hanging open.

"You did the right thing. I forgive you. For everything. Just...forgive yourself too."

Marcus skidded to a halt beside Zara, eyes wide with shock. Paige followed, standing further back, her mouth tight and posture fragile. Ed pawed the ground and whined nearby.

Lyn stepped beside Zara, in her human form now. Rags of clothing pulled around her. She rested a hand on Zara's shoulder.

Zara released the sword in his chest and stepped back.

Oscar welcomed its heat. Everything else felt cold in comparison.

Oscar felt pressure building behind him. Tugging. A few bones fell from above where the gate's crown rested.

Time to go.

He held his smile.

"Look after each other." His voice was failing.

Paige's lip shook, and she stifled a sob, covering her face with both hands.

"I love you."

Oscar struggled; the weight was too much. More bones fell around him.

His eyes travelled across them all, his friends, his family. His everything. Until they rested on Dmitri. "I love——"

He felt himself being pulled away.

He saw Dmitri jumping to his feet, rushing forward with his hands outstretched.

But he was gone before they ever touched him.

❦ 40 ❦

THIS FIRST PARTING AMONG US

Zara watched as the world shuddered.

The willblade hummed in Oscar's chest, and then its hilt shattered, glowing pieces burning into the air like fireworks and shrapnel.

In that same moment, it all collapsed.

Oscar was lost amidst a cascade of darkness and bones, the crackling shadow and energy swallowing it all.

It seemed the world took a long breath out.

Dmitri grunted, staggering through the space where Oscar had been only a moment before. Now there was nothing.

He fell to his knees, one hand outstretched, the other clutched to his chest. His downturned face was empty.

He had nothing left in him.

He screamed.

The deepest, loneliest scream of loss she'd ever heard.

A howl of a thousand years alone.

Ed was a thin and shivering grey whippet. He crawled, whining, body close to the ground and ears flat to his head, to be close to his master.

"You did the right thing," Lyn said softly at her shoulder. "It was him or...everything."

Zara shrugged her hand away, wiping her eyes. "Shut up." She turned her back on Lyn and walked away. Walked toward what was left of the car.

"Zara." Marcus struggled to keep up. His eyes shone with tears, and his bottom lip shook.

"I know," Zara said. Everything inside of her wanted to come out. Everything.

But she couldn't.

Not now. Not here.

The bleeding had stopped, and the Ghatokacha was so quiet it might have been gone, smothered by her crushing sorrow.

"What happened?" Paige's voice was hysterical. She swallowed. "Where did he go?"

Zara stopped, taking a deep breath and closing her eyes. Trying to hold onto herself before she turned around to answer. "I'm sorry. He's gone."

Paige let out a stunned sob.

Zara reached out and took Marcus' hand. Her voice sounded hollow in her own ears. "We need to leave."

DMITRI HAD REFUSED TO COME. He refused to get up or even speak.

He still knelt on the ground on the spot where Oscar had disappeared, face blank and hopeless. Like a statue in memoriam. A dark stain of blood had blossomed on his chest, and Zara wondered when he'd been hurt, but didn't ask. Instead, she sat in the front seat of Paige's ruined rental with Marcus and Ocampo in the back, the shattered remnants of the gaeant in the boot, and they left him there. Ed would not leave his master's side, but other than the mimick-dog, Dmitri was alone.

Paige drove them to their apartment. She was pale and silent with shock. When they arrived, Zara got out and helped Marcus from the back. Song's buzz in the air was subdued and weak, but clung to him gently. The night had taken a toll on him, and whatever powers the ethernal gave him didn't reach to heal wounds like this. Zara wondered if Song would take his grief. If Marcus would let them.

She wondered if Song would be willing to take hers too.

Lyn opened the passenger side door.

"No." Zara raised her hand.

"I—" Lyn swallowed, her angular features battling to convey her thoughts. "I am sorry, Zara. Truly, it is a great loss. I wish it could have been any other way. Please, let me know what I can do to help."

Zara pulled Marcus close to her, standing up straight. "I think...I think it's best if we don't see each other again, Lyn."

Lyn's face slackened in shock.

Zara met her eyes. "I have to figure everything out, and you're not the one to help me do that. We're not good for each other, Lyn. Like you said, what needs to be done isn't always the easiest thing."

Lyn blinked sadly. "Zara..."

"Be good for yourself, Lyn. I mean it. That's what needs to be done."

Ocampo sat back in the car, her shoulders sagging, and closed the door.

"Paige..." Zara swallowed. She'd almost asked if she was going to be okay.

Of course she wasn't.

None of them were.

"What are you going to do now?"

Paige's eyes were bloodshot, her smile sad and distant. "Who the fuck knows?"

"Call me," Zara said. "For anything you need."

Paige chewed her lip for just a moment in a familiar way that made Zara's heart break all over again, and then she nodded and drove into the night.

ZARA DIDN'T HAVE the heart to contact Dmitri or go to the house for a few weeks, not until Marcus was fully recovered with a newly formed Song sitting beside him.

Song was different now.

Those burnished gold eyes were the same, as were their delicate features and large lips. But there was something wiser about them, more wary perhaps. Their short hair was now platinum, a wild and beautiful contrast with their onyx skin.

Zara travelled to the house alone, trying to decide what to think the whole way or, at the very least, what to say.

She hadn't contacted Dmitri. She thought he would need his space as much as she needed hers. He'd been around long enough that he could take care of himself, but now, she needed to know for sure.

Every night while she slept, she saw Oscar's eyes.

'Forgive yourself.'

Forgive yourself for driving a magickal sword through your best friend's heart to save the worlds?

Yeah. Fat chance.

As she slammed the cab door shut and wandered up the long-overgrown drive of one-hundred-and-thirty-eight Kinmount street, she wondered if Dmitri would be angry. She didn't imagine he would. If they had done nothing, he still wouldn't have been with Oscar, because then they wouldn't have existed. But she did not know if she would be able to look him in the eye.

Not with what she had done.

His car wasn't there.

The rebuilding of the front of the house had been completed

and new windows installed. Zara pushed the door and found it locked. She knocked.

No answer.

She walked to the fence at the side of the house, where Marcus had clambered through a broken slat and fallen under the house seemingly forever ago.

It was new now, complete. But with a little spiritual boost and her increased strength, she scaled its eight feet easily and clambered down the other side, half falling to her feet with a thud.

The Ghatokacha roiled inside her resentfully, pulling away from her fast as she released it, leaving a burning tingle running across her flesh. She'd barely used its powers since Stonehenge, and something had changed. It felt...*closer* somehow. Less like it was waiting to help her, and more like it was waiting for an opening, a chance to take control. It wouldn't be so bad if it didn't feel stronger, too. She needed to ask Nani about it, about what she'd meant.

You don't know what it is you bear.

She just hoped Nani had another lucid state again soon.

The garden was overgrown, though not in the state it had been when they first found it, and the side of the house was long since repaired.

She found the back door unlocked, just as she had hoped.

Ed came trotting out into the hallway, an overweight and creased bloodhound whose jowls practically dragged on the floor. She'd always wondered if his changes reflected his emotions.

"Dmitri?" she shouted as she began to check around the house.

The living room was repaired but still filthy. Deep cracks ran down the wall, in need of re-plastering. The door still hung off its hinges, its frame mashed and in need of replacement. She checked in the basement first and found that all the gaeant parts were gone, though there was no sign of a breakout.

Next, she checked the attic and found, it too, had been

cleaned, the bloody ceiling repainted or replaced, though the contents appeared somewhat reduced, and the faint smell of sulphur remained.

She did not bother calling his name again or checking any other rooms.

She knew he was gone.

She sat for a time on the sofa in the living room, wondering if she could call him, and decided against it.

It wasn't until she passed through the hallway again that she spotted it on the side table. A bunch of keys with a hastily scrawled tag on them that said 'ZARA.' She picked them up as Ed leaned against her legs.

Beneath the keys was a folded note, written in a tidy hand.

Zara read it, then read it again, before she folded it carefully across the same lines and pushed it inside her pocket. Then she made her way to the back door and locked it up. Ed followed closely behind as though he knew his master's last instructions. As she opened up the front door, and he followed her out, Zara wondered if the cab would object to her bringing a dog home with her.

Zara locked the door of one-hundred-and-thirty-eight Kinmount street behind her, and took a moment to look up at the house one last time.

She touched her fingers to the note in her pocket, and smiled.

Zara,

All of the years I have been alive, all of the tongues I have spoken, yet I struggle to find words now.

Thank you.
I know you did what I could not.
you did what must be done.
you did what Oscar would have wanted.
Thank you.

use the house as you wish. All its affairs are in order, and I do not know if I will ever return. Please, care for Ed. I did not wish to subject him to the path I plan to walk.

I cannot stay in this place. Not without Oscar. In truth, I do not know I can stay anywhere any longer. I was not prepared to let him go. I am not. I have a long way to go before I am ready to surrender myself to his loss. Something the Bean-Nighe said has been smothering my mind since that night. A thread that when I pull it may lead to nothing but death, but a thread I must pull nonetheless.

I may not deserve a happy ending, but he does.

Take care of each other, and fate willing we will meet again.

with love,

Dmitri

ACKNOWLEDGMENTS

I'm sorry.

You probably didn't expect things to go this way.

Here we were, having a lovely time and making silly jokes, then all of a sudden, *that* happens.

This book came out of me like the Zburator form might tear out of Dmitri's flesh. I had no choice in the matter of how fast it was written, or how it ended. All I can say is, you've probably gotten this far because you had faith in Oscar; now I'm asking you to have faith in me.

The series will conclude in the next book, THE TORN EARTH. Stay with me, you won't regret it.

First of all, thank **you**, for sticking with me through this wild book. I write first and foremost for myself, but if even one other person finds enjoyment in my stories, that means the world to me.

Charlie Knight, my amazing editor, thank you for lending me your amazing mind and talents. Without you, this book would make a lot less sense and have about two thousand less commas. Dean Cole, my ever patient cover designer, and incredible author himself, has all my gratitude for facilitating my difficult requests. Axel, your artistic vision always seems to fit with my imagination, and i'm so happy and proud to have you illustrate for this series. Jayme Bean, whose amazing debut novel 'Untouched' is out now, thank you for your hours of support and talking me off all those author-ledges. I look forward to years more of us clinging together through our bizarre storytelling journeys. Thanks to Shimaira, who along with Jayme and William spent hours lovingly combing through these words to provide feedback and fixes, you both have my eternal gratitude for this (everyone knows I can barely use a full stop). Ash Knight, my alpha to omega reader, thank you so much for everything, I wouldn't even be writing books if not for you. Halo Scott, A.C. Merkel, Mario Dell'Olio, Chris Durston, Rue Sparks, M.E. Aster, Lou Willingham, Tizom Vanclief, and so many others in the writing community have provided incredible support. Thank you to Matthew and Queer Lit, such love and kindness from a great bookshop has been really special, and I can't wait to work together more. Reading this book back, I don't remember even adding all the pop culture references, but here they are: from 'The Wizard of Oz' to 'The Lord of the Rings' (and my personal favourite, 'the cock-destroyers'), so I guess thank you to the decades of creators living rent free in my brain.

Finally, a special thank you to my fiancé, for taking care of me, and supporting me with everything I do. If anyone ever tried to keep us apart, I would pull the moon from the sky to guide my way back, and tear the earth in two to find you.

ABOUT THE AUTHOR

Rory Michaelson is always doing too many things, and rarely the ones that they ought to be. They spend their time reading, watching anime, and trying to convince their fiancé to let them have a pet cat (this is forbidden due to them being too 'cat-like' themself, and said fiancé not wanting to be 'outnumbered'). Rory is easily bribed with cookies, and aims to be one of the many queer authors continuing the fill the world with infinite sparkling rainbow-coloured towers of beautiful queer books.

Find Rory on Twitter for fun nonsense @RoryMichaelson, or you can join their newsletter at RoryMichaelson.com.

THE LESSER KNOWN MONSTERS SERIES
WILL CONCLUDE IN

THE TORN EARTH

ON FRIDAY 13TH MAY 2022
E-BOOK AVAILABLE FOR PRE-ORDER NOW.